Praise for *Upside Down in the Middle of Nowhere*

"A story that will grab avid and reluctant readers alike."
— *School Library Journal*

"Accomplished debut . . . full of touching, distressing detail."
— *Booklist*

"An honest, bleak account of a national tragedy sure to
inspire discussion and research."
— *Kirkus Reviews*

"Lamana's writing is like poetry."
— *The New Orleans Advocate*

"Does a marvelous job of describing . . . the horrors of those
first moments when water sweeps into the Ninth Ward."
— *Reading Today*

A Junior Library Guild selection

UPSIDE DOWN IN THE MIDDLE OF NOWHERE

BY JULIE T. LAMANA

chronicle books · san francisco

For all of the storm-tossed children everywhere.

First Chronicle Books LLC paperback edition, published in 2015.
Originally published in hardcover in 2014 by Chronicle Books LLC.

ISBN 978-1-4521-2880-1

The Library of Congress has cataloged the original edition as follows:

Lamana, Julie T.
Upside down in the middle of nowhere / by Julie T. Lamana.
p. cm.
Summary: At the end of August 2005, ten-year-old Armani is looking forward to her birthday party
in the Lower Ninth Ward of New Orleans, where she and her extended family live, but Hurricane
Katrina is on the way, bringing destruction and tragedy in its wake.
ISBN 978-1-4521-2456-8 (alk. paper)
1. Hurricane Katrina, 2005—Juvenile fiction. 2. African American families—Louisiana—New
Orleans—Juvenile fiction. 3. Survival—Louisiana—New Orleans—Juvenile fiction. 4. Lower Ninth
Ward (New Orleans, La.)—Juvenile fiction. 5. New Orleans (La.)—Juvenile fiction. [1. Hurricane
Katrina, 2005—Fiction. 2. African Americans—Fiction. 3. Family life—Louisiana—Fiction.
4. Survival—Fiction. 5. New Orleans (La.)—Fiction.] I. Title.

PZ7.L15956Ups 2014
813.6—dc23
2013003262

Manufactured in China.

MIX
Paper from
responsible sources
FSC™ C101537
www.fsc.org

Design by Kristine Brogno.
Cover photograph by Jennifer Hale.
Typeset in Electra.

10 9 8 7 6 5 4 3 2 1

Chronicle Books LLC
680 Second Street
San Francisco, CA 94107

Chronicle Books—we see things differently.
Become part of our community at www.chroniclekids.com.

"The oak fought the wind and was broken,
while the willow bent when it must and survived."

— ROBERT JORDAN, *The Fires of Heaven*

CHAPTER 1

I was on my tippy-toes, bouncing up and down on the first step of the bus, stuck behind my second cousin, Danisha, and her melon-sized butt. My little sister, Sealy, was up in there sobbing, but there wasn't a dang thing I could do about it, 'cause I was all squished between the biggest fifth grader in the Lower Ninth Ward and a clump of sweaty kids all but killing each other behind me.

Danisha hit me square in the chest with a booty-bump and glared over her shoulder. "Girl, you best stop pushin' me!" Her bottom lip was rolled out so far, I couldn't help that my eyes went straight to the shiny bubblegum-pink underside.

"Hey, hey, hey, now, you girls stop all that messin' around," my bus driver mumbled all slow in his old-man voice. Mr. Frank had drove my daddy to school when he was a kid, using the same old bus, except it was new and shiny back then, not all beat-down and rusted-out like it was for us. Daddy said he guessed Mr. Frank had to be close to a hundred and twenty years old.

"Sorry, Mr. Frank," I said to Danisha's giant backside. The girl was standing on the step in front of me, so all I could see was how her khaki school pants were stretched so tight, it was only a matter of time before they'd bust open at the seam right in my face. My nerves had wore down about as thin as the pants on my oversized cousin.

Sealy's crying had turned to blubbering. I was flat-out done waiting. I tried to push my way into the aisle so I could at least see her.

"Armani, what is your problem?" Danisha swung around and stomped her foot. She was at least six inches taller than me and everything about her was big, even her head. When she looked down at me, with her fat lips flapping and her big head rolling from side to side, I knew she could kill me easy if she set her mind to it. But I didn't care. Sealy was crying.

"Shut up, Danisha, an' get out the way." I slipped past her before she had a chance to say something else stupid.

I knew where Sealy would be sitting, because we always sat in the same seat, right up front. I didn't like sitting in the back of the bus. Seemed to me, the further back you went, the crazier the kids were.

Danisha shoulder-bumped me when she passed me up heading to her seat—in the back where she *always* sat.

Sure enough, Sealy was doing the ugly cry. Her face was all puffed up, her eyes were pouring water, and her arms were folded up tight across her chest. "What's goin' on? Why are you cryin'?" I asked, all out of breath.

Sealy looked up at me with her head hiccupping up and down. She ran the back of her hand up under her nose, smearing all that wetness across her face. "Bugger took my book," she sobbed. I ain't never seen no one look so pitiful.

"He took your book? *That's* why you're fussin'?" Sealy nodded about fifty times. I hated seeing her not smiling, but I couldn't believe all this drama was on account of a dumb book.

I looked around for Bugger. I don't know what his mama named him, but ever since that kid was born five years ago, he's been Bugger, simple as that. I don't even think he knew his real name. Then I seen him. He was standing on the very last seat in the back of the bus, jumping up and down like a fool, waving my sister's book in the air, just as proud as he could be.

I marched toward the back to pry it out of his grimy hands. Stupid Bugger seen me coming, and he squealed like a stuck hog. He threw the book. It almost went flying out an open window.

I kept heading straight for Bugger, never minding the book. At this point I just wanted to knock that boy upside his head. But I never got the chance. Danisha stepped in my way with both hands on her wide hips and her big head cocked to the side.

"Where you goin', Armani?" *To kill your little brother*, I wanted to say, but my good sense kept the words from leaving my mouth.

"Nowhere," I lied.

Some little kid leaned over the seat next to us and handed Danisha my sister's book. As soon as I seen the swirly green and white cover, my hands squeezed shut—Sealy's journal. No wonder the girl was having such a fit.

Danisha started flipping through the pages. She opened her mouth to say something, but just then the oldest Boman kid reached in front of her and snatched the book out of her hands.

"Boy, you crazy!" she squawked.

The shaggy blond-headed Boman kid never even looked at my cousin or said a word. He just held the book out for me to take.

I grabbed the journal from the boy's smelly hand and whipped around. "You best tell your brother to leave Sealy alone," I hollered over my shoulder at Danisha. My heart was about to jump out of my chest. I rubbed the book on the seat of my pants, hoping to wipe off any germs it might've picked up being passed around like gossip on the crazy side of the bus. I walked fast back to my seat.

"Whatever," Danisha hollered back. "You need to tell your sister to stop bein' so triflin' and weird!" She started laughing, and lots of the other kids laughed with her, slapping high fives behind me, but I didn't care.

"Whatever," I grumbled to myself.

I tossed the journal onto Sealy's lap. She went to hugging that book and looked up at me. The tears left in her eyes looked like specks of twinkles dancing around. "Oh, thank you, Armani! Thank you!"

"Just put it away," I said. "Don't be takin' that thing out on the bus no more. Why can't you just keep it home, anyways?"

"Because I never know when I might need it, silly." She was back to being her normal, strange self. I stood there watching her put the book into her small book sack. Not her regular book sack for carrying school stuff. This was her other book sack, the one she used for carrying her special books and whatever else she had stashed down in there. After she zipped it up, she went to hugging the dumb sack. Danisha was right. My sister was weird.

"Move over, girl, an' let me sit next to the window."

After I sat down, Sealy laid her head on my shoulder and sighed. "I love you, Armani."

I wiggled my shoulder to get her head off me. I looked at her with my lip curled up, praying that nobody else had heard her. "Shut up, Sealy." Then, while I was staring out the window, I reached over and gave her hand a little squeeze.

Ol' Mr. Frank always had his soul music pumping out of the home-made speakers he'd rigged up with fishing line. They hung crooked up over the huge mirror he used for spying on us kids while he drove. Most times, I could barely hear the music on account of the kids hootin' and hollerin' about a whole lot of nothing, everyone talking at the same time. Some days it got so bad that by the time we finally made it to our stop, I'd used up all the nerves I'd been given to help me make it through the day. The noise wasn't the biggest problem, though.

Nope, it wasn't the ride, the noise, or even the tore-up seats and sticky floors that pulled the nice out of me. I didn't even care that they had us stuffed three or four kids to a seat.

What *did* bother me was the smell. The smell wasn't so bad in the morning. But by afternoon, the August sun had been beating down all day, cooking up the smells. By the time school let out and we loaded onto the bus, it was like stepping into a big stinky sock. It didn't help matters none when all the sweaty kids piled into the bus and started spreading their smells around, especially the older kids coming straight from P.E.—and them white Boman kids.

There was four of them in that family, and they always walked together and sat together. Every day when they got on the bus, I'd keep all my fingers crossed that they wouldn't sit nowhere close to me. I ain't trying to be hurtful, but them kids smelled like their mama was bathing them in pure onion water. I don't know how anyone can smell that bad and not be bothered by their own stink. If they sat even kind of close to me, I'd bury my nose in my own armpit and suck in the scent of the lavender soap Mama made us bathe in twice a day. I was always grateful when they walked on by and headed to the back of the bus. I only had to hide my nose for a quick minute.

———

When Mr. Frank made his first stop, about twelve kids got off. That's when the rest of us shuffled around, jumping into open seats, so we wasn't all so squished up.

While the bus sputtered and bounced down the road, I looked out the window and counted things. Mostly I took to counting to keep my mind from noticing the canal. I hated the canal. I hated it because Mama hated it, and she hated it because Memaw hated it. Somewhere in that stinking canal was the bones of my two dead uncles, Mama's brothers—Memaw's sons. Story goes that one day when they were kids, one of them tried to save the other from drowning when the canal decided to take them both. My bus went by that liquid graveyard every day—so I took to counting.

Once, I tried counting folks sitting or standing out front of houses, but I lost track and had to start over two times. Memaw said most of them were loafers, and they needed to get off their rear ends and make themselves useful. That's when Daddy reminded her that we needed to mind our own business, and leave the loafers to their loafin'.

The week I started the fourth grade, I took to counting all the pink houses. Light pink, dark pink, it didn't make no difference, so long as there was some kind of pink to its color I went on and counted it. I'd counted nine pink-colored houses when we turned the last corner before the stop where we got let off. I was used to seeing window fans shoved up in windows—anybody with good sense had one. We had three real nice ones ourselves. Well, except for the one in Memaw's room that made a chirping bird sound every time she turned it on. But I was *not* expecting to see the new, clunky metal box sticking out of the side window on Danisha's mama's boyfriend's house.

She seen it too, and went to hollerin' and singing in the aisle, "We got us some air, we got us some air. . . ." the whole time swinging her big butt, doing some kind of happy dance.

All week long she took to saying stupid things like, "Well, I guess I best be gettin' back to my *air-conditionin'*," or, "It's sooo hot, y'all wanna come sit awhile in my *air-conditionin'*?" Stuck-up Danisha and her lame air conditioner got on my last nerve.

———

After letting out kids here and there across the Lower Ninth Ward, Mr. Frank let us off in front of the tire shop where my Uncle T-Bone worked part-time. From there, it was just a short walk to get home. Eight kids got off at our stop: the Boman kids, Danisha and Bugger, and me and Sealy. Danisha and Bugger got off because their mama's boyfriend, Mr. Charlie, worked at the shop too. I don't know why they liked going in that nasty place. It reeked of gasoline, motor oil, cigarettes, and rotten ol' men. The only good thing about that shop was Mr. Jasper Junior Sr. and the sound of his saxophone pouring out into the air. We could hear the sweet sound of his horn playing clear down by our house every day of the week except Sunday, when the shop was closed up and Mr. Junior Sr. was at church making his music for Jesus instead of for the rest of us.

"Y'all have a good weekend," Mr. Frank said, and pulled the bus door open. "Don't forget to watch the five o'clock news, now."

Sealy was on the step in front of me. She stopped so fast I almost plowed right into the back of her. "Why do we need to watch the news, Mr. Frank?"

He took a second to chew on the toothpick sitting between the couple of teeth he had left, then he pulled the dirty ball cap off and rubbed his bald head. Staring out the bus windshield, he said, "There's a storm brewin'—a big one—out there in the Gulf." He let out a whoosh of stale old-man air. "Reminds me of Betsy."

"Who's Betsy?" I asked.

Mr. Frank put his cap back on his head and looked me in the eye. He plucked the toothpick from his mouth. He squinted up his already wrinkly eyes and said all serious, "Betsy was the storm that sucked the life outta me. She took away everyone I ever loved."

Sealy gasped. "That's so terrible, Mr. Frank."

"Yes it is, child," he sighed. "All right, then," and just like that, he turned and looked straight out the bug-spattered windshield. "Y'all have a good weekend. Tell your daddy an' them I said hey."

I got a whiff of something that smelled ripe as rotten gumbo, and I knew right off them Boman kids had to be coming up behind me. Scared that the smell was contagious and could possibly stick to my clothes and skin forever, I gave Sealy a nudge.

————

Once we were off the bus, Danisha and Bugger went on into the tire shop, the oniony Boman kids took off running to Lord knows where, and me and my sister crossed over the road to walk home.

Sealy pulled out one of her books and started reading.

"How can you read an' walk at the same time?"

She shrugged, never taking her eyes off her book. "I guess it's because my feet know the way home."

"Yeah, but ain't you worried about trippin' over somethin'?" I almost wished she would trip, just to prove my point.

She stopped and looked at me over the top of her book. She rolled her eyes real big and took a slow, deep breath. "I can walk and read at the same time, but I sure can't talk and read at the same time." For a split second she reminded me of Mama, with that soft, sweet, *I-feel-sorry-for-ya-face, 'cause-you're-so-cute-and-young-and-ain't-smart-enough-to-know-yet* look. She gave me a little sympathy smile, then went to reading and walking again. I was left there, just staring after her with my mouth hanging open.

While Sealy walked on ahead of me, I let my eyes wander up to the sunshiny sky. I couldn't help but notice that there wasn't one tiny cloud up there. Mr. Frank was a nice man and all, but I got to thinking that he must be getting really old—maybe even too old to drive a bus. There wasn't no storm coming, even *I* could tell that. It was a perfect day. And it was Friday. *And* it was my birthday weekend. I smiled to myself and hollered, "Wait up, Sealy!"

CHAPTER 2

"Mama Jean, turn off that TV and come sit for supper," Mama called for Memaw from the kitchen. Memaw had been glued to the nothing-but-weather television station and barely even looked up to say hey when we got home. The year before, she was so fixed on not missing a single episode of that genius man on *Jeopardy!* that she straight-up broke one of Mama's biggest suppertime rules and took to eating her meals right from the comfort of her TV-watching chair.

Memaw clicked off the television and shuffled on over to the table, mumbling under her breath about needing the good Lord to do something. "I sure don't like the looks of that storm," Memaw said to no one in particular. She sucked in her belly so she could scoot past the twins' high chairs lined up on her side of the table.

It didn't make no difference to Mama what else might be going on: If there was eating to be done, she wanted us sitting at her table. Mama loved that oversized, scuffed-up table, especially when the eight of us were taking up space around it.

"Well," Mama said, "I don't think that storm is anything we need to fuss about at the supper table, Mama Jean." She scooched her chair up to the table and went straight to fixin' plates for all us kids.

Baked macaroni and cheese, pan-fried pork chops, collard greens, Memaw's sugar-topped cornbread, and a big ol' pitcher of iced-down sweet tea. Mama had outdone herself again. We were all sitting around the big table Daddy had made out of the old high school gym floor, eating and talking like always. With the high chairs pushed up to the table and the rest of us all gathered around in our mismatched chairs, it was all shoulders and elbows. There wasn't even room for a night crawler to shimmy through.

I was fixin' to tear into my second pork chop when I remembered an interesting fact I'd learned at school.

"Daddy, ya know what my teacher told us today?"

"Armani, don't talk with your mouth full," Mama said without even looking up. She kept right on cutting up meat and tossing it onto the table in front of Khayla and Kheelin. They didn't use the high chair trays no more, not since springtime when they made three.

"What'd your teacher tell you?" Daddy asked.

I swallowed and sat up a little straighter in my chair. "Well, she said that yesterday, somewhere in Idaho, a cow gave birth to a chicken."

Georgie, my older—*not* smarter—brother, spit a wad of half-chewed chop across the table. He put his fist up to his mouth and started cracking up. He threw hisself back in his chair so hard, he just about fell over backward. "Oh, my gawd! You're so stupid, Armani!" The boy was laughing so out of control, tears were streaming down his ugly face.

"I ain't stupid!" I yelled. "*You're* stupid!" Heat filled my cheeks. My head throbbed. I slumped into my chair wishing I was an only child so I didn't have to be in the same room with thickheaded people like Georgie.

"That's enough, Georgie," Daddy said, trying to stifle his own laugh.

Memaw and Mama chuckled and shook their heads. My whole face was on fire.

"I'm sorry, Daddy," Georgie said, shaking his head back and forth, wiping tears and holding back more laughs. "But that's the dumbest thing I ever heard. A cow having a baby chicken! What'd they call it, Armani—a cow-icken?" Everyone at the table was laughing—except Sealy. "Or, wait, wait, I got it . . . how 'bout a chick-ow!"

"Chick-ow! Chick-ow!" Khayla and Kheelin sang, moving their shoulders up and down. They were banging away on the tabletop doing some kind of chicken high chair dance, singing the ridiculous word. My whole family was acting like fools.

"Why are y'all smilin' an' lookin' so crazy?" I whined.

"Is that true, Armani?" Sealy asked with big puppy eyes. She was interested in what I had to say.

"Yes, Sealy, it *is* true. My teacher even said it was on the news."

"Lord, have mercy," Memaw said.

"Then your teacher's a dummy," Georgie said, shoving a pile of collard greens in his mouth.

"Mr. Curtis, I think that will do," Mama said to Daddy. But her head nodded at Georgie.

"Shut up, Georgie! You think you know everything!" I hollered.

Daddy wasn't laughing no more.

"Well, I know more than you do," Georgie mumbled under his breath, still feeding his face.

"Yeah, right, that's why you barely made it to the sixth grade," I said, putting sass behind my words and a slide to my head.

Daddy stood up. I can't speak for Georgie, but I'm smart enough to know that when Daddy goes and stands up like that, it's best if I just shut up altogether.

"Your mama's right. That's enough," Daddy said. "Understood?"

"Yes, sir," we fussed at the same time.

Daddy sat back down. Before he went to eating he turned to Georgie. "I don't ever want to hear you speak disrespectful toward a teacher again. I know Armani's teacher and she's a good woman."

"A good woman with a vivid imagination," Memaw said into her napkin. Mama bit down on her bottom lip, shaking her head at Memaw.

I seen my opening and took it. "You need to speak respectful to your sister too."

"Oh, Lord," Memaw coughed. "Here we go."

"In your dreams," Georgie said. His voice sounded like a whiny little girl's.

Sealy leaned in so close to me I could see food stuck in her back teeth. "I can't wait to get to fourth grade," she happy-whispered. "Y'all learn so many interesting things."

After supper Daddy handed out chores. Georgie had to cut the grass, and I had to clean up the kitchen. I didn't care. I'd rather clean ten kitchens than push that rickety ol' contraption across the yard.

The blades on that ancient thing were so dull, it took going back and forth over the same spot at least twenty times before the grass looked even close to cut.

Mama had Kheelin in the bath, and Daddy was outside, most likely supervising dimwit Georgie. Memaw was sitting in the living room, watching her sacred Weather Channel, talking with Sealy about some book called *Roll of Thunder*. I couldn't hear exactly what they were saying, but it didn't surprise me none that the two of them would waste their time discussing a book about storms. Memaw would be getting Sealy all worked up about the weather. It was only a matter of time.

I was done washing, except for the big ol' black cast-iron skillet Mama used for frying up the pork chops. I still couldn't believe how stupid Georgie was, and I sure wasn't in no mood for scrubbing that skillet. Every time I washed that heavy thing, I got a crick in my neck. It had to weigh at least a hundred pounds. I was fixin' to start on the bothersome blob of iron when one of Kheelin's little cars rolled right up over my bare toes.

Khayla was tucked up under the gym-floor table playing with the cars Kheelin had got for his birthday present. It didn't make no difference to Kheelin that his twin had them, because he never played with them anyhow. He was always too busy being snug up against Mama. If Khayla was wearing pockets, you could bet good money the girl had a tiny car shoved into one. Mama had washed cars in the laundry more than once by accident.

I used my foot to roll the tiny car back to Khayla. She looked at me and gave me one of her famous chubby-cheeked smiles. I smiled back, and gave her the "I love you" sign with my soapy fingers. My cousin, TayTay, had taught me how to do it when we were out on summer break. I'd been trying to teach the sign-language symbol to the twins, but they couldn't get their pudgy little fingers to stand up straight.

I was fixin' to walk over and help Khayla situate her fingers when she stopped me cold and looked me dead straight in the eyes singing, "Chick-ow! Chick-ow!" She scooped up the itty-bitty cars and took off running scared like a fat little bunny.

I grabbed the wet, red-checkered dishrag out of the soapy water and threw it at her. But she scooched quick around the corner. Just then, Memaw came walking toward me around that same corner. The slopping-wet rag slapped her smack in the middle of her face and stuck there like flypaper.

My hands flew up to stifle the scream that wanted to leap out of my mouth. Memaw froze. She stood there, with the rag covering her whole face—dirty dishwater dripping down her housedress. We were both still as statues, like all the clocks stopped ticking, and the earth stopped spinning.

"Memaw, oh my gosh . . . I'm so sorry."

Slow as a slug, Memaw took hold of the bottom edge of the rag. The wet cloth inched down off her forehead slower than cane syrup. The first thing I seen was her eyes. They just stared at me. My heart pounded harder. I was fixin' to get a whipping for sure.

Then . . . real slow-like, I seen her nose pop out. You can't tell nothing about how a person feels by looking at their nose. Even still, seeing half her face uncovered like that made my knees wobble. Then, with one final tug, she pulled that dishrag all the way down, and I seen her mouth. She was smiling! I couldn't believe it! I thought for sure Memaw was gonna tear me up. But there she was, just smiling. I gulped down a sigh of relief. We both took to laughing.

She walked over and gently swiped me upside my head. She tossed the dishrag into the sink, grabbed a towel, and patted her face dry.

"You're lucky," she said, in a pretend-serious voice. "I s'pose I'm gonna go ahead and let ya live to see your double digits." She swatted me a good one on my butt when she strutted by, grabbing a cold pork chop off the leftovers plate.

"Now, hurry up and finish your chores, child," she said over her shoulder. "I'll be waitin' for ya."

———

Sitting on the porch swing with Memaw was always my favorite time of day. Whether I was doing my homework or finishing my chores, I always did them without dragging my feet if I knew Memaw was waiting for me on the swing. Evening time, after supper, was the best time for swinging. The smell of honeysuckle strong in the breeze, crickets singing their never-ending song, June bugs flickering about, and neighborhood after-supper music spilling out into the still evening air. I never even cared about the little pieces of white paint chips peeling off the swing and sticking to my clothes. Mama kept asking Daddy to sand that ol' swing down and paint it, but the truth was, Daddy was scared that if he messed with the thing too much, he might ruin the names on it.

My PawPaw, Mama's daddy, had made that swing with his own bare hands for Memaw when they first got married, back before there was such a thing as microwaves or computers. Every time they had a baby, he'd go and carve their names on it, making the swing even more special. Then when Mama and Daddy got married and started having us kids, Daddy took to carving our names on there too.

When Georgie was about to make eight years old, he snuck one of Mama's favorite butter knives and did his best to dig out the I sitting up between the last G and E of his carved name. But all he managed to do was leave behind a big ol' ugly, sloppy fat letter I instead of the nice skinny one Daddy had put there. He said he did it because he wanted to be just "George" like Daddy—not Georgie. From then on, it just looked like his name had a big ol' scratch. Daddy was mad for two or three days after that.

There's names scattered all over that chair swing, but most times I sat resting my back on my own name. It's been a special chair for a long time, all right. So I sat there, never minding the specks of white, and rested my head on Memaw's shoulder.

"Memaw, why don't we call you Grandma, or Nana, or somethin'?" I asked.

She took my hand and sandwiched it all sweet between hers. I reached over and played with the loose skin on the back of her hand. It felt soft and buttery, like the leather cover of Daddy's ol' wore-out Bible. I took to wondering how her veins could move back and forth like that without hurting.

"Well," she said, "I always called my grandmother MawMaw, and your mama called her grandmother MawMaw. So it seemed natural when my first grandbaby was born, I'd be MawMaw too."

"Georgie was your first grandbaby, right?"

"Yes, he was. And when that sweet child started talking, he gave me the name Memaw."

"Why?"

"I think he was tryin' to say 'my MawMaw.'" There was a smile in her voice. "But it came out Memaw. I've been Memaw ever since."

"It don't bother you that he messed up your name?" Seemed to me, Georgie sure did like messing up names.

"No, indeed, I think it's a fine name. He didn't mess it up. He just named me special, that's all." She patted the top of my leg. "Now, I have a question for you." She paused a good long minute. "That cow of yours in Idaho—are you suggestin' that it laid an egg or did a whole chicken pop out?"

I let go of her hand, sat straight up, and planted my feet down firm on the cracked concrete, bringing the swing to a stop. "Memaw . . ." I whined, giving her my full-face pout. All of a sudden, I got a picture in my head of a cow laying an egg. I seen the laugh around her eyes. I tried to cover my mouth before it broke into a big smile, but my hand was too slow.

She reached up and put my head back on her shoulder. "I'm just askin'. You know, sometimes we've got to think for ourselves before we start repeatin' the foolishness of others. That's all I'm sayin'."

We went back to the business of swinging. We weren't talking or nothing—just swinging. My right foot was wrapped around her left foot, and it was like we were one big ol' foot pushing down on that square of concrete. When the swing slowed down, we knew at the exact same minute that it was time to push again. The high-squeak, low-squeak, high-squeak, low-squeak sound of our rocking just made the feel-good feeling better. Being with Memaw was easy.

Every time the huge fern hanging from the porch above Memaw's head brushed against her updo, she'd reach up and slap herself in the head. I tried hard not to laugh. It looked like she was swiping a fly, except there wasn't no fly—it was just that overgrown plant hanging outside Mama's kitchen window.

Right when I thought that she might've forgot, Memaw reached into the half-torn pocket of her favorite yellow housedress and plucked out one of them hard caramels she knew I'd walk all the way from New Orleans to Jackson, Mississippi, for. She handed that little piece of Heaven to me, and then she pulled out a second one.

She opened hers, I opened mine, and just like we'd been practicing for years, I plopped the candy I was holding into her mouth, and she plopped hers into mine. We rocked and sucked on our candies, watching the trees sway side to side, like they knew our secret.

"My, my, my, now ain't this nice?"

"Umm-hmm," is all I said.

Long after my candy was gone but while the sweetness of it lingered, I stared up at the honey-colored sky, tilted my head back, and settled into Memaw's shoulder. I closed my eyes and listened to the wind. It was stronger and thicker than usual, moving from here to there, blending in just so with the sound of Memaw softly humming a hymn from church last Sunday. The porch swing added rhythm, with its high-squeak, low-squeak.

The screen door smacked open. "Memaw, they're coming on the TV after the commercial break with an update about that storm," Sealy rudely interrupted.

"Girl, are you serious?" I said, sliding my head with my lip curled up to one side, making sure she knew with more than my words how aggravated I was. "Can't you see we're busy?"

But just as quick as a swat, Memaw scooched herself to the edge of our swing. Bearing most of her weight down on my thigh, she umphed herself up and out of the chair. Her sweet caramel breath floated down and settled in my deserted lap, leaving me to swing half-crooked by myself. She tapped the loose arm of the chair without even so much as looking back at me. "Hold the door, Sealy, baby. I'm comin'."

The plump purple muscadines hanging from the vine called my name. The grapevine was another one of Mama's babies. It spread from one end of the chain-link fence clear to the other side where Daddy kept his homemade charcoal grill.

I lifted a few of the top vines, because the fat dark grapes are almost always hiding up underneath. Everybody knows that the darkest ones are the juiciest and the sweetest. I found what I was looking for and plopped the yummy grape in my mouth. I about choked on the dang thing when Georgie tapped me on my shoulder.

"Hey, whatcha doin'?"

I rolled my eyes and ate another grape. "Makin' a pie." 'Course, I wasn't, but a stupid question deserved a stupid answer. I spit a seed over my brother's shoulder.

Georgie plopped his own grape—from a *top* vine—into his mouth. He wiped muscadine drool on his shoulder and said, "The Babineauxes are out front, loadin' their car with suitcases."

The Babineauxes were our neighbors.

I plucked another grape from Mama's vine. "Why? Are they takin' a trip or somethin'?"

"I guess. Mr. Babineaux told me they're evacuating 'cause of the storm." He picked another grape.

I all but sucked an entire grape right into my lung. A tiny thump started up in my head. "Evacuate?" I said, like the word smelled bad.

"Yep. He says I should tell Daddy. They're headin' north, probably to Mississippi. He says we should pack up and head north too, while we still can."

Without even thinking about it, I grabbed hold of Georgie's shoulders and got up in his grinning face. My heart was thumping like a snare drum at a jazz funeral. "You didn't tell Daddy that, did you?"

Georgie pulled his face as far away from mine as he could. His big ol' grin shrunk right up, and his glasses were hanging on to the tip of his fat sweaty nose.

"Not yet."

"Georgie, you gotta promise me you won't tell Daddy."

He wiggled out of my grip and pushed his glasses back into place with his finger.

"Why shouldn't I tell him? Maybe we *should* evacuate."

I couldn't believe my ears. My brother was so slow. "Georgie, it's my birthday weekend. My party's *the day after tomorrow.*"

"So?" he said. He might as well have slapped me upside my head.

"So?" I did the best head slide I've ever done in my whole life.

He plucked a half-green grape off the vine and started walking for the back door.

I scooted in front of him, forcing him to a stop. He rolled his eyes and folded his arms up across his chest.

I took a deep breath and forced a smile that most likely showed too many teeth. "Please don't tell Daddy. Please? Just don't say nothin' till after my party Sunday—*please*, Georgie?"

His eyes softened. He opened his mouth to say something, but the screen door squeaked.

"There you are. Your mama's looking for the two of you." Daddy stood in the doorway, holding the screen open.

Me and Georgie stood there froze like a couple of fools.

"Is everything all right?" Daddy stepped out of the doorway. All the muscadine juice in my mouth dried up and sweat beads popped out across my forehead.

"Sure, Daddy, everything's fine. We're just eatin' some grapes." Georgie play-slapped my arm and walked over to the screen door. "You better come on, Armani, before them mosquitoes eat you up!"

Daddy put his hand on my brother's shoulder and the two of them held the door open, waiting on me. "Your brother's right. We don't want the birthday girl covered with bug bites."

"Yeah," Georgie said over the top of his glasses. "You don't wanna show up at your party on Sunday looking like you dragged yourself up outta the swamp." He laughed. Daddy shook his head from side to side, a nice smile shining across his face.

I smiled so big I could feel it in my ears.

CHAPTER 3

Tap, tap, tap. Someone was knocking on me and Sealy's bedroom door.

"Come in," I loud-whispered. It was early, and Sealy was still asleep beside me. I moved her arm from across my face. I hated sleeping with my sister. It wouldn't have been so bad, except for the fact that instead of her occupying her side of the bed, like she was supposed to, she felt inclined to find new ways of sleeping on top of me.

The door creaked open a few inches, and Daddy stuck his head through. "Good morning."

"Mornin', Daddy," I said in my lazy morning voice. The smell of cinnamon and warm chicory brewing in the coffeepot floated into our room.

"I'm headed to Pete's. Do you want to ride along?" At the end of every month, when Daddy got his paycheck, him and Georgie made a run to Mr. Pete's doughnut shop and got us a couple dozen fresh doughnuts. I knew without even asking that the reason he was offering for me to ride with him instead of my brother was because it was my birthday weekend.

Sealy rolled over, but kept on sleeping. I was out of bed before I answered, "I'll be out in a minute."

I always liked the way Saturday mornings smelled. That was the day Mama made her pies. Everybody in our neighborhood called her The Pie Lady. Anyone needing a pie for any reason would be a fool if they didn't get it from my mama. Last Christmas there was a lady who drove four hours from Lake Charles for five of my mama's pies. They're that good.

Mama would get up while it was still dark as tar outside and the rest of the world was still sleeping. She'd start out by rolling the dough. Most times, there'd be flour from one end of the counter to the other. After she got her piecrusts all fixed, she'd start slow-cooking the fillings on the stovetop.

By the time I'd come walking into the kitchen, the sun had only been up a short while, but the whole house already smelled of cinnamon apples, sweet potato with extra nutmeg, and the sugary-sweet perfume of heavy syrup simmering in the big silvery pot.

Mama was standing at the stove stirring one of them pots with a big wooden spoon. I came up behind, and stood on my tippy-toes so I could kiss her cheek. "Mornin', Mama."

She's pretty, my mama. But I think she's always been the most pretty real early in the morning when she has her pie-making glow. I knew that's when she was the happiest. I guess she loved her pie-making the way Sealy loved her books.

"Good morning," Mama said, putting the spoon down on the countertop. She wiped her floury hands on her apron and gave me a warm morning hug. Then she took my face in both her hands and rubbed my nose with her nose. "Did you sleep well?"

"Yes, ma'am." I reached past her and dipped my finger in the thick goop puddled on the wooden spoon. Mama lightly slapped the back of my hand. I smiled and put my syrupy finger in my mouth, knowin' right away it was the fixins of a pecan pie.

Memaw was sitting at the table cracking pecans. There was a bowl for the shells and a bowl for the nuts, but Memaw was missing both of them. Nuts and shells and nut dust covered the table. Hardly nothing was in the bowls.

"Well, now, aren't you an early bird," Memaw said, squinting at me. Her eyeglasses were hanging from the gold-colored cord around her neck. I unfolded the glasses and slid them onto her face, careful not to accidentally poke an eye out.

"Oh, my—look at this mess," she said, looking around at all the nuts and nut dust. I giggled.

"Mornin', Memaw." I leaned over and kissed her forehead. She reached her hand up and hugged my head.

The back screen door slapped shut and Daddy's heavy footsteps came toward the kitchen.

He wasn't smiling like he usually did on a doughnut Saturday. Long creases were planted across his forehead. "You ready to go, baby girl?" Daddy asked. His pleasant voice didn't match the look of trouble on his face.

"Uh-huh," I said, picking up nutshells and wondering if his look had anything to do with the Babineauxes skipping town.

"Excuse me?" Daddy cocked his head at me. Both Mama and Memaw stopped what they were doing and looked at him.

"I mean *yes, sir.*" I had to stop my lip from wanting to curl.

He relaxed a tiny bit. "Why don't you wait for me in the truck? I'll be there in a minute."

"Yes, sir." I looked to Mama and Memaw and gave my finger sign for *I love you.*

I almost made it out the door when Memaw shuffled toward me in her wore-out fuzzy slippers.

"Here." She shoved two dollars into my hand. "Get me two of them apple fritters."

"But Memaw, you ain't supposed to be eatin' too many sweets on account of your sugar bein' high." I held out the dollar bills for her to take back.

"You listen to me, child. There's nothin' wrong with my sugar that a warm apple fritter can't fix. Now go on." She shooed me toward the door.

I let out a big sigh and stuffed the money into the pocket of my shorts. "You're gonna get me in trouble." She stared at me over the top of her glasses, holding up two fingers with one hand and rubbing her belly with the other. She looked silly, and it made me smile.

"You're bad, Memaw. You're gonna get us *both* in trouble." I went out and got in Daddy's truck. I sat there trying to figure out how I was gonna sneak that ol' woman her apple fritters.

————

The truck smelled like Daddy, or maybe Daddy smelled like the truck. I really ain't sure. It was one of them aromas made up from a whole collection of smells.

Daddy never smoked in front of us kids. I don't even think he did in front of Mama, neither. But we all knew that when Daddy drove by hisself, he would smoke on a skinny cigar. I liked the smell it left behind—a smoky, thick sweetness of leaves burning at Christmastime.

The truck door creaked and stuck on the hinges when Daddy opened it. He sat down heavy in his driver's seat and let out a long sigh. I think he might've forgot I was there. His hand sat there holding the keys, and he stared at something I didn't see out the windshield. He shook his head, shaking his private thoughts loose, and then he turned to look at me. His mouth was smiling, but his eyes looked far away.

"Are you buckled up?"

"Yes, sir." I wanted to ask him what was troubling him, but I knew that whatever it was, he'd feel better as soon as he had some of Mr. Pete's fresh doughnut holes.

He picked up the little metal can that held his peppermints. He flipped the lid and held it out to me. I smiled and took one of the tiny candies. He winked at me and took one for hisself. I had a feeling that he was aching for a cigar right then, but he went to sucking the mint instead.

Once we got moving, I was relieved to see that whatever was upsetting my daddy seemed to fly out the open truck widow and into the muggy morning air.

"Daddy, hurry up!" I pointed out the window. I could see the flashing blue and white light on the pole next to the building, even though the doughnut shop was still more than a block down the road. That bright, spinning light let everybody know that a new batch of doughnuts had come out of the oven. It was like the light was screaming, "Come an' get 'em while they're hot!"

My mouth started to water thinking about biting into the hot, fresh, melt-in-your-mouth fried, sugary dough.

"Daddy, drive faster!"

Daddy didn't say nothing. He just grinned and sucked on his peppermint. I bounced up and down in my seat.

The truck finally made it to the sandy parking lot. A big ol' dust cloud whooshed out from underneath us. I jumped out before Daddy even had a chance to shut off the engine. I slammed my door shut and slid around the front of the truck.

I was running for the shop's bright red painted door when I seen a playpen like the one Mama used for the twins sitting up in the alley between Pete's and the pawn shop next door. A cardboard sign reading "free puppies" was taped to the rim. I skidded to a stop, temporarily forgetting all about doughnuts.

I whipped around and gave Daddy my most convincing sweet-as-pie face with my hands folded in prayer up against my chest.

"Oh, Daddy, please?" I hadn't even looked at the four-legged creatures yet, but I'd been wanting myself a puppy for as long as I could remember. I knew he'd say yes, it being my birthday weekend and all.

Daddy was shaking his head "no" before he even took the time to ponder the possibility.

I approached the filthy playpen holding the free puppies. I was fixin' to open my mouth to remind him of all the benefits of a free pet when a stench flew up my nose, making my stomach do a flip-flop.

Daddy yanked me back. A mangy beast leaped up out of that pen made for babies like it was gonna tear me to shreds. It took to barking and growling and flinging thick dog spit everywhere.

"Hey, keep back, girl!" snarled a toothless old white lady. She came swaggering from around the corner of the doughnut shop carrying a long, thick stick in her gnarled hand. Daddy swept me behind him and took a step toward the skinny, dirty, hunched-over woman.

"We were just looking at your puppies, ma'am," Daddy said. The devil dog and two more like it were all yapping and having a fit.

"These here puppies ain't for you." The words got lost in raspy phlegm rumbling around in her saggy throat. The woman's eyes were watery-yellow, and her face was dry and cracked, like gator skin. Even though I was safe up behind Daddy, I could smell the sourness of the old woman's breath.

Without any warning, that ugly ol' witch swung her stick and hit one of them dog-monsters upside the head so hard the stick splintered. The animal screamed a dog scream, and the other two yelped and ran to huddle in a corner of the pen.

"Now go on," the evil woman grumbled, waving her stick. "Get on outta here."

Daddy put his arm around my shoulder and guided me toward the red door of the doughnut shop. I couldn't tear my eyes from the old woman's heartless face. I pulled loose from Daddy and went marching right up to the woman, getting as close as my good sense would let me.

"You should be ashamed of yourself," I said slow and clear to the wicked witch. "How would you like it if I took a stick an' hit *you* upside your fool head?" My voice was beginning to rise and my whole body took to shaking.

"That's enough, Armani," Daddy said.

I walked back to Daddy and slipped my hand into his. I glared at the woman with my face all puckered up in disgust and stuck my nose up in the air. I didn't blink, not one time.

The woman finally tore her eyes away from mine. She lowered her head, nodding it from side to side, grumbling to herself. She lifted the front of her long, stained gypsy-looking skirt and shuffled on back around the corner where she'd come from. The poor messed-up puppies got quiet.

I took a deep breath and my heart took to beating again. "Sorry, Daddy."

He squeezed my hand. "You don't have anything to be sorry about, baby." Then he kissed the top of my head.

—————

The friendly little bell rang above the thick red door when Daddy opened it. The warm, Saturday morning baking smell filled me up and brought my mind back to doughnuts.

Just like the blinking light outside promised, piping-fresh sugar-dusted doughnut holes and beignets filled the glass case. The shop was full of people, but not one of them seemed to be interested in the goodness of fried dough. More than one person said the name Katrina, and I knew right then the talk was about the stupid storm.

Mrs. Louell was standing smack-dab in the middle of the room, preaching to everyone. I ain't trying to be hurtful, but the woman was so large she took up more than her share of the tiny shop.

"Well," Mrs. Louell went on, "alls I'm sayin' is, soon as that storm hits them warm waters in the Gulf—humph. Well, y'all know it ain't gonna be good." One hand was firmly planted on her generous hip and the other one was waving here and there, with the underpart of her arm wobbling like a bowl of brown Jell-O.

"Yup, yup," is all her scrawny, soft-spoken husband said. It was probably the only thing he ever said, what with being around Mrs. Louell and all.

"Y'all best mark my words. We ain't ready for no big hurricane— humph. That's all I'm sayin'—humph." She kept blowing out air like it was helping to make her point. I was bored to death with Mrs. Louell's rantin' and ravin' about that dumb storm.

Daddy and ol' Mr. Leroy were over by the red door in the corner that takes Mr. Pete upstairs to his living area. Mr. Pete's the best-smelling white man I've ever known. He used to live in a real nice butterbean-colored house with his wife, till she died from cancer a few years back. That's when he moved, and started staying above his doughnut shop. Memaw said he was never gonna find him a new wife living up there like that, but I didn't agree. I told her that someday I'd love to marry a man that came with his own built-in doughnut shop.

The corner door creaked open and Mr. Pete hurried through it, tying his blue apron strings behind his back. He stopped to shake Daddy's hand. "Mornin', George. Leroy."

"Good morning. You doing all right, Pete?" Daddy said.

"Oh yeah, you know—just trying to get ready for this storm," Mr. Pete said, and headed my way. "Hey, George, while you're here, go on upstairs and grab one of those tracking charts off my desk. I have plenty. Grab one for Leroy too." He took his place up behind the counter and went to lining up a fresh batch of doughnut holes in perfect straight lines.

"Good morning, Armani," said Mr. Pete.

"Mornin', Mr. Pete." My eyes scanned the doughnut case. Mr. Pete picked up one of the hot sugar-dusted doughnut holes off the counter and offered it to me. I set it on my tongue where it dissolved, barely needing any chewing at all. I closed my eyes. "Mmm . . ."

Mr. Pete chuckled. "What can I get for you, young lady?"

"Well." I looked over my shoulder. Daddy opened the red door in the corner. He seen me looking. He smiled and gave me the *I'll be back in a minute* signal by pointing his finger up in the air. I nodded and smiled back real sweet-like. He ducked so he wouldn't smack his head on the low door frame and he disappeared up the stairs. *Finally.*

I cleared my throat and turned back to the counter. I stood tall on my tippy-toes and said in my best hushed voice, "Actually, Mr. Pete, I'll be needin' two of your apple fritters, please."

—----

Smuggling the dang fritters out of the store and into the truck was only successful because Daddy was so distracted. I was gonna strangle Memaw for making me turn to criminal-type behavior just because she had a sweet tooth. I prayed I'd make it all the way home without the little white bag falling from under my shirt and landing on the truck floor. I got real nervous when I seen that Daddy was going the long way home.

"Why are we goin' this way, Daddy?"

"I need to stop and get gas. It'll just take a minute."

I shifted in my seat, and the bag holding the fritters made a crinkle noise. It sounded like my stomach was made of crumpled newspaper. I froze and held my breath. Sweat left the top of my head and ran down past my ears.

Daddy started whistling some tune that only made sense to him. He smiled and looked sideways at me.

Before he got out of his truck at the gas station, Daddy said, "Armani, why are you hiding your Memaw's apple fritters under your shirt?" He smiled and winked and walked off to pump gas.

I seriously felt my heart stop right then and there.

CHAPTER 4

Memaw was wearing a hole in the front porch, pacing back and forth. She was fussing—close to tears—looking all crazy, like she'd gone and lost her mind. All I could think was how much she must've been wanting them apple fritters. The little white bag felt like a brick wall sitting on top of the big white box of doughnuts on the seat between me and Daddy. If the fritters had caused her to get that worked up, we were gonna have to have a serious talk about the importance of pastries.

Memaw's hands flew up to her cheeks when she seen us pull up. I knew right then from the look in her eyes that whatever was happening, it sure wasn't about no apple fritters. My stomach twisted into a hard knot, and my heart went to pounding in the sides of my head.

Daddy flew out of the truck, leaped up over all four steps, and had Memaw in his arms before I could even get my stupid stuck door open.

"What is it, Mama Jean? What's wrong?"

"Oh, thank the good Lord you're home!" Memaw held a hand to her heart. "It's the baby."

Kheelin.

The ambulance people about knocked me down the porch steps when they ran past me with the oxygen tank. Ever since the twins was born, Kheelin had been sickly and Khayla stayed as healthy as could be. Kheelin had at least twenty asthma attacks a week till the doctor gave Mama the inhaler. That thing was always with Mama, and Mama was never more than a holler away from Kheelin.

I tried to avoid Kheelin, 'cause I was afraid to love him. It seemed he was living with only one foot this side of Heaven. I ain't proud of it, but it was the truth. All that baby boy had to do was sneeze sideways, and my nerves would get set in motion. When he was first born, I wouldn't even hold him. Not that I would've had a chance to even if I'd wanted—not with the way Mama was always fussing over him twenty-four-seven.

Memaw was huddled up in her TV-watching chair with her hand wrapped tight around the silver compass-locket she never took off. A layer of sweat covered her face. Sealy stood beside her.

"Are you okay, Memaw?" Sealy asked, loud enough for everyone in the room to hear. A lady paramedic on her way out the door stopped and looked down at Memaw. "Ma'am, are you feeling all right?"

Memaw forced a smile and nodded her head. "I'm fine, darlin'," she said, waving the lady away. "Don't mind me none. I'm just an old lady who needs a rest, that's all."

The ambulance lady took Memaw's wrist and checked her pulse.

"Is she havin' an asthma attack too?" I asked. Nobody ever told me asthma was contagious.

Memaw pulled her wrist away from the helpful lady and said, "No, indeed. I'm not havin' an *attack* of any kind!" She slapped her hands down—one on each arm of her gold-flowered chair. She planted her feet firm on the floor and stood up, no grunts or nothing. She didn't even take time to let the blood flow down to her toes like usual.

As she strutted past me, Memaw put her hand on my shoulder and whispered, "I'll be in my room if ya need me." She snatched the white bag holding her apple fritters off the edge of the counter where I'd put it. She stuck her nose into the air and disappeared around the corner.

———

My cousin TayTay, whose real name is Quantayvea, came over after the ambulance left. She's been my best friend since the day I was born. She used to live down the road from us, but when her mama—my daddy's stepsister—ran off the year before, TayTay moved across the river to Chalmette to stay with her grandma. Since then, I only got to see her on the weekends when she came to stay with her dad on the south side of the Nines. I didn't like calling him *Uncle* Alvin, on account of the way he treated TayTay. He was always passed out drunk somewhere, leaving his only child to fend for herself. And besides that, he was mean to her—real mean.

TayTay knew when *not* to ask too many questions. I liked that about her. I never did care much for anyone trying to get all up in my business. Like my second cousin, Danisha. That girl was messy, always acting like you was her best friend, then going around talking all kinds of trash about you behind your back.

It was fixin' to be lunchtime, and all us kids were scattered here and there in the living room. Georgie was helping Kheelin build a city out of blocks for his little cars to drive through, but as fast as the boys could stack them, Khayla knocked the blocks down. Georgie pretended to be upset by throwing hisself on the floor in a tizzy fit each time.

After a good while, Memaw came wandering out from her bedroom and sank into her chair. She let out a long, sleepy-sounding sigh.

Mama looked in from the kitchen. "Armani, get Memaw a glass of water."

"Y'all better stop all this fussin' over me! Now, I mean it! If I want a glass of water, I'll get myself a glass of water!" Memaw was known for speaking her mind, but she didn't usually raise her voice like she did just then. She turned the TV on with the clicker but left the volume down.

"We're just worried about you, Mama Jean," Daddy said, walking into the living room. He stood with his arms folded up across his chest.

Memaw let out an aggravated sigh. "Well, all this carin' an' lovin' has plumb tuckered me out." She noticed we were all staring at her. She clapped her hands together so fast and loud that everyone jumped. You would've swore lightning had just gone and struck the house!

Everyone stopped staring, looking anywhere but at Memaw.

"All right then. That's better. Now let's eat some lunch. I'm starvin'."

———

38

Daddy showed us the tracking chart that he'd got from Mr. Pete. He explained that it was a map to help people follow the path of storms.

"When I spoke to Leroy this morning at Pete's, we agreed it's wise to track anything that comes into the Gulf—like Hurricane Katrina."

"Yeah, but it's not comin' here, right, Daddy?" I asked, after swallowing a mouthful of chicken and biscuit.

"Well, according to the latest coordinates, it looks like it's still headed toward Florida." His finger moved slowly through the Gulf of Mexico and into the upper left side of Florida.

"Oh, those poor souls in Florida," Mama said, wiping lunch goo off the twins' faces.

"Better them than us," Georgie piped in.

Mama's hand stopped wiping and her eyes tore into Georgie. "George Joseph Curtis Jr., don't you ever wish harm on others!" Whenever Mama used someone's full name like that, it meant she was mad as a hornet in a pickle jar.

"Sorry, Mama." Georgie sat back in his chair, quiet for a change. If you asked me, that boy needed to grow up and stop acting like such a child.

CHAPTER 5

Daddy was staring for way too long at the cardboard map again.

"Are you gettin' worried about the hurricane, Daddy?" I asked.

"We need to keep an eye on it," Daddy mumbled mostly to hisself. Then he looked up at me and smiled. He folded up the map. "But we'll be fine." He stuck the folded map chart in his back pocket.

"Lord willing," Mama said to no one in particular. She was standing at the sink with Kheelin holding onto her leg.

I started bringing the dirty lunch dishes to the counter by the sink. Daddy came up behind Mama, careful not to step on the baby, and put his arms around her waist. She looked at me and shook her head. A sweet smile lit up her face. Daddy buried his face into her neck. She squirmed a little, and I seen the rose-color creep into her cheeks. But she kept right on washing dishes, and he kept right on nuzzling her neck.

TayTay sat on the kitchen stool with her glass of sweet tea resting on her bottom lip, just grinning with dreamy eyes, like she was watching magic. I smiled inside and out, loving my parents so much right then I could've burst.

Mama cleared her throat and said, "Mr. Curtis, I am trying to wash dishes."

He rested his chin on her shoulder and said, "Mmmhmm."

Mama grinned and shook her head again.

"You know," Daddy said, looking at me but talking into Mama's ear, "we don't have time to worry about that storm. Tomorrow's a big day. Someone I know is making ten, and we're not going to let some storm ruin one of the most important days of the year." *Finally*, Daddy was talking some sense.

He reached in front of Mama and dipped his finger into the soapy dishwater. She playfully slapped the back of his hand, but a clump of bubbles still clung to his finger. He stretched out his arm and put the glob on the tip of my nose. It tickled.

"Daddy," I whined with a giggle.

TayTay quiet-laughed behind me.

Mama grabbed a dry dishtowel and gently wiped the bubbles off my nose. Daddy kissed the top of my head and gave Mama a play-slap on her backside before he left the kitchen.

When I looked down, I seen Kheelin sound asleep, still holding tight to Mama's leg.

———

Me and TayTay grabbed pickles from the giant jar on the counter and went outside. The wind had picked up. We found us a shady spot in the crabgrass, under a peeling crepe myrtle. We tried hard not to move around too much while we finished our pickles, 'cause it was hotter than a jalapeño bathing in Tabasco, and muggy as all get-out. The wind wasn't helping none, neither. It just felt like swirling hot oven air.

I noticed TayTay sitting there doing nothing while I picked through the grass trying to find a four-leaf clover. "Hey, are you okay?"

"Yeah," TayTay shrugged. "Me and my dad had a huge fight." She went to picking at the grass. "I love being around your mama and daddy." She lifted her head, and the wind caught hold of the hair coming loose from her braid. I scooched over behind her and took her braid down so I could fix it.

"Someday I wanna marry someone who looks at me the way your daddy looks at your mama."

"Yeah, I guess," I said, trying to get her uneven ends to stay put up inside the braid. "But sometimes it's embarrassing, y'know?"

She tried to turn her head to look at me, but I nudged her back around to the front so I could finish fixin' her hair.

"So, what did y'all fight about this time?"

She shrugged again. "I don't know. He just yells and screams. He don't need a reason. He could start an argument in an empty house."

"Yeah, he's a mean ol' snake, all right," I said, tapping her shoulder in a way that let her know I was finished messing with her hair.

"And ugly too." TayTay tried to hide a grin behind her hand.

"Yeah, an' his breath smells like armadillo poo!" I said, with real attitude, sliding my head with my chest puffed out.

TayTay threw a handful of grass at me and smiled. She had the prettiest smile out of everyone I knew, and when she smiled like that, it spread all the way to her eyes.

"He's not always like that, you know." TayTay sifted through a clump of clover.

I raised one eyebrow and cocked my head. "Well, he sure is every time I see him."

"Yeah, I know." She shrugged and kept her eyes glued on the clover. "But most times he's normal, you know, when he's not . . ."

"Drunk?" I went on and said the word 'cause I knew she wouldn't.

"Yeah."

"Do you miss livin' with your mama?"

TayTay lifted her head and looked me straight on. "No."

We'd never ever talked about any of her family business before, and I was trying to think of a good way to change the subject so it didn't look like I was meddlin'. But the truth was, I wanted to understand why my cousin was always sitting wrapped up in all that sad.

Right then, she got a little smile on her face and shook her head. "I remember one time when they had a fight about somethin' stupid, and Mama threw a whole super-sized order of french fries at my dad." She gazed off into the air, and the wind blew that same chunk of hair loose again. She smiled big and looked at me. "I'll never forget that—seein' all them fries flying through the air like that." She reached up and tried to tuck the loose hair behind her ear, but it was too short and wouldn't stay put. "Girl, it was like the sky opened up and let loose french fries!" She let out a quiet laugh. "It was crazy all right." She was back to picking through clover. Without looking up she said, "I remember Mama slapping me hard, just 'cause I ate a couple fries off the floor."

I ain't trying to be hurtful, but I'd seen the inside of TayTay's house when her mama was still staying there. I got a picture in my head of my cousin eating food off them disgusting floors. "Girl, that is *nasty!* You ate *fries off the floor?*"

"Yeah, but I was a little kid, you know? Don't tell nobody." We looked at each other in a way only real friends know how, and we knew I'd never tell.

We went to picking through the clover some more. "Mama was the mean one," TayTay said, right out of nowhere.

"She was?" I barely got the words out. TayTay never talked about her mama—never.

"Yeah," she said. "Lots of people think it's 'cause of my daddy that she left, but it's not. Mama left 'cause she wanted to, plain an' simple. *She* was the mean one, Armani. She turned my daddy mean."

I wanted to hug her and tell her I was sorry that anyone would ever be mean to her. But I kept looking at clover and crabgrass instead. I swiped at the beginnings of a tear in my eye.

TayTay let out a long sigh. "I wish he'd find someone like Auntie Katherine. It'd be nice to have a new mama."

"Yeah," I said, "but it would have to be someone who don't mind kissin' a man with poo-breath."

TayTay tried to hide her smile, but it spread too big.

"And if your daddy an' his new wife had a baby . . ."

"Oh my gosh, Armani! Look, a four-leaf clover!" Sure enough, the girl was holding a big ol' four-leaf clover. I could barely believe my own eyes.

TayTay looked all cross-eyed at the little green plant. "That's exactly what I'm gonna wish for—a new mama and a brother or sister!"

I sat smiling and nodded, not having a clue how to tell my cousin that a clover ain't for making wishes. Everybody on the planet knew a four-leaf clover is for bringing good luck.

The screen door screeched open and Georgie popped his head out. "Hey, TayTay, your daddy just called. He says you need to come home." His fat head disappeared and the screen door slapped shut.

TayTay's smile slid off her face. *So much for luck.* She sighed and got up real slow, brushing herself off.

"TayTay," I said in a deep, silly voice, "Poophead called an' wants you home." I fell out laughing.

She shoved a handful of grass and clovers down the back of my shirt and took off running for the screen door, laughing the whole way.

———

Memaw came huffing into the kitchen. Mama was braiding Sealy's hair and I was washing more dishes. Mama had braided mine earlier and it was so tight my whole head throbbed. I could barely blink my eyes.

"Katherine, I've got a bad feelin' about this storm." Memaw picked up a towel and started drying the clean dishes. She looked over at me, covered all of her face with the towel except her eyes, and gave me a secret wink. I smiled, shook my head, and went back to scrubbing something dried and stuck on a sippy cup.

"Mama Jean, I think you're just worrying too much," Mama said. "The last weather report has the hurricane going east of here. Mr. Curtis says we'll probably get some wind, and Lord knows we need the rain." I knew why my mama called *her* mama Mama Jean—it was so us kids wouldn't get all confused with too many mamas in the house. But I never did understand why she called Daddy Mr. Curtis, like they weren't married or something.

"Well, I know what those fancy folks on the television are predicting, but I'm tellin' you what my *bones* are sayin'! I have a bad feelin'." Memaw set her dishtowel down and turned in a huff to face Mama.

I got a good look at her. I knew that look on Memaw's face. She was worried.

I stopped scrubbing.

Mama shook her head with a smile and kept on braiding. So I shook my head too, and went back to washing and scrubbing.

———

After supper, me and Daddy were sitting outside on the front porch steps when ol' Mr. Scott from down the road came over and told Daddy that the store was running out of water and we'd best hurry up and get some before it was gone.

After the man wandered off to go inform someone else about the disappearing water, I asked Daddy how come people were buying water when all they had to do was go to the faucet where, it seemed to me, there was plenty of water.

He took a deep breath, "We need to be prepared, Armani. Mother Nature can be unpredictable."

"But Daddy, I thought you said that storm ain't comin' here."

He looked up at the dusky sky for a minute, and I seen worry pass over his face like a dark cloud causing a shadow. Then he smiled his handsome smile and bumped his shoulder into mine. "We're going to be fine, Armani."

I giggled and shoulder-bumped him back. He looked at me with his milk-chocolate-colored eyes and shook his head real slow. "I can't believe my little girl is having another birthday already."

"I'm not little, Daddy. I'm fixin' to be ten." I wished he would real-ize I was practically grown and *not* a little kid no more.

"You're growing up, all right." He put his arm around my shoulder and pulled me in close for a big bear hug. "Too fast, if you ask me." It was one of them cozy hugs that last a long time.

"I love you, Daddy."

"I love you too, Armani. Now, stop worrying about that storm. Let your Memaw do the worrying. She worries enough for all of us."

"I'm not worried, Daddy."

"Good," he said, and stood up. He grabbed hold of my hand, help-ing me to my feet. "Now run along and tell your mama I'll meet her at the truck."

"Yes, sir." I headed for inside when Daddy called my name.

"Armani, you'll always be my little girl, you know." He winked and walked off to his truck.

I folded my arms up across my chest and stomped off to go find Mama.

CHAPTER 6

A hot breeze swirled through the air, strong enough to blow some Spanish moss off the neighbor's huge oak tree. It plopped right down on top of me and Memaw's bare feet that were pushing off the concrete, keeping the chair to swinging.

The moss was nasty and tickled. I kicked my feet in a hurry to get the stuff off me before a spider or some other creepy-crawly creature ran up my leg. Memaw didn't seem to care one way or the other that the spaghetti-looking weed had made itself comfortable sitting on top of her foot.

I laid my head on Memaw's shoulder and stared at the pillowy white clouds scooting across the blue-green sky, trying my best to ignore the kids running around the yard like fools.

"Memaw, can I ask you somethin'?"

"What's weighin' on your mind, baby?" She fanned herself with a flyer from the Pentecostals who'd come knocking earlier trying to sell us Jesus, not realizing we already had Him.

"Well, TayTay says that her daddy used to be nice before her mama turned him mean."

"Uh-huh."

"Well, is that true?" I raised my head up off her shoulder.

She reached up and pushed my head back down. "Alvin Brown was a good boy till the devil's juice took hold of him."

"Yeah, but is it true that TayTay's mama was mean?"

The slap of Memaw's hand on the arm of the swing cut me off. She looked at the palm of her hand before wiping the bug guts on the bottom part of her housedress.

She stared at me over the top of her glasses, her eyebrows coming together in a perfect letter V in the center of all them wrinkles. "I'm gonna say this, and then I'm done."

I sat on the edge of my seat.

A big ol' clump of Spanish moss landed up on top of Memaw's head. It took a scat up there like a cheap wig fell right out of the beauty shop in the sky.

Georgie went to hollerin' and pointed a finger at Memaw. "Look at Memaw, y'all!" The boy was so full of stupid, it wouldn't have surprised me none if he went and passed out just from being so full of it.

Sealy and Khayla were laughing and hopping and hopping and laughing. Memaw brushed a couple of the scraggly pieces of moss hanging in her eyes off to the side like she was adjusting her hairdo.

I stood up too fast and the swing went crooked, forcing Memaw to plant her feet down on the concrete.

"What is wrong with all of y'all?" I screamed and stomped my foot down. Both of my hands were knotted up in fists. "I am trying to have a grown-up conversation with my own Memaw, and you're so pea-brained, Georgie!"

My brother was laughing harder than ever. I wanted to march over there and knock some sense into him. My sisters were acting about as simple as their big brother. "Y'all are so . . . so . . . *immature.*"

I whipped around to face Memaw. She sat there blowing poofs of air out of the side of her mouth, making the stringy moss flop up, then settle back down in front of her eyes again.

"Do you like my hairdo?" Memaw couldn't keep a straight face.

"I like it, Memaw," Georgie hollered from across the yard.

"Me too," giggled Sealy.

"Me too," said Khayla.

Memaw looked at me with her bottom lip forced out in a pout. I rolled my eyes and curled up my lip. She blew out another loud poof and the moss-hair flew up again. It *was* funny the way she sat there with the gross clump on her head. I couldn't keep from smiling no more.

Memaw smiled with me and started pulling the mess of moss off her head. I helped her. I threw a handful of it into the air when the wind caught hold of it. The moss sailed up toward the roof and settled there. "This is nasty, Memaw."

"Yes, indeed," she said. I picked the last few strands of muck out of her hair. She reached up with her hand and refluffed her real hair till it looked normal. "Come sit back down," Memaw said, tapping the seat beside her where Kheelin's name was carved in the wood.

"I want to sit with you too, Memaw." Sealy came butting right in, like always. Memaw scooched over and made room.

Memaw leaned in close to my ear and whispered, "We'll talk about your cousin's mama later." She rubbed my leg and pushed off with her feet, sending the chair into a swing. I let out a loud sigh. Memaw pushed Sealy's head down onto her other shoulder and went to waving her fan again. *Whatever.* Sometimes I hated having brothers and sisters.

I took my finger and traced the letters of my dead Uncle Shelton's name carved into the arm of the swing. S-H-E-L . . .

"How many hurricanes have you been in, Memaw?"

Sealy and her stupid questions.

"Oh, my, more than I care to remember."

"Really?" Sealy sat up and faced Memaw. "What's it like?"

I kept on tracing the letters, but I put my focus on my ears.

"Well, every storm is different," Memaw said. "They've all got their own personality, I guess you could say. Some aren't so bad: Ya get some rain, some wind—might even lose electricity. And others, well, others you just get down on your knees and thank the good Lord ya came out on the other side alive." Memaw had that faraway look in her eyes. Her body somehow got heavier on the swing.

"What kinda storm do you suppose Katrina's gonna be?" I asked. "You figure it'll be one of them get-down-on-your-knees storms?"

Memaw planted her feet so fast I had to grab hold of the arm of the chair to keep from flying out and landing on my head. "Child, don't you even *think* that!" Memaw looked straight into my eyes with her face all ugly-scrunched. She squeezed her eyes shut, mumbled some words to the Lord, took in a big suck of air, and pushed it out with such force it caused her lips to vibrate.

Then, just as quick as ice melts in August, she settled back in the chair. The fan went back to fanning, and her face smoothed out. She gave the concrete a nudge and we went to swinging again.

Memaw pushed my head down on her shoulder, forgetting to be gentle about it, and patted my leg. "We're gonna be fine. Yes, indeed. We're gonna be just fine." I blinked about fifty times and breathed in some of that thick, muggy air.

———

After Mama and Daddy got back from the store, the sky felt alive. It had turned a dark, pink-orangey-brown color. It was pretty, but I got to thinking how I ain't never seen that color painted across the sky before. It was like God was right on the other side of them colors. I shivered.

———

Looking at the black of the night through my bedroom window made me worry about what might be out there that I *couldn't* see. Usually I don't like sharing the bed with Sealy, but right then, I was grateful to have the feel of her up next to me.

I was all but sound asleep when Sealy threw back the sheet, hopped out of bed, and grabbed her book sack off the stack of stuffed animals piled in the corner. She opened the sack, looked inside, zipped it up, put it on her back, then jumped back into bed.

"Sealy, what are you doin'?" I yelled in a whisper.

"Nothing, Armani, go to sleep."

"What do you mean *nothing*? You can't be bringin' that ol' dirty bag of yours in my bed!" I started pulling back the sheet to make it easier for her to get up. But Sealy wasn't moving.

"First of all, my book sack isn't dirty, Armani. And, second, it's my bed too. Just go to sleep."

Sealy must've bumped her head. She took that bag with her everywhere, but she sure never brought it to bed. "As long as it don't come on my side. You hear me, Sealy?"

Sealy made a huge yawn sound, "Yes, I hear you. Good night, Armani. I love you."

"Yeah, whatever." I flopped to the left, then flopped to the right, trying to find a comfortable position, making sure Sealy knew that dumb bag was making the whole bed uncomfortable. It didn't work, though, 'cause she fell asleep faster than Mama could fry an egg and I was left wide awake, listening to the sounds that were bringing in the storm.

I tried to force my brain to think about my party and what I might be getting for a present. But all I could do was think about the colors in the sky. Daddy buying water. The scrunched-up worried look on Memaw's face. Sealy sleeping with her stupid book sack.

The Babineauxes evacuating.

CHAPTER 7
Sunday, August 28, 2005 - 8:18 A.M.

It was finally my birthday morning.

I ain't lying when I say my feelings were hurt when I realized Memaw didn't even seem to notice. But then I seen that Memaw wasn't noticing much of nothing. She acted like whatever the triflin' weather people were blabbing about was more important than acknowledging the fact that it was my birthday morning.

Instead of fussin' about whatever Memaw was fussin' over, I went for breakfast—my first meal being ten.

Sometime after breakfast, Memaw asked if she could talk to Mama and Daddy in private. Every time she did that, us kids knew something was wrong. What I couldn't understand was why they thought we weren't gonna be able to hear them, just 'cause they walked off to the kitchen. There wasn't nothin' but a corner separating the two rooms. They acted like the kitchen was some kind of soundproof room or something.

So when Memaw told them they should consider canceling my party, I heard her plain as day. I flew around the corner and slid into the kitchen the second the crazy words came out of her mouth.

"Oh, please, *please* don't cancel my party!"

"Armani, this discussion doesn't concern you." Daddy didn't sound normal.

"Of course it does, Daddy. It's *my* birthday! I don't understand why . . ."

Memaw walked over, took hold of my hand, and pressed it to her chest. "NeeNee, there's a *terrible* storm comin'." She hadn't called me by my baby name in a long while, and right then, I didn't much like it. I pulled my hand loose from hers.

"But Memaw, Mama made my cake, and Daddy said we could do the Slip'n Slide. And, and . . ."

"That's enough, Armani. Take the twins and go on outside." Daddy pulled off his glasses, squeezed his eyes shut, and pinched the top of his nose. My brain knew it was time to shut up, but the message didn't make it to my mouth.

"But . . ."

Daddy slapped his hand down on the gym-floor supper table, catching me so off guard I jerked backward. My eyes went to blinking. Mama's hands flew up to her mouth and Memaw turned away altogether and stared out the window up over the kitchen sink.

"I'm sorry," Daddy said in a tired voice. "Just get your brothers and sisters and go outside." He finally looked at me. His sagging eyes matched his voice.

"Yes, sir." I rolled my eyes and let out a heavy sigh.

I stopped before going all the way around the corner to the living room. I turned and looked at the three people who could ruin my day if they saw fit to do it. I didn't say a word, but I sure did give them the most pitiful pout I could get my face to make. My shoulders were all rolled forward and my arms just dangled there, hanging as low as they could go.

Slow as a slug, I made my way to the next room, never taking my droopy eyes off Mama and Daddy and my troublemaking Memaw's back.

———

I sat on the swing, flicking paint chips, and watched Khayla and Kheelin try to keep up with Georgie and Sealy while they all ran around like fools, chasing leaves that were blowing off the trees. The whole while, I was thinking that this was turning into the worst birthday ever. Didn't anyone understand the importance of what day it was?

Everything was headed in the right direction when Mama made me birthday biscuits for breakfast, and Sealy woke up singin', "It's your birthday, it's your birthday!" over and over again. But, just 'cause of some annoying storm, everyone wanted to go half-stupid and cancel my party. I hated Hurricane Katrina. I didn't care where the idiot storm went. People can't just go around canceling other people's birthdays.

I was fixin' to go back inside to point these things out to Daddy when he opened the screen door. As soon as the twins seen him, they ran to him with their pudgy arms reaching for the sky. He scooped one twin up in each arm, giving each of them a raspberry on the fat part of their necks. I pretended like I wasn't dying on the inside to know if I was still having my party or what.

Daddy sat down on the swing beside me. I scooched the tiniest bit away from him. The twins slid down off Daddy's lap and went back to running about.

"Today's important to all of us, Armani." I let myself look over at him. "We're going to have your party."

"Oh, Daddy! Thank you!" I threw my arms around him the best I could from a sit, smiling as big as my mouth would go. Relief spread through me from my head to my toes.

"Let me finish, Armani." *Uh-oh.* I settled back on the seat. A big chunk of the happy I was feeling fell like concrete to the bottom of my stomach. I had to fight the urge to cover my ears to block out whatever he was fixin' to say.

"Your mama's on the phone calling your friends. We've decided that it'd be best for them to stay home."

"Stay home?" There went my head—throbbing again. "But why, Daddy?" The answer popped in my head. "It's because of Memaw, ain't it?" I was so mad at her! I had never in my life been mad at Memaw, and I didn't like how it felt. It reminded me of how my stomach gets all tangled up and twisted right before I puke.

"You watch your tone, miss, or there won't be a party at all. And stop saying 'ain't.'" Now Daddy was mad at *me.* "It's my decision, Armani, so if you want to be mad at someone, be mad at me."

"But, Daddy, seriously, it ain't—I mean—it's *not* gonna be a real party without my friends. I don't understand." Mama's wind chime was just a-clanging around. We both turned and looked at it.

Daddy stood up. He took a long, deep breath and pushed it out slow. "The hurricane's changed its course, Armani. It's coming closer to Louisiana now." Daddy walked over and took Mama's chime down.

"What does that mean? Is it coming here? But . . . you said we didn't need to worry." Some of my mad blew away with the wind when I seen the way Daddy flinched when the words came flying out of my mouth.

"It means that we'll definitely be getting some bad weather." He paused and glanced up at the swirly sky. He sat back down beside me. I scooched closer to him. "It would be irresponsible for us to have your friends over when the weather's so unpredictable." He put a hand on my bouncy knee. "Uncle T-Bone's still coming, and of course TayTay will be here." He gave my knee a ticklish little squeeze. I swiped at his hand and bit my bottom lip, holding in my smile.

He stood up and brushed teeny bits of white chips off the back of his faded jeans. "Your mama's right. I need to paint this old chair." He stole another look up at the busy sky. "Don't waste too much time out here pouting. It sure doesn't make a whole lot of sense to waste a minute of your birthday being mad about something we can't control."

He hollered for the twins. They came hopping over. Daddy scooped them up, but didn't let out his usual big ol' belly laugh. Khayla and Kheelin giggled most likely 'cause they were too little to see what I wasn't seeing in my daddy's normally happy eyes.

I watched them all go inside, leaving me there with myself. I tilted my head back and stared up at the sky. I couldn't remember a time when I'd seen the clouds move so fast.

The hurricane was coming closer. Stupid storm. I considered the possibility of running inside to tell Daddy about what Mr. Babineaux had said. I decided right then that I'd tell Daddy as soon as my party was over.

———

"Happy birthday, Armani!" TayTay held the giant pickle she was nibbling on up in the air and gave me a one-armed hug. I wondered if she could feel the light-green juice running down her arm. She flashed me her famous smile, letting me know that she didn't care one bit about whatever might be running into her armpit.

I looked over where Daddy was standing at the big black burner and cooking pot. Him and Uncle T-Bone and Georgie were all standing around, watching steam rise. It never did make no sense to me that some people like to stand and watch food cook. Uncle T-Bone's newest girlfriend was off by herself, smoking near the bushes.

"Uncle T-Bone looks happy," TayTay said, pointing over that way with what was left of her pickle.

"Yeah, I guess." I watched my uncle and the way he was grinning from ear to ear, just a-flashing that shiny gold tooth of his all over the place. TayTay was right—it was good to see him happy. After he first got back from Afghanistan, he was acting messed-up in his head. Memaw said that being in a war and seeing people die like that can make a person completely lose their mind. Lucky for us, that didn't happen to Uncle T-Bone—he just lost his mind for a little while.

Course, I thought he'd lost it again when he went and hooked up with Miss Shug.

Just looking at the way she stood there in her stupid, huge, floppy tangerine hat got on my nerves. "Ugh, I can barely even look at that woman," I said, and turned away.

"I like her," TayTay said.

"Who?"

"Miss Shug. I think she's pretty." TayTay had lost her mind.

"Tay—*seriously?* Miss *Shug* ain't even her real name. Uncle T-Bone says we gotta call her that 'cause she's so sweet—like a big spoon of sugar." I pretended to stick my finger down my throat. "There ain't no one that sweet." I curled up my lip and stole a look back over there at the woman and her fake laugh. "Whatever. I think she's gross and her hats are obnoxious."

"Girl, you need to stop." TayTay smiled and shook her head from side to side, licking her pickle fingers. "Don't be so mean."

"Mean? I ain't mean, I'm just keepin' it real. I know one thing: You ain't gonna catch me calling her *Shug* or *Sugar*. I'm calling her Miss. That's it, just plain ol' Miss."

"You're so funny, Cuz," she said. "Oh, I almost forgot to tell you. Last weekend me and my dad were driving by the church, and there was Georgie standin' outside Uncle T-Bone's, practically up in the bushes, staring in the window."

"For real? Are you serious?"

"Yep. But why? I mean, what's the point in lookin' in Uncle T-Bone's window?"

A tree somewhere made a cracking sound. I seen Daddy turn and look over his shoulder.

I kept my eyes on Daddy. "I'll tell ya why—'cause Miss walks around that house with no clothes on all day, an' Georgie's so desperate, he's gotta sneak peeks when he can."

TayTay busted out laughing.

Georgie must've heard me say his name 'cause his head whipped around and he looked at me with a big question mark all but painted on his face. I gave him a whatcha-lookin'-at stare and hoped he hadn't heard us talking about him.

Uncle T-Bone and Miss lived six blocks over, right next door to our church. Wasn't none of my business, but it sure did seem to me that if you lived right next to the very place where you worshiped, you should at least put all your clothes on before you went walking in front of big ol' windows.

"Hey," I tried to whisper, "I wonder if she wears her tangerine hat when she does her naked walkin'."

TayTay went to laughing again and a cloud of pickle breath flew up my nose.

"I'm glad you're here, Tay," I said, holding my hand up under my nose.

"I'm surprised I got to come. My dad almost didn't let me."

"What's wrong with everybody? They act like the end of the world's comin' or somethin'."

We walked over to where Mama had laid out some Zapp's potato chips and Jell-O squares. And pickles. There was a whole lot more food than there was people. TayTay was loading up a plate with chips when Miss headed our way.

Me and Memaw rolled our eyes at the same time when Miss walked by, just a-swaying her apple booty and fanning her over-painted face with a tangerine-colored clutch purse. The woman smiled all fake-like and twirled the ends of her cheap-looking too-long-to-be-real slick black weave. She grabbed a pickle between two tangerine-painted claws.

I covered my mouth and turned my head quick before the laugh flew out in a disrespectful way. TayTay grabbed me by the arm and pulled me out into the yard. Mama shot me a look that told me I might not be acting my age. I couldn't help it. Just knowing that the next time my poor uncle tried to get him some sugar, all he was gonna get was pickle vinegar, had me all but rolling in the grass.

Memaw swatted me upside the head with her Pentecostal fan and winked when she walked by on her way inside to check the latest update on the weather station again. I smiled to myself knowin' I couldn't stay mad at my Memaw—not with her swatting me like that and all.

— — — —

The little kids were runnin' and slippin' and slidin' all over the backyard. Over summer break, me and Sealy seen one of them Slip'n Slide commercials on TV. The next day, Daddy had made us one in our backyard. Course, ours wasn't yellow like the one we seen on TV.

Ours was dark green, and a lot bigger than the lame yellow one. Mama told Daddy, "Mr. Curtis, I don't want those trash bags all over my backyard!"

All I know is, when Daddy turned the hosepipe on full blast, ours was the slipperiest slide ever!

"Armani, look," TayTay said. "Uncle T-Bone's fixin' to take a slide!" He was always acting like one of the kids—well, since he'd started being happy again. Every time he smiled, that shiny gold tooth flashed for everyone to see. He was handsome, my Uncle T-Bone was.

Me and TayTay were headed over to do some sliding ourselves when I overheard Georgie ask, "When are you gonna give it to her, Daddy? It can't stay in that box much longer."

Daddy seen me looking. He smiled. Something good was fixin' to happen—I could feel it. Daddy whispered in Georgie's ear. Georgie took off running for the house with a big sloppy grin on his face. He stopped to whisper in Mama's ear. Whatever he said to her made her look over at me, then she started smiling too.

I was bouncing on my tippy-toes. Georgie ran in the house, letting the screen door slap him in the butt. Mama whispered in Memaw's ear.

When my brother came back outside, he was holding the shoe box that my new school shoes had come in. He walked fast over to Daddy and handed him the box.

"Y'all, come see! We're gonna give Armani her birthday present!" Georgie jumped up and down like some kind of fool.

I walked across the yard to where Daddy was standing. We never, not one time, stopped looking at each other. Daddy stood straight and tall with the biggest, most happiest smile in the whole world. Right then, I knew he had to be the most handsome daddy in all of Louisiana.

"Happy birthday, Armani," he said. He hugged me and handed me the present.

As soon as he put that box in my hands, the top popped off! I was so surprised, I about fell over backward. Everyone clapped and took to laughing. Poking out of that tiny box was the cutest thing I'd ever seen.

"A puppy! Oh, Daddy, it's a puppy!" The box fell from my hands when the puppy jumped up on my shoulder and started licking my face. She licked and licked like I was a big ol' chicken bone. Her stubby little tail thumped up against my heart. I loved her already.

"Thank you, Daddy!"

Mama cleared her throat behind me. "Last time I checked, you had *two* parents, Armani," she said, with her head turned to the side. I could tell she was pretending to be put out, 'cause she had a smile up in her eyes.

I ran over and thanked Mama too. "Oh, Mama, ain't she just the cutest thing you've ever seen?" That little puppy was wagging and smiling at everybody.

Memaw patted the puppy on the head. "This dog looks just like a little black cricket, with those beady eyes and long whiskers."

"Memaw, that's a great name!" I said. "Hello, Cricket. Welcome to the Curtis family." I buried my face in her soft black fur and made a silent promise to her that I'd always love her and keep her safe.

CHAPTER 8

"I wanna see puppy, Ah-mani," Kheelin said.

"Her name's Cricket." I sat the puppy down on the ground and she went to Kheelin right away. She sniffed his little pudgy, barefoot toes, then came running back to me. Cricket ran to each person and sniffed, every time coming to me afterward like she needed to make sure I was still there.

Everyone was laughing, and I was having the best birthday ever.

Out of nowhere, a small dead tree branch flew right in front of my face. If I wouldn't have ducked when I did, that splintered branch would've hit me right upside my head.

That's when I first noticed how hard the wind was blowing. The same trees that had been swaying and bringing me comfort the day before were looking like giant, dancing, house-crushing monsters. Pin prickles spread across the back of my neck.

"Goodness gracious," Memaw said. "Katherine, I think we should take these children inside."

Mama looked up at the sky. "Mr. Curtis," she said, never taking her eyes off the changing sky, "how much longer until that jambalaya's done?"

Before Daddy could answer, a paper plate full of chips flew off the table and danced across the yard, getting lost up in Mama's grapevine.

Just then, Danisha and Bugger's gonna-be-stepdaddy, Mr. Charlie, came running into the yard, breathing like he'd run all the way from Mississippi.

I scooped up Cricket.

"T-Bone!" Mr. Charlie hollered. He ran over to where Uncle T-Bone was stirring the jambalaya pot.

"Hey man, what's up?" my uncle said.

Mr. Charlie looked around the yard at all of us.

"Don't y'all know what's goin' on out there?" He pointed with his thumb toward our fence. Spit flew out of his mouth every time he said something. His eyes got narrow, like little slits, and he started shaking his head back and forth.

"Charlie, calm down," Daddy said, stepping closer to the man.

Mama walked over with Kheelin planted on her hip. "Are you hungry, Charlie? Armani, get Mr. Charlie a plate."

Mr. Charlie mumbled, "No, ma'am, I won't be stayin'." He kept fidgeting with the dirty ball cap on his head. "I need to get on back to my place. They're all waitin' on me so we can head out." He turned away from Mama and looked real hard at Daddy and Uncle T-Bone.

I scooched all quiet to the other side of the big tree.

"Ain't y'all got no sense?" Mr. Charlie whisper-spit at Daddy, looking over his shoulder at us kids. In a lower, not so spitty voice, he said, "Look, man, I ain't tryin' to scare y'all, but the mayor's tellin' everyone to get out of N'awlins. Ain't y'all been watchin' the news?"

Like the weather was trying to help make the man's point, the wind gushed through the yard, causing half our slide to blow and flap and make slapping sounds. I held Cricket a little tighter.

Out of the corner of my eye, I seen Memaw and Mama gathering up the little ones and shooin' them inside. Miss was standing off by herself, smoking a cigarette, trying to hold on to her tangerine hat.

TayTay turned off the hosepipe and stood over by the screen door. She waved her hand for me to come on. I gave her the *I'll-be-there-in-a-minute* signal. Little Cricket's nose was all snuggled up against me.

Daddy took hold of Mr. Charlie's elbow and led him to the other side of the jambalaya pot. I put all my focus on my ears.

"Slow down, Charlie, and tell me what's happening." Daddy's voice was calm, but his words came out in a hurry.

Mr. Charlie took a deep breath. "About an hour ago, Mayor Nagin came on the TV and ordered an evacuation of the entire city."

My stomach twitched and tightened up. I seen Georgie. I could tell by the way his mouth was hanging open that he'd heard the *evacuation* word too.

"They're tellin' everyone to leave. The hurricane's a *cat five*, bro! Y'all best get them kids outta the Nines. There ain't much time!" Mr. Charlie was talking fast and spit was flying all over the place. I could barely keep up. Something bad was happening—something really bad.

"*Category five?*" Daddy asked. "Are you sure, Charlie? A category five would wipe New Orleans off the map!"

I started to breathe faster. The trees started to bend further.

"Man," Uncle T-Bone said, shaking his head from side to side. "This happens every time! They tell us it's gonna be the big one and it turns out to be nothin' but a storm. It don't do nothin' but cause con-fusion, and cost money I ain't got. You know what I'm sayin'?"

I felt a tug on the back of my shirt. Sealy was standing there behind me. The girl was wearing a bathing suit with that silly book sack strapped to her back.

Her whole body was shivering, and her teeth were chattering, even though it was about two hundred degrees outside. I wanted to yell at her to get on in the house with Mama, but I didn't want Daddy to know I was listening in on his conversation. I took hold of her hand instead.

Uncle T-Bone put his head down and walked in a tight circle, kick-ing at the ground. He stopped and looked at Mr. Charlie. "E-vac-u-a-tion. You mean to tell me they expect *everybody* to evacuate the city? You gotta be kiddin' me. I'm so sick of this bureaucratic crap, man." He went back to walking in the tiny circle, the whole time shaking his head and kicking grass.

I gave Sealy's hand a squeeze and snuggled Cricket up under my chin.

"That's what I'm sayin', T," Mr. Charlie said. "It don't look good, man. I'm serious, y'all need to get them kids somewheres safe."

"I can't." Daddy was rubbing his head with his eyes squeezed shut. "I don't have room for Katherine and all the kids in my truck. And I've got Mama Jean to think about."

"Look, man," Uncle T-Bone said. "We can load up my car too. You know I ain't gonna leave you hangin', bro."

"T-Bone, George—look, y'all don't understand." Mr. Charlie shook his head. "The mayor can say 'Leave N'awlins' all he wants. Y'all won't never get out of the city now. It's too late." The man sounded pitiful, standing there, shaking his big ol' hanging head, talking in circles, looking at the ground.

Daddy nudged Mr. Charlie's head up real gentle-like, so he could see the man's face. "Charlie, what do you mean, it's too late?"

"There ain't no leavin' N'awlins, George. Nobody can get outta the city. Not nobody. Ever since the mayor ordered the evacuation, there ain't nothin' but wall-to-wall cars on the interstate." The longer Mr. Charlie talked, the higher his voice got. "I talked to a buddy of mine from Gentilly 'bout thirty minutes ago. He left at ten o'clock this mornin' an' sat still so long, he 'bout ran outta gas. The interstate's deadlocked, man. He turned his car around an' came back. The only ones who made it out is the ones who left yesterday. The smart ones left Friday."

A gasp came from the bushes. There was Georgie with his hand over his mouth and his eyes all bugged out. I knew he was thinking about the Babineauxes by the way he looked at me. My heartbeat was pounding up in my head.

No one said a word. Daddy stared up where the dark clouds raced across the sky.

"They waited too long to tell us this time," Mr. Charlie said, and let out a long sigh.

"Why did you say you're leaving, Charlie, if no one can leave?" Daddy sounded tired.

"Oh, I'm leavin' all right. I ain't gonna be caught with my pants down. I'm takin' my ol' lady an' the kids an' gettin' somewhere safe while I can. We ain't stayin' down here in the Lower Nines, man. Do y'all know what's gonna happen if them levees break?"

Daddy cleared his throat. His eyes were heavy. "I still don't under-stand where you're going."

"To the Super Dome, bro!" Lots of spit went flying. "They're call-ing it the Refuge of Last Resort. Can you believe that?" He nervous-laughed. "Radio says anyone who can't get outta the city can come hang out there till the storm passes. My ol' lady packed us some food an' drinks. She figured it'd be best to stay at the Dome, ya know—just to be safe—with the kids an' all." Mr. Charlie shook Daddy's hand. "Look, man, I best be goin'."

He gave Uncle T-Bone a handshake-hug and patted him on the back. "Don't stay here, T. It ain't gonna be good, man. Seriously. Go to the Dome." Then the man left as quick as he'd come.

Nobody moved or said a word. We all stayed put, pondering on what Mr. Charlie had just said.

The ol' screen door slammed shut. Khayla hurried into the yard, all but tripping over her own clumsy feet. "The lights runned out, Daddy! The lights runned out!"

"Oh, no," Daddy said. "I think we just lost power."

CHAPTER 9

It didn't take but a minute for it to get so hot and thick and sticky up inside the house, the floors were even sweating.

Georgie kept pestering Mama for one of the bottles of water stacked across the table, but Mama said no, they was for later—for *just in case*. So we were all stuck sipping on boring faucet water and the sweet tea, but it didn't taste right without ice. Mama wasn't letting nobody open the fridge for nothing, 'cause we'd let out all the cold air. I guess we were saving that for just in case too.

The wind was banging the screen door like a drum while Daddy told us how he remembered having hurricane parties when he was a kid.

The uneasy feeling up inside me was as constant as the sounds of slapping and creaking in the air.

Georgie announced that Mama was fixin' to bring out my birthday cake. Everybody gathered in the living room. Sealy giggled and ran over to switch the lights off. The surprised look on her face when she remembered there wasn't no power made us all laugh.

I set Cricket in her shoe box bed, and she went right to sleep. I stood with my hands folded behind my back, bouncing on my tippy-toes.

Mama came into the room carrying my cake. She looked extra pretty, smiling big behind the glow of my ten birthday candles. She was wearing a new lime-green colored dress that she'd made special just for my party. The color of the dress showed off the flecks of gold in her eyes.

Mama real careful placed my beautiful double-decker birthday cake right on top of the two milk crates stacked in the middle of the living room. I don't much care for pink and other foo-foo colors, so Mama decorated my cake with buttermilk icing in every shade of blue under the sun. It was more beautiful than anything that had ever come out of my mama's kitchen. I was glowing right along with all them candles.

"Happy birthday to you, happy birthday to you . . ." I stood next to the flickering candlelight and looked at all the people I loved—even Georgie—singing loud and happy as they could *for me*.

Kheelin was walking in a slow circle, doing his best to sing the birthday song. Khayla was still eating jambalaya. Poor thing was trying her best, but the rice fell off her spoon every time she lifted it to her mouth. The sight of it made me giggle.

Sealy was sitting on Daddy's lap, swinging her legs to the beat of the song—the two of them grinning like possums. Out the big window behind them, the trees were even dancing to the rhythm of my birthday song.

Miss rested her oversized backside on Uncle T-Bone's skinny knee. He sat in one of the metal folding chairs, just a-flashing that silly gold tooth, trying to watch the presentation of my birthday cake over the top of his girlfriend's gigantic tangerine hat. Georgie stood as close as he could to Miss without actually touching her, his usual goofy grin stretched across his face.

Mama looked at me with eyes soft and sweet as butter and her cheeks full of rose color. She had her arms around TayTay's shoulders. It might've been 'cause of the way things looked in the warm candle-light, or maybe it was her happy shining through. Either way, TayTay looked extra beautiful sitting there wrapped in Mama's love.

Cricket had tipped out of her box and was running full speed off in the corner, chasing her own fuzzy black tail. Even my sweet puppy was celebrating.

Then I seen Memaw. She was smiling from ear to ear, singing the birthday song louder than everyone, holding up the *I love you* sign. I smiled and gave her the sign back. My heart all but exploded with all the love I was feeling.

The song ended. I squeezed my eyes shut and made my secret birthday wish. I used my wish on TayTay. Right then, I couldn't think of one single thing to wish for except for her wish to come true—even though she'd made her wish on a clover.

I opened my eyes and blew out my candles. At the exact same time, a loud *toot* came from over where Khayla was sitting. The room got quiet. Cricket stopped running in circles. The puppy tilted her little head and made a tiny whine.

"Oops," Khayla said, and reached her hand back to grab her bottom.

Georgie went into hysterics. "Oh no she didn't!" He waved his hand in front of his nose like there was actually a bad smell.

"Khayla, say 'Excuse me,'" Mama said.

"'Cuse me," Khayla said, and kept on eating.

"Shush!" Memaw said, and stomped her foot. She finally found whatever station it was that she'd been looking for on the battery operated radio, but the man's voice kept cutting in and out, like he had the hiccups.

Daddy got up from the table where he was staring at the tracking chart again. He went over and fiddled with the radio's antenna till the sound came in clear. Memaw planted herself back in her chair.

Me and Sealy were playing a clapping game. TayTay hummed along, smiling big with her mouth full of my birthday cake.

"Hey," Uncle T-Bone said, holding his cell phone and nodding in Daddy's direction. "Alvin just called. Says he just found out about the storm." My uncle rolled his eyes and glanced at Tay. "He's been drinkin', there ain't no doubt about that, George. Says he's on his way over to pick up his daughter."

Daddy shook his head and rubbed the back of his neck. "All right." He looked over at Georgie. "Son, why don't you and T-Bone come help me wash this pot outside before the weather gets any worse."

Georgie jumped up, "Sure, Daddy."

A quiet fell over the room, like we were all just sitting there while the seconds ticked by, waiting for *him* to come. Mama and Memaw stared at the radio, listening. I had never noticed till that minute how much they looked alike. They had the same curve to their noses, the same high cheeks, and the same exact worried eyebrows—eyebrows that looked like frowns hanging over their eyes. But it was Mama's hand that caught my attention.

Her hand was rubbing on Memaw's shoulder and I could see Mama giving little squeezes. Every time lightning flashed and lit up the room, or a clap of thunder rumbled somewhere off in the distance, Mama'd give a shoulder-squeeze, and Memaw'd let out a heavy sigh and reach up to pat the back of Mama's hand. This went on for a good while.

Then Memaw grunted, trying to stand up quick, and said to Mama, "I'll go fill the tub."

I was fixin' to ask her why when the front door flew open and the wind blew in TayTay's dad. The door went to smacking up against the side of the house. Sealy ran over and tried to pull it shut, but the wind was blowing too hard. I slid past *him* and went to help her.

TayTay's dad brought the stormy weather with him. Shadows filled the living room, and it turned three shades darker inside and out. The temperature inside the house felt like it went up by fifty degrees on account of the heat pouring off my cousin's dad.

Memaw came back in the room. "Alvin," is all she said with a nod. Then she went and took a heavy seat back in her chair.

"Mama Jean," he slurred and slow-blinked.

I smelled the whiskey on my uncle's breath, and the sourness of it was making my stomach do flip-flops.

He stared down at his only child with his lip curled up, like he couldn't stand her. If my daddy ever looked at me that way for even a second, I'd shrivel up and die from sadness right on the spot.

"Get your butt up, girl," TayTay's dad spit out. He pushed hard up against the side of her leg with his grimy ol' work boot. "Weather's bad. Gotta get you home." He burped and swayed.

Anger started rising up inside me—a heavy burning that started in the bottom of my belly. It worked its way up past my heart and caused a throb in my head, turning my hands into fists.

I jumped up off the floor without thinking. Cricket ran and hid up behind Memaw's feet and started a low puppy growl. The man was drunk, mean, and huge. But I wasn't gonna sit there and watch him bully my TayTay no more.

"Sealy, honey," Mama said all calm, but in a hurry, "go get your daddy."

"Yes, ma'am." Sealy ran like a scuttlebug.

"It's all right, Auntie Katherine," TayTay said to Mama in a voice I hardly recognized.

TayTay set her plate of cake on the floor in front of her and started to get up. She was almost standing when her dad pushed again with his foot and knocked her off balance. She fell forward and her hand came down, landing smack-dab in the middle of her plate. Globs of thick, creamy blue buttermilk frosting flew up in the air and landed with a plop all over Mama's wood floor.

I barely remember winding my arm up like one of them girl softball pitchers and bringing my fist up as hard as I could square into his big, hard, bloated belly. The man barely moved. A hot poof of sour air shot from his mouth. Hatred poured out of his eyes and straight into mine. A shiver ran through my hair. His giant hand flew up over his head. I squeezed my eyes closed and covered my head.

"What in blazes is going on in here?" Daddy's voice came rushing into the room. I opened one eye and seen Daddy holding tight to the man's raised arm. Daddy looked around the room. Mama was standing right close, clutching Khayla to her chest, rocking back and forth with Sealy hiding behind her. Memaw was mumbling with her face buried in her hands.

Daddy looked down at TayTay and seen her crying, with blue frosting everywhere.

"Stupid girl made a mess on your floor, man," TayTay's dad said.

Daddy's eyes landed on TayTay's dad.

I took a step toward the stinking bully.

"Armani." Daddy held his arm straight out in my direction.

"Sir?" I said, never taking my eyes off the man.

"Armani," Daddy said again. "Look at me."

I turned my head toward Daddy, but kept my eyes locked on Tay-Tay's dad. He looked away with slow, bouncy, beady eyes. Daddy took a step to the left, blocking me from my enemy.

"That's enough, Armani."

Tears puddled up, stinging my eyes.

Mama helped my cousin to her feet.

"I'm so sorry, Auntie Katherine," TayTay sniffled.

"Oh, sweetheart, it's not your fault," Mama said. "Come on in the kitchen and let's clean you up." Mama put her arm around TayTay and led her toward the kitchen.

My fool-headed uncle grabbed Tay's arm. "She can clean up at home," he slurred, his fingers digging into the softness of her arm.

Mama kissed TayTay on the cheek and walked away. I was mad all over again. How could Mama just leave TayTay to fend for herself?

Real calm-like, Daddy looked TayTay's dad straight in the eye. "I don't think this is necessary, Alvin." Without moving his eyes, Daddy peeled each one of the man's fingers, one by one, away from TayTay's arm. He took the man's hand in his like they were fixin' to shake. Daddy put his other arm around the man's shoulder. And just like that, Daddy walked him to the door. "T-Bone's going to take you and TayTay home in my truck."

TayTay rubbed her arm where her dad's fingers had dug in. She stared down at the floor. I stood beside her, not knowing what to say. A tear slipped from her eye and landed on the floor.

"Sorry for ruining your birthday, Armani."

"You didn't ruin it. Ol' poo-breath did," I said, with my lip curled up and my head sliding to the side.

TayTay's head was hanging, but she turned it up enough so she could look at me. A tiny smile found her eyes. "Yeah, poo-breath," she whispered. Another tear ran down her cheek. I reached up and wiped it with my thumb.

"Well, I better go." She shrugged.

The thought of her going home with that man made me feel sick. "You should stay here, Tay. Let me ask Mama if you can sleep over!"

Memaw walked up behind me. "She needs to go on with her daddy now, before the storm gets worse. Your Uncle T-Bone's already out there waitin'." Memaw had both hands on her hips, looking over the top of her glasses.

"But, Memaw, that man is gonna kill her!" I argued.

"Nobody's gonna kill nobody. You listen here." Memaw looked from me to TayTay. "My own daddy was a mean ol' dog when he drank, just like that one. You do as you're told and don't give him no reason to have to correct ya. Do you hear me, baby girl?" Memaw took TayTay's face in her hands.

"Yes, ma'am." TayTay nodded.

"But Memaw . . ."

Memaw shook her finger up in my face. "Nope, that's it." She gave TayTay a big hug, then shooed her toward the door. "Go on now."

Memaw turned on the switch for the hall light, forgetting that the power was out. She slapped the wall and scooted off toward her room. "And as for you, Miss Muhammad Ali," she hollered at me over her shoulder, "you and me's gonna have a talk later."

I rolled my eyes as far up into my head as possible. "Who's Muhammad Ali?" I hollered after her.

Mama's hanging plant came crashing through the kitchen window and shattered glass flew clear into the living room.

I never made it to the door in time to say bye to my best friend.

CHAPTER 10

Rain was coming down sideways. Thunder and lightning filled the sky. And the wind had a mind of its own.

There was still a hint of light making its way in from the outside world, but the usual golden colors of Mama's living room in the late light of the day was missing. A stillness and a gray had took over the whole house.

Mama never said one word when she swept up the broken glass and dirt and pieces of her favorite hanging plant into the dustpan that Memaw held for her. The little ones didn't even wander in there and get in the way. Somehow they just knew to stay put and not be whiny.

Daddy and Georgie had stretched thick silvery tape crisscrosses on all the windows while I laid out the papers that Memaw gave me. She showed me how to put them down for Cricket, since we wasn't gonna be able to take her outside to do her business.

Miss had herself stuffed into the corner of the couch. She looked lost and uncomfortable without Uncle T-Bone to hang on. Her eyes were fixed on the floor, and her shiny knees moved up and down as fast as her feet could bounce. I almost went and sat next to her, but I went into the kitchen instead.

Mama was sitting at the table with her head in her hands. Memaw was keeping herself busy wiping down the counters with a rag. The trash bag covering the hole where the window used to be was flapping loud and poofing like it was gonna tear loose any minute. I couldn't take my eyes off it.

"Mama, can I have a water?"

Mama never looked up at me. "Just one." Her tired voice got lost in the sounds of the storm and the noisy trash bag window. "Make it last," she said.

I took a bottle off the table. "Here," I said, holding it out in front of me.

Miss slowly stopped staring at the floor. Her gaze met mine and I froze. Her caramel-colored eyes were sad, scared, soft, and sweet.

I blinked and swallowed. "I thought you might want a water or somethin'."

She took the bottle and pressed it against her chest. "Thank you, Armani. This is so thoughtful of you." She smiled, but her eyes filled with tears. "I'm so scared." She stared at me in a way that sucked me in. "If anything happens to T-Bone, I don't know what I'll do." Tears fell from both of her eyes at the same time.

Her crying made my eyes sting. I sat down beside her on the couch, not knowing if I should touch her or not. Finally I laid my hand on her shoulder and patted a couple times. "He'll be okay" was all I could think to say.

She fell into me and went into a full-blown ugly cry, all but suffocating me with her tangerine hat.

The front door slammed open and a soaking-wet Uncle T-Bone fell in.

———

Listening to Uncle T-Bone go on about the ride to Uncle Alvin's and how he had to practically carry the grown man into his house in the pouring rain turned my stomach.

I gathered up my new puppy and went to my room. Of course, Sealy followed. I didn't mind 'cause I knew she'd let me be.

Quicker than Memaw could crack a nut, Sealy had one of her books out. She sat down on the floor and folded her legs up under her with the book spread across her lap.

The curtains above Sealy's head fluttered the tiniest bit even though the window was closed up good and tight. It made me nervous.

I plopped facedown on my bed with Cricket. I ran my finger up and down in the space between her eyes and down the top of her short, round little nose. She stared at me with her shiny jet-black eyes and thump-thumped her wagging tail up against my arm. Every couple of seconds, she'd stare at the window and whimper, cocking her little head to the side. I wondered if she was hearing the same wind-whistle as me.

I was admiring the beauty of her when there was a quiet knock on my door. It opened a couple of inches and Georgie's wide, fat nose peered in at me. "Armani, can I come in?"

"No," I said, with no energy.

Georgie walked in anyway.

He sat on the edge of the bed. I scooted over, making sure no part of my brother was touching me.

Cricket left my side and crawled up on Georgie's lap. He bent his face down and she licked him on the chin. He laughed and petted her. She went to licking faster all over his face.

I'd seen enough. All I could do was pray that Cricket hadn't picked up some dreaded disease from that ugly boy's face.

I sat up. "Come here, Cricket," I called in my baby-talk voice. "Come here." I clicked my tongue a couple times.

Cricket hopped over to me and sniffed my hand, all the while wagging her stumpy tail. Then she turned around and hopped back to Georgie, picking right back up with the licking.

"She likes me!" Georgie said. He kissed my puppy on top of her head.

"Whatever," I mumbled. I folded my arms across my chest. Sealy smiled at me over the top of her book.

"Anyway," Georgie said, still playing with Cricket. "I just wanted to tell you that I thought it was cool the way you stuck up for TayTay."

"What?" I said.

Georgie jumped to his feet, dancing on his tippy-toes around in a circle, boxing the air.

I rolled my eyes and unfolded my arms.

In a really high, squeaky voice he said, "My name's Armani Curtis. Mess with me or my cuz and I'll kick your butt!" Georgie laughed at his own self, like he was the funniest person alive.

A boom of thunder shook the house at the exact same time a huge, bright flash of lightning lit up my room like someone was shining a spotlight. The three of us stopped breathing and stared at each other. Sealy grabbed her book sack and leaped onto our bed.

Georgie cleared his throat. He reached over and gave Cricket a quick belly rub.

"Anyway," he said.

"Yeah, anyway," I said, just 'cause.

"Well, happy birthday, Sis." And before I realized what he was fixin' to do, that crazy boy bent down and kissed me on my cheek.

I swatted at him, but Georgie moved too quick. He was out the door, bouncing off walls in the dark hall.

"What an idiot," I grumbled.

I threw myself back on the bed. Sealy snuggled up next to me and opened her book sack. She put her book inside and pulled out her journal and fluffy feather pen.

I lay there with Cricket, feeling sticky and hot. The room got darker and darker as the gray light of day faded away. I watched my sister's pen move across the pages of her journal. I couldn't hear the scritch-scratch sound that her writing usually made on account of the whistling winds and pouring rain pounding down on our roof.

But the rain and wind couldn't cover up the cracking sound that made me and my sister jump clean out of our skin. It was like God was tearing the whole world in half in one big, long *riiiiiipppp*. . . .

CHAPTER 11

The whole house shook with one quick, loud *thwack*! I ran out to the living room with Sealy on my heels. It was dark, and I didn't see Khayla sitting there in the hall playing with the cars and Cricket's shoebox. I ran right into her, almost dropping the puppy. Sealy plowed into the back of me and screamed. Khayla fell flat to the floor, squashing the little box. She started wailing.

I grabbed hold of Khayla by one arm and pulled her off the floor. "It's okay, Khayla, it's okay . . ." I kept saying in huffs of breath, trying to calm her down. It wasn't working, though, 'cause I was as close as I've ever been to a full-blown panic myself. Everyone was shouting and running around. The room was spooky with candles flickering and shadows running across the ceiling.

"Katherine!" Daddy shouted. "Get the children and take them to our room! Stay away from the windows!"

"Come on, y'all, you heard your daddy!" Mama was scooping up babies and still managed to grab hold of Sealy's hand.

A bright white light streaked through the checkered curtains and poured into the room. In that split second, I seen Memaw's face, her mouth wide open and her eyes all bugged out. The air got sucked out of me.

An explosion of thunder rattled the whole house. I screamed and covered my ears. Another bolt of lightning lit up the shadowy room. There it was again—that look on Memaw's face. A cry that started in my belly flew out of my mouth, blending in with the screams of the wind.

Cold prickly shivers ran up my back and down my arms. A sour taste burned in the back of my throat.

Daddy had his arm around Memaw and led her off to the bedroom to be with Mama and the kids. I didn't want to see her looking that way—all full of fright. My breathing was coming fast and hard. My heart raced almost as fast as my brain.

Another clap of thunder. The creaky, broken screen door made one last loud slap up against the house before I heard it rip right off, flying to who knows where. The house moved beneath my feet. "Daddy!"

"I'm here, baby!" The lightning flashed and there he was—my daddy was right there just on the other side of Memaw's TV-watching chair. The wind shook the windows like an airplane was fixin' to land on our roof.

Even with Memaw and the kids all up in the bedroom, I could still hear them crying and screaming and begging Mama to make it stop.

Uncle T-Bone was huddled on the couch with his arms wrapped around Miss. She was wailing louder than the kids in the bedroom, waving the only flashlight in the room every which way.

More lightning and more thunder. The constant sound of rain dumping down in buckets so hard it sounded like we might as well've been standing up under a waterfall.

I didn't even realize I was holding onto Georgie till he screamed in my ear. It was a high-pitched scream that sent terror running through me. He covered his head with his hands. I dug my fingers deep into his arm and screamed with him.

It wasn't no normal thunderstorm. The sky had fell out, and the world was ending.

Daddy stood by the front window and looked out. He shook his head back and forth. He took off his glasses. His right hand came up and held the top of his head and then slid down. He rubbed his eyes. He put his glasses back on. Then his hands fell heavy to his sides. Daddy looked straight up at the ceiling, and squeezed his eyes shut. In a whisper-cry he said, "Protect us, sweet Jesus."

A tree branch crashed through the big window and knocked Daddy to the floor.

CHAPTER 12

"Daddy!" me and Georgie both screamed. We ran to him.

Daddy looked up at us. He had a thin line of blood trickling down his forehead and his glasses were missing from his face.

Miss Shug shined the flashlight in Daddy's direction. She seen the blood streaming down the side of his face and went to hollerin'. The whole while, she kept right on fanning herself with the tangerine hat, blinking her eyes a mile a minute.

Uncle T-Bone looked at Georgie. "Go calm Lorraine down."

Me and Georgie looked at each other like maybe Uncle T-Bone was the one who got knocked in the head. "Who's Lorraine?"

"Shug! Go calm Miss Shug down!" The woman was wailing louder than ever by now.

My brother looked over at the woman so sweet they called her Sugar. "No, sir," Georgie said, pushing his glasses firm up on his nose. "Daddy needs me."

Georgie walked across the broken glass that was covered with stuck globs of sticky gray tape. He scooted past my uncle and put his arm around Daddy's waist. He helped Daddy get over to the sofa.

A long-lasting flash of lightning lit up the room. In the white light that shined on my brother, I caught a glimpse of the way I think Georgie'll look when he's a grown man. He looked just like Daddy.

——————

The rain had let up and the lightning and thunder had rolled on out. It didn't take long to figure out what had caused that first loud cracking sound.

The big oak tree from next door had come up out of the ground, roots and all, and slammed into the top of Daddy's truck. Ruined. The truck was forever ruined. I couldn't remember us not having that ol' truck. It was practically the only thing I'd ever ridden in, except for my school bus.

Daddy kept shaking his head back and forth. A couple times he said, "Thank God no one was killed."

"Daddy," Georgie said, "what're we gonna do?"

"Well, son," he said, lifting his head and sitting a little taller, "the first thing we're going to do is make sure your mama knows that every-thing's going to be all right."

"But Daddy . . ." Georgie looked at the broken glass that was still catching light from far-off lightning.

Daddy stood up. I was happy to see him standing. I felt safer with him standing.

He put one hand on Georgie's shoulder and his other hand on my shoulder. He looked at the two of us with soft eyes. "I need the two of you to help me clean up this mess so it doesn't upset your mama."

"Yes, sir," we both said.

"Good, because it's going to be a long night. I don't want your mama to worry more than she has to."

I don't remember Daddy ever talking like that to us before—like we were grown. *This must be what it's like when you make ten.* I was all grown up. And to think, the day before, I had been just a child.

———

Mama and her flashlight came around the corner and into the living room. She was toting Kheelin on one hip and Khayla on the other. Mama stopped and looked at the broken window and the mess all over the room. Khayla slid down her leg and went running to Daddy.

Mama's hand covered her mouth. Fear filled her eyes. "You're hurt." She went to Daddy and took his face into her hands.

"I'm fine, Katherine. Are the children all right?" He smoothed her hair with his thumb.

Memaw came into the room. "Well, we might as well hunker down an' get ready," she said to no one in particular.

Suddenly, a huge gust of wind came blowing through the broken window.

And just like that, the minute of calm was over.

We all let out a gasp and covered our faces.

"T-Bone," Daddy hollered over the roar of the wind, "help me find something to cover this window!"

Misty bits of rain moistened my skin.

"Mr. Curtis!" Mama yelled. The panic in her voice caused the hairs on the back of my neck to prickle. "My black-velvet Jesus!"

There, sitting all cockeyed on the wall next to the broke-out window was Mama's pride and joy. A huge black-velvet painting of brown Jesus Hisself. No matter where you walked in the room, the eyes on black-velvet Jesus followed. Even in the dark, with nothing but a candle and flashlight lighting the room, His shiny gold halo glowed— and His eyes followed.

The picture was about to fall and Mama was about to lose her mind.

For the first time in my whole life, I felt unsafe in a place where I'd always known, no matter what, I was gonna be safe.

Daddy grabbed hold of the picture and took it down from the wall, real careful-like. He sat it up on top of the gym-floor table next to the leftover jambalaya and birthday cake. About fifty bottles of water were standing in a row, like soldiers keeping watch.

Seeing black-velvet Jesus lying there, with Mama's food all around Him, gave me an unsettling feeling. For years Jesus had been hanging high on the wall, always watching over us—and now He was lying flat on the table with us looking down at Him. I fought the feeling of wanting to pick Him up, and stand Him upright.

I wondered how Jesus would feel about being surrounded by leftovers stuffed into plastic baggies, and a half-eaten blue birthday cake practically sitting on top of His head.

After a while, the constant whipping of the swirling wind and pounding rain caused a quiet calm to fall over the inside of our house.

My eyes got heavier and heavier, till I couldn't keep them open no more.

Howling winds interrupted that peaceful feeling when the night-time hum turned to shrieking crashes and rattles just past midnight. The house was swaying. Part of the roof was flapping and slapping in the gusty, roaring wind. I thought for sure the roof was gonna let go.

We all sat squished together on the sofa, listening to the wind wail, watching the flicker of a candle make crazy, scary shadows dance across the walls and ceiling. The house shuddered and moaned with noises that made us all shut up, like we was waiting to see if something was fixin' to fall and bury us alive. I sat there knowing that *something* was coming. Maybe next time a tree was gonna fall and crush *us* instead of a truck. I couldn't help but wonder if the roof got pulled off, would we get sucked out?

Memaw was humming church hymns. The sound made my eyes droopy. It was a nice sound, a familiar sound. Memaw had the best hum this side of the Mississippi River.

With my eyes closed and Cricket breathing heavy on top of my belly, I started to fall asleep with Sealy pressed up against me.

The rain fell from the sky like marbles, and the wind whooshed through the house like the walls were made of cheesecloth instead of drywall.

Minutes felt like hours. Hours felt like days.

Crashing sounds. Popping noises. Something getting crushed. Each time I'd hold my breath, close my eyes, and wait for it to pass. I hugged my knees and rocked myself, trying to ignore the rush of wind and rain slapping everything I knew to bits. Our house never felt smaller.

The darkness slowly changed from black to gray. As the room grew lighter, the more settled and quiet we all got. The only sleep I grabbed was right before the sun came up. I just knew once the sun started shining and we were out of the dark, everything would be all right.

But that feeling of peace came to a quick end.

CHAPTER 13

The creak of the front door and the gush of outside coming in had me up and on my feet. Daddy was standing at the open door, looking out into the early gray of the day. He said he wanted to go outside to see if we had any other damage from the storm—besides his smashed-up truck.

"Daddy, can I come with you?" I asked.

He looked over at Mama, who nodded.

"I suppose," Daddy answered, "but stay close to me, you hear?"

"Yes, sir." I ran to my room for my shoes. I could only find one. I searched everywhere. I ran back out to the living room. That's when I seen Cricket all snuggled up, sleeping with Georgie.

"Sealy." I shook her awake.

"What?" she said, not even opening her eyes.

"Have you seen my other shoe?"

"No," she said, and rolled over to go back to sleep.

"Armani, if you're coming with me, you need to come on," Daddy hollered from the kitchen.

"Oh, no!" Sealy said, sitting straight up. The look on her face had trouble written all over it.

"What?"

"Well, I'm not sure, but I think I saw Cricket playing with it."

I remembered too. I ran back to our room. Sealy was on my heels.

Sitting over in the corner, where Sealy did all her reading, was a shredded pile of what used to be my new white left tennis shoe with triple blue stripes.

"Cricket, what did you do?" I fell to my knees on the floor. "Mama's gonna kill me."

Sealy put her hand on my shoulder. "No, she won't, Armani. It's just a shoe."

"My *only* shoes, Sealy! Mama just bought these for school." Tears started to build up in my eyes. "What am I gonna do, wear one shoe?"

"You can wear mine if you want."

"Don't be dumb, Sealy. I can't wear your little-girl shoes." I stood up and glared at her.

She wasn't smiling no more. She looked down at the floor with her bottom lip all puffed out.

"What's wrong with *you*?" I said, annoyed. "*I'm* the one who's gonna be hopping around on one good shoe." I started picking up the chewed-up pieces of my used-to-be-shoe. Sealy bent down to help me.

Memaw walked in our room. "Your daddy's waitin' for you, child." Her eyes zoomed in on the pieces of white rubber and canvas. "What is goin' on up in here?"

We explained to her what happened and begged her to pinky-promise not to tell Mama or Daddy.

"The only reason I'm not gonna bother them with this today is because they've got enough on their plate already." She bent down and helped us pick up the chewed pieces. "But," Memaw grunted as she bent over, "you're gonna tell your mama first chance you get. Understood?"

"Thanks, Memaw," I said.

"Now, let's get somethin' to put on those feet of yours," Memaw said, and walked off toward her bedroom. Me and Sealy followed.

———

The shoes that Memaw gave me to wear weren't shoes at all. They were boots. The most horrible, ugly rubber boots ever made. They were navy blue with baby-pee-yellow polka dots. Memaw said they used to be her garden boots. I wanted to know why she didn't bury them in the garden when she'd had the chance.

I clomped into the living room.

Sealy walked behind me, stiflin' a laugh. Mama must've heard me coming, 'cause she looked up, then straight down at my feet.

"I like you boots, Ah-mani," Khayla said. She bent down and rubbed her chubby hand across the toe part of one of the obnoxious boots.

Mama stopped sweeping. She looked from me to Memaw, then back at the boots.

"Why are you wearing those dirty old boots, Armani?" Mama asked.

"Those boots are not dirty, I'll have ya know," Memaw piped up. "I told her to wear 'em. She doesn't need to be outside sloshin' around through Lord knows what in her school shoes."

"Do they fit?" Mama asked, looking at me sideways.

Not really, I wanted to say. I looked away and waved "Hey," at Kheelin sitting up in a big-person chair.

"They fit good enough," Memaw said.

That was that. I headed outside to see for myself what kind of damage the storm had caused.

———

The air. It was thick. Muggy. Heavy when I sucked it into my lungs. The skin on my arms turned wet with humidity. My hair tried to curl, even up inside my braids. Steam seeped off the blacktop of our road.

I looked up at the sky. There were cracks of the bluest blue I'd ever seen. But the clouds surrounding them patches of blue were strange and scary. Some clouds were big white, fluffy puffs and others were dark, almost black. I could tell just by the looks of them that they were filled with trouble. Some clouds moved to the right, and some moved around to the left. It was like I was standing there in the perfect center of a whirlwind.

An unexpected shiver made its way up the middle of my back. I stood there with myself soaking up the beauty of the mesmerizing sky. But then, without no kind of warning, the blue gave up and let the dark, thick clouds move back in. A soft rain started falling.

I seen the tree.

The tree lying across Daddy's truck was one of Mama's favorites— the big tree that shed a shadow as big as Texas across our whole front yard, keeping the blistering sun out of the front of the house in the afternoons. Mama wasn't gonna be happy when she found out. I wondered if the clovers covering the ground under that tree would still be there for me and TayTay to pick through.

A big gust of wind came whooshing by, throwing hard bits of rain into my cheeks and all but knocking me off my own two feet. I threw my arm up and buried my face up in my armpit.

The wind settled back down and I lifted my head.

A bird's nest.

Up toward the top of that dying tree covering the entire top of my daddy's truck was a bird's nest.

The nest was somehow still resting between the branches that surrounded it. But the tiny bluish eggs inside were all cracked and broken. I stared at what had to be the little dead bodies of half-made baby birds poking out through the ruined shells.

The winds picked up again, blowing rain-needles sideways.

A beautiful blue and black bird circled in the dark sky above me. The bird swooped down and landed on the edge of Daddy's shattered truck mirror. It stood there, chirping and chirping, with its head moving in little jerks from one side to the next. Then it hopped across the scattered branches till it reached the tiny nest.

The bird touched one of the cracked eggs with its pointy beak, then turned and did the same thing to the next lifeless egg. The bird started squawking louder and faster, moving its head from side to side. And then it stopped. It just froze. And it looked straight at me.

Its solid black, watery eyes grabbed hold of my heart and started to pull, causing a heavy feeling up in my chest, like someone reached in there and laid down a cinder block. Then the bird let out one last loud, squeaky caw sound that sent fast prickly bumps down my arms.

The bird leaped into the air and flew away. When I lifted my head to watch it fly off—disappearing into the dark sky—a dreadful feeling came over me.

"Armani!" Daddy hollered.

I about jumped out of them ugly, oversized boots at the sound of his bellowing voice. I wiped the back of my hand across my face, taking one last look at the nest holding the ruined bird family.

"I'm right here, Daddy," I hollered back, turning away from his truck.

"Armani, I want you to get back in the house! It's too dangerous out here!"

"But Daddy, I wanna stay out here with you," I shouted into the falling rain and gusts of wind.

"Go inside, Armani."

I tilted my head up so I could look at him. Just past Daddy's shoulder, I seen that the roof on our neighbor's house was gone. It wasn't half off, or messed up. It was *gone*.

Mrs. Tilly, the ol' lady who lived in that house with her twelve cats, was running around between her yard and the road, crying and waving her arms up and down. Uncle T-Bone and Georgie were over there with a few other people.

I tore my eyes away from the poor lady gone crazy and looked back at Daddy. I noticed for the first time how different he looked without his glasses. The cut across his forehead was bleeding again. The blood was watery and thin on account of mixing with the rain washing over his face.

I was about to tell Daddy he was bleeding when Uncle T-Bone came running over.

My uncle pulled off his soaking wet shirt. He rolled it up, squeezed as tight as he could, wringing out rainwater.

"George," Uncle T-Bone shouted, "your head's bleedin' real bad!"

Daddy took a wobbly step closer and tipped his head a little to the left. He pointed to his ear and stared at Uncle T-Bone.

"What?" Daddy hollered. The rain changed directions. The wind blew harder than ever, making me feel like I could be lifted up any minute and just swooped right off the face of the earth.

In one quick move, Uncle T-Bone ripped the shirt in half, like it was made of paper. He folded one half into a large square and then he used the other half to tie around Daddy's head.

"Your head," he pointed, "it needs stitches." He grabbed Daddy's hand and made him press it against the T-shirt bandage. "Keep pressure on it, George."

"Thanks, T," Daddy said, and did a thumbs-up.

Then everything stopped. It was like the storm had wore its own self out with all that huffing and puffing.

"Armani," Uncle T-Bone said, taking a big breath, "go inside and tell Shug to come on."

I turned to run inside. "Hang on, Armani," Daddy said, and held his hand up. "Where're you going, T?"

"George, I gotta go home, man." Uncle T-Bone's eyes were jumpy.

"I could use your help here, brother," Daddy said, with sad sitting heavy in his eyes.

"I know." The sadness was contagious, 'cause it filled my uncle's eyes too. "Look, I'm gonna go home and check on things. I'll be right back."

Steam started rising out of the road again.

Sirens filled the air. They weren't close, but they were *everywhere*.

Daddy and Uncle T-Bone gave each other a look, like they were talking without words. I grabbed hold of Daddy's hand. He squeezed tight. I took hold of Uncle T-Bone's hand too.

We stood there, not saying a word. The wind, sirens, people shouting, rain dripping, the sight of Daddy's tore-up truck—right then the only thing for us to do was stand there and hold tight to each other.

A tree cracked somewhere over on the other side of the street. The three of us jumped and turned our heads.

"Georgie!" Daddy hollered. "Come on!"

My brother came running over, almost tripping over a mangled bicycle.

"Be careful, son," Daddy said. "You need to be careful too," he said, looking at Uncle T-Bone.

"I will," my uncle said. "I just gotta go make sure my house is all right, George, but I'll be back."

"I know," Daddy said, giving Uncle T-Bone a handshake-hug.

"C'mon, Georgie," I said, "let's go get Miss Shug."

We turned to run inside when the old oak tree fell with a *crraacckk* and a *thunk* smack-dab into the middle of our road with poor Mrs. Tilly up underneath.

CHAPTER 14

"Lord, have mercy," Memaw said for the hundredth time in five minutes.

Poor Memaw. Her and Mrs. Tilly had been in choir together since before I was born. I sat on the floor next to where Memaw was collapsed in her chair. I hugged her hand, wishing I knew something I could say to help her feel better.

Daddy was outside trying to help move the huge tree. None of us talked about what had happened. But we all knew. I was thankful right then that we couldn't see through the trash bag covering the window. Upset fluttered around in my belly.

Mama wouldn't stop cleaning and wiping the little ones down with a wet rag. She passed out waters and told us to drink them, whether we were thirsty right then or not. She went on and on about staying hydrated and keeping our strength up. It didn't seem to me that we needed a whole lot of strength to stay put in the living room while the world got flipped on its head outside.

I hoped Mama was drinking water too.

Sealy sat on the floor in front of Memaw and went to reading out loud. Memaw rocked in her chair. Tears fell. She didn't wipe them off. Me and Sealy did the best we could to help Memaw with her grieving—my sister with her reading and me with my hand hugging.

––––

Daddy stood still as a statue, taking up most of the space inside the doorway, his hand held tight to the doorknob. The Heaven-like glow coming from behind him cast a shadow, making it impossible to see anything but the dark outline of his body. The way the light surrounded and held him all but took my breath away. It was the most beautiful I'd ever seen my daddy.

I ran to Daddy and wrapped my arms around his waist, grateful to have him back inside with us. As I hugged him, I could see that the outside world had took on an orangey-pink look. It was a color I ain't never seen in no crayon box before. It was beautiful. The half-gone trees, the sky, the beat-up houses, even the people I seen roaming around outside—*everything* had took on the swirly orangey-pink color. I stepped to the side of Daddy with my mouth wide open, just gazing at the sight of it all.

"Armani, get in here and shut that door!" Mama shouted.

"But Mama, it's so beautiful. Come see." I couldn't tear my eyes from the sight.

Sealy and Georgie were at my side squeezing in to take a look. Both of them said, "Whoa . . ."

"It looks like Heaven," Sealy said in her whispery voice.

I was fixin' to agree with her when Daddy stuck an arm in front of us and swooped us back so he could slam the door shut.

"Daddy . . ." we all whined, looking up into his face.

He looked down at us with watery eyes and crinkled eyebrows. "There's nothing *beautiful* about what's happening on the other side of that door."

———

Daddy wouldn't sit still. He paced back and forth, pulling back a corner of the trash bag covering the front window and peeking out. Then he'd walk all quick to where the back screen door used to be and stare into the backyard.

Cricket took to whining so loud she'd wore down everyone's nerves. Daddy stopped his pacing. "Armani, please do something with that dog."

"She probably needs to go outside to do her business like a real dog, right, Daddy?" Georgie jumped to his feet so fast he nearly fell right back down again. "I'll take her."

When Daddy opened the door to let them out, everything outside was soft and quiet—all drippy and thick and *peaceful.*

"The storm's over," Georgie said with a grin. "Looks like we dodged a bullet! Uncle T-Bone was right, Daddy—we didn't need to evacuate. It wasn't *even* the big one." He smirked and walked out of the house with Cricket.

"Do you think the storm is really over, Armani?" Sealy asked, standing squished up against me.

"Looks like it is." I just wished that Mama and Daddy or Memaw would smile or something, so my nerves could take a rest.

But then Georgie screamed at the top of his lungs from the front yard.

Sealy's fingers dug into my arm.

Memaw and Mama gave each other the most frightful look.

Daddy took off running.

CHAPTER 15

We all jumped up and ran outside behind Daddy.

"What is it, son?" Daddy asked, out of breath. Georgie pointed. We all saw it. No one said a word. Everything was going in slow motion. The air sat in perfect stillness.

A wall of water. A black rumbling, swirling, groaning wall of water was crashing toward us.

I looked down where the tire shop sat, except it wasn't where it was supposed to be. It'd been knocked clean off its blocks and was floating sideways in the direction of the doughnut shop.

I could hear windows shattering, houses breaking, and people screaming.

The trees left standing fell like toothpicks, disappearing altogether.

The ground hummed and vibrated. The water rose as it rolled closer and closer.

Mama picked up Khayla and Kheelin in one scoop and ran back inside the house. She let out a long, constant stream of "No, no, no, no, no."

Sealy squeezed my hand so tight it hurt.

I stared at the nightmare barreling toward us.

"Get inside!" Daddy's words boomed into the still, thick air. We turned and ran for the house.

Georgie slammed the door shut and stood with his back pressed up against it, like he was pushing hard to keep the water out. Then I seen he was crying. I ain't never in my whole life seen Georgie cry. My heart pounded harder.

The roar and rumble got louder, closer.

Daddy put his arm around Georgie. He pulled him gently away from the door. "I want you all to listen to me. I only have time to say this once. The levee must've breached—that's what this has to be. We have to go upstairs, and we have to go *now*."

"But Daddy, we don't have an upstairs," Sealy squeak-cried, her lips quivering.

Before Sealy finished, Daddy had the rickety ol' ladder to the attic pulled down. He was already helping Memaw up the loose-looking steps. Mama was next, with one of the twins in her arms and Sealy behind her, holding tight to the hem of her dress.

I ran over and tore down the trash bag so I could see out the broken window. I couldn't believe what I seen. That wall of churning black water was at least as tall as Daddy and was so close I could feel its heartbeat. I couldn't stop staring at it. The loud, rumbling sound of the water monster filled my head.

"Armani!" Daddy yelled. He had me in his arms and was forcing me up the attic ladder. I was still wearing Memaw's rubber boots and my feet kept slipping off the steps. Daddy's body pressed against mine to keep me from falling.

I was almost to the top of the ladder when the front door and all of the windows exploded at the same time! A tidal wave came plowing into our house! Everyone in the attic screamed and sobbed. Daddy pushed me hard from behind, forcing me to move from where I was froze on the ladder.

I looked behind me and Daddy was shoulder-deep in the inky-black foamy water. Then I seen it. Mama's black-velvet Jesus, smeared with sky-blue buttermilk frosting, floated out the window and into the rolling darkness.

CHAPTER 16

Daddy slammed the door shut to our horrible tiny attic. It was hot. So hot, the air felt like it was on fire when I sucked it in. It even *smelled* hot.

It was dark.

We coughed.

We cried.

And we didn't talk. We waited.

We huddled together in one big Curtis clump on the attic's crooked plywood floor, squished into a corner as far as possible from the door that held the water back.

———

The roar of raging waters destroying our house had stopped. But for a long while, the water rushing below us churned and pushed—the sound of everything we called home being washed away.

The roof rattled and shook, giving me the constant unsettling feeling that the wind was gonna rip it clean off.

The scariest time was when everything got all quiet and still. None of us was crying or talking. I was scared to make any noise. I didn't want the water to find us.

Then the sweetest sound filled my ears. Memaw went to humming one of her hymns real soft. Sitting there in the dark, all wrapped up in fear, came the angels' music. A calm settled over me—settled over all of us. We stayed that way for a good while, letting Memaw's voice carry us from one long minute to the next.

———

"Mama, I hot." Khayla broke the spell.

"I know, honey," Mama said in a normal voice, like we weren't stuck in the attic.

"I'm hot too, Mama," Sealy said.

Cricket was breathing fast. Her tongue lay out across my arm.

"Yeah," Georgie's voice came out of the dark. "It's two hundred degrees up in here, Daddy. Feels like we're runnin' outta air."

"Mr. Curtis," Mama said, "what should we do?" The twins started fussing.

Memaw's humming got louder.

"Everyone hang on and try to stay calm," Daddy said, moving around. There was a *thunk* and he mumbled, "Ouch."

"Daddy, are you all right?" me and Georgie asked.

"I'm fine. I hit my head on the ceiling. What I need is a flash-light."

Sealy fooled with something next to me. "Here, Daddy." And just like that, a bright beam of light shot across the attic, shining right in Daddy's face. Memaw's humming stopped.

Daddy put his hand up to block the light. "Sealy, where'd you get a flashlight, baby?"

"From my book sack."

"Well, I'll be," Daddy said, like he was admiring a straight-A report card.

Memaw was soaked in sweat. She looked more tired than I'd ever seen her in my whole life. "Are you okay, Memaw?"

She took hold of my hand in both of hers and squeezed. Tears rolled down my cheek. I wiped my face on my sleeve. I fanned her the best I could with my other hand.

Daddy took the flashlight from Sealy and made his way to the attic door. I knew what he was fixin' to do. Part of me was excited that our horrible time in the stiflin' attic was about over. Daddy would open that door, we'd climb back downstairs, and start cleaning up whatever mess the water had left. I'd run the whole way to TayTay's. . . .

But my good sense wanted to scream, *Don't open it, Daddy!*

Daddy pulled on the door's handle. Nothing happened. The door didn't budge an inch. His forehead scrunched up. He reached up and adjusted his bandage. He gnawed on his bottom lip.

Daddy gave the flashlight to Georgie and told him to shine it so that he could see what he was doing, then he heaved so hard his arms shook. The door let out a creak and then popped. It flew open. Daddy fell backward onto his butt.

The stink of floodwater slammed into the stuffy attic. A strange gray-white, flickery light came rising from below. Someone let out a gasp. My heart sank down to my toes. Invisible hands reached deep down inside me and stole the air right out from my lungs.

Water. Dirty, oily, foamy water—all the way up to the top of the attic steps—sloshed back and forth.

Mama whimpered and shushed the twins. Or maybe she was shushing herself.

Sealy had her head buried in Georgie's lap.

Memaw started humming again. It wasn't the soothing sound like before. It sounded more like hum-crying.

Daddy stood with his head hanging as low as a head could go. All the tallness of him was gone.

"Are we gonna die?" I almost-whispered.

Daddy barely lifted his head. He looked at me. One tear left a wet line down his face.

"I'm serious." This time I shouted. My heart was about to leap out of my chest. "Are we gonna die? I wanna know!" My whole body shook.

Sealy was sobbing.

Daddy came to me and wrapped me in his arms. I buried my face against his chest. He stroked my hair and rocked me. "Shhh . . . it's all right, Armani," he said, with a sniffle. "Nobody's going to die."

"But, Daddy, the water. We're stuck up here *forever*."

He took my head in his big hands and looked at me straight on. "Now listen. I want *all* of you to listen." He cleared his throat. "We're going to be all right. We're not stuck up here forever. The water's not rising anymore and it should start receding soon. Now, let's all try to stay calm." He took a deep breath. "We're going to be fine."

"Are you sure, Daddy?" I asked.

"I'm sure, sweetheart," he said, and he smiled. But the smile didn't reach his eyes.

"Promise?"

His smile faded. He pulled my head up against his chest with my ear pressed to the spot where his heart beat the loudest. He kissed the top of my head and whispered in my ear, "Promise."

CHAPTER 17

The dim, shimmery gray glow coming off the water gave us enough light so we could see most of the attic. I was mesmerized by the sight of it.

I got lost staring into the water that filled our house like a fishbowl. All our things drifted by. I seen a sippy cup, my math book, lots of clothes, and Mama and Daddy's gold-framed wedding picture. Memaw's TV-watching chair was down there, just a-bobbing up and down—almost dancing in the murky water. I even seen a paper plate still holding jambalaya float by real slow. But when I seen Khayla's pretty little baby doll float by with one eye open and one eye closed, I jumped back from the sight. I tore my eyes away from the water and the sadness below.

I gave Cricket a hug and poured water into my cupped hand for her to drink. Daddy and Georgie fished out maybe ten or twelve bottles of water that Mama had been saving for just in case.

I closed my eyes and drifted off to sleep.

———

Kheelin. Kheelin wheezing. Kheelin wheezing loud.

I pushed the annoying sound away so I could keep sleeping. The wheezing stopped. I sat straight up.

"Dear God, he's not breathing!" Mama screamed.

"Lay him down!" Daddy hollered back. "Here, Katherine! Lay him here!" Daddy patted the wood floor with the flat of his hand.

"Why is he having so many attacks?" I screamed at no one and everyone. Nobody answered. Memaw turned her head away and stared at nothing on the floor beside her.

Daddy did CPR while Mama rubbed Kheelin's head, begging God to let her baby live.

Kheelin let out a cough and started to cry.

"Okay, that's it," Daddy said, and got to his feet. He couldn't stand all the way up 'cause the ceiling was too low. But he sure seemed tall right then. "You children get in that corner." He pointed to a dark area on the far side of the attic. "Katherine and Mama Jean, get over there too."

We squished together the best we could in the crowded space.

"I want y'all to look down and cover your eyes."

"What are you fixin' to do, Daddy?" Georgie asked.

"We're getting out of here. Now close your eyes." And with that, Daddy went to pounding on the ceiling of our attic. I was scared that Daddy might've suffered some kind of serious damage with all the blows he'd been taking to his head. He looked like a crazy man, punching the heck out of that ceiling with his bare hands.

Georgie was on his feet, scuttling around. He picked up something and went over by Daddy. "Here, Daddy, try this."

Daddy took it. "Where'd you find this, son?"

"Over there by them boxes."

"What is it?" I asked.

"It's your PawPaw's old walking stick," Memaw said. Hearing her voice sent a wave of happy through me. "You're gonna like this, George—unscrew the end of it."

Daddy twisted the end. "Like this?"

"Um-hmm," she said, with a twinkle in her eye. I hugged her arm. Memaw was back.

The wooden end fell to the floor. Out of the end of PawPaw's walking stick was a sharp metal spike.

"Well, I'll be," Daddy said.

"What is it, some kind of secret sword?" Georgie asked.

Memaw sat up as straight as she could against the hard, two-by-four wood beam. "Well, somethin' like that. Your PawPaw called it his poker. He never left the house without it." There was a look of remembering in her eye. "It wasn't safe for an old man to go off walkin' by hisself in the streets of New Orleans. Your PawPaw sure did enjoy his long walks after supper."

Memaw took a long deep breath and coughed. "One day he up an' asked ol' man Riley to fix him some *assurance* onto the end of his dern walkin' stick. And, don'tcha know, good ol' Riley did. PawPaw called it his poker. And from that day on, he never went nowhere without it."

She looked over at me and Sealy with the little grin that always made me smile. "Ya know what else he never left home without?"

"What?"

"A kiss from me, that's what." She sighed a happy sigh. "Yes indeed, a kiss from me."

Daddy poke-drilled about fifty quarter-sized holes in the ceiling, making it so I could get a good fix on the sky. The gray of the sky matched the gray everywhere else, but seeing outside reminded me that there *was* something besides the attic.

The wind was gusting so hard, it whistled as it blew in and out of the flute holes all over the ceiling. I swear it felt like the house was gonna flip over, or maybe even just take off sailing into the sky like Dorothy's house in *The Wizard of Oz*. It creaked, it groaned, and it rattled so bad it most likely shook the nails loose.

A constant drip fell from the holes, making a *tink, tink* sound on the lopsided plywood floor. Water was under us. Water was falling outside. Water was coming in—and there was nowhere to go.

Memaw patted her shoulder, letting me know she wanted me to rest my head there. She gently rubbed my leg with her fingertips, causing a tiny tickle. She slipped one of them hard caramels into my hand and held her finger to her mouth. "Shh . . ." She winked.

I unwrapped the candy and plopped it into my mouth. It was the best piece I'd ever had. It was sweeter and juicier than usual. I was gonna ask her where hers was, but I didn't wanna give away our secret.

"How you doin', child?"

"I'm okay, Memaw. Are you all right?"

"Oh, I'm gonna be fine, darlin'." We sat like that—just being close, for a good while.

"Armani, I have somethin' I wanna give you." Memaw reached down inside the neckline of the yellow housedress and pulled out her locket. "Would you be so kind to unhook me, dear?"

"But, Memaw . . ."

She shook one crooked finger at me. "Please do this for your ol' Memaw. And don't argue." Her eyes were watery and tired. I reached behind her and unlatched the necklace. She kissed it before putting it on me.

Memaw patted the locket resting near where my heart sits and said, "Yes indeed, that is *special*."

"But Memaw, why are you giving this to me? This is *your* special locket."

"I know what it is, child, but it's not mine no more. Truth is, it never really was mine." Memaw opened the locket. Inside was a tiny dial under glass with a needle that bounced around and finally settled on the letter N sitting off to the left. I rubbed my thumb careful-like across the little glass dome protecting the compass. Memaw lifted her glasses up off her nose to swipe the sweat that had pooled up there.

Nested up inside the lid of the locket was a tiny little speck of a picture of Mama about my age, sitting on the porch swing with Memaw.

"You an' Mama are so beautiful."

"Thank you, baby. I like to say we come from a long line of beautiful women. Legend has it the women in our family keep gettin' more beautiful with each new generation." She smiled. Happy, warm love spread from my heart to my cheeks.

"I put that picture in there for you the day you were born, NeeNee. I've been waitin' for the right time to give it to ya. My mama gave this compass-locket to me when I married your dear PawPaw. She said it would help me if I ever lost my way home." Memaw's eyes got that far-off look and she let out another long sigh. "I wanted to give it to ya yesterday on your birthday, but everything got so . . . busy."

A huge, pounding rumble of thunder shook the house like we needed reminding as to why yesterday got so . . . *busy*.

I wrapped my arms around her, the best I could from a sit, and squeezed tight. "Thanks, Memaw."

"Keep it close to your heart an' know that's where I'll always be." Memaw kissed my forehead.

Mama swiped at a tear sliding down her face. She smiled and blew me a kiss across the shadowy attic.

———

The sky turned dark and ugly again, wrapping us up in darkness. The rain poured down sideways—the winds keeping most of it from coming straight down and into our pitiful, tore-up, leaky attic.

I rested my head on Memaw's shoulder with the locket tucked safe inside the palm of my hand. Her shoulder was wet from sweat. My eyes got heavier and heavier.

CHAPTER 18

Shadows danced and shifted from one wall to the other. It scared and confused me. It took me a minute or two of looking around to remember that we were in the attic, and why we were there.

Sealy and Georgie played with a flashlight, making finger shadows on the dirty plywood floor and vibrating walls.

My neck was stiff. I needed to stretch, but Memaw's heavy ol' head was lying on top of mine. I tried to get out from under her without waking her up.

I got frustrated. "Memaw," I whispered, nudging her with my trapped arm.

She didn't move.

"Memaw," I whispered again, but louder.

She still didn't move.

I patted her cheek, and real quick jerked my hand away. Something was wrong. Her skin didn't feel normal. I touched her cheek again. Instead of feeling her usual silky soft skin, it felt like I was touching the outside of a chilled watermelon.

My breathing came faster—harder.

I didn't care if I interrupted her sleep or not. I pulled my head out from under the weight of hers. Her head flopped down. Her chin rested on her chest at an unnatural angle.

I jumped to my feet. My heart raced. Panic spread up from my toes. My mouth went dry and I couldn't swallow. "Memaw," I said, poking her shoulder with my finger.

She still wouldn't wake up.

My whole body took to shaking from the inside out.

I didn't see Daddy come up beside me, but I felt him there.

Mama was sobbing.

I just stood there.

I didn't move.

I didn't cry.

I couldn't breathe.

I just stood there.

Georgie paced back and forth with Cricket pushed against his chest, punching jabs at the empty air in front of him.

The wind was blowing fierce. Howling. Screaming. Something crashed down onto the roof. *Thud!*

Sealy was crying louder than anyone. The twins fussed and wanted to be picked up. Mama was down on her knees. Daddy hovered over her, with his head all slouched down.

"Do something, Daddy!" I shouted, in a voice that didn't sound like me.

"It's too late, Armani. She's gone," Daddy said, through his own tears.

"What're you sayin'?" I shook so hard my teeth chattered. "Save her like you did with Kheelin!"

Daddy still didn't move. He just fussed over useless Mama.

The house shifted under my feet. The world rattled and whooshed.

Why wouldn't he at least try *to save her?*

I all but pushed Mama out of the way. I grabbed hold of Memaw's shoulders so I could lay her down and do CPR like I'd seen Daddy do for Kheelin. But she was heavy and wouldn't move. Sweat poured off me. I was shaking and clumsy. I needed to hurry.

Daddy tried to wrap his arms around me.

I wiggled free, never taking my eyes off Memaw. Daddy put hisself between me and Memaw. I swung at him and landed a good one somewhere in the middle of his belly.

"Leave me alone!" I screamed at him. "Someone's gotta save her!" I kept trying to move her.

"Armani, please stop," Daddy said, wiping his tears away with the bottom of his shirt. "It's too late, baby, she's gone."

"No, she's not! Stop saying that." I couldn't catch my breath.

I tried again to move her, this time with a big heave, but Memaw's lifeless body fell sideways, to where she looked like she was kissing her own kneecap.

Everyone gasped. Sealy cried louder.

Mama came to me. She stood beside me, barely placing her hand on my shoulder.

"Memaw's with Jesus, Armani," she said, with tears streaming down her face. Everything was blurry through my own tears that wouldn't fall. My head throbbed.

Mama gave my shoulder a little squeeze. She walked away and went over to tend to Sealy, who fell into her arms like a rag doll.

Daddy was over in the corner, trying to get Georgie to stand still.

I took Memaw's hand into mine. I kissed the top of it where it was extra soft. I pressed her hand to my cheek. A tear fell and rolled across her hand. "I love you, Memaw," I said, sucking in hot, thick air. I looked down at her crumpled body. My tears started flowing.

Without saying a word, Daddy came over and scooped up Memaw like she didn't weigh more than Sealy. He carried her to the far side of the attic and laid her down, careful not to let her head bump the floor.

I crawled over and sat beside Memaw, losing control of my crying. It came in long, loud sobs.

Daddy kneeled down and put his arm around me. "I know, baby, I know," he said softly near my ear. My head started to fall toward his shoulder.

His arm went around me tighter. "It's going to be all right, NeeNee."

A bolt stabbed into my heart. I pushed him away, all but knocking him to the floor. I jumped up, trembling, and glared at him. "Shut up! Don't *ever* call me that!"

He stared at me, his mouth half open, his eyes all puffy and wet.

After a few solid stomps in the clunky boots, I stood over by Mama. I whipped around and gave him a serious head slide, my eyes burning and glazed over. From the bottom of where all my meanness is stored, I said in a slow and even tone, "*No one* calls me that but Memaw." We locked eyes for only a second, till Daddy slowly turned away with his head hanging down.

Tears streamed down my face as I watched Daddy bend down to kiss Memaw on her forehead. Then he unbuttoned his thin ol' shirt.

He took it off, and covered my Memaw. All the air, and happy, and knowin', and . . . *everything* got pulled out of me and left me standing there empty on wobbly legs.

I threw myself into Mama's arms and cried till I had no tears left inside me. Daddy was holding Georgie the way Mama was holding me.

We stayed like that till the tree broke through the roof and landed in the middle of our attic, separating me from Memaw.

My brothers and sisters were all screaming and crying—I could see it on their faces. But I didn't hear anything.

I looked up through the huge hole in the roof. The black of the night fell into me and took me in. I closed my eyes. There was finally gonna be enough air to breathe.

CHAPTER 19

The night was close to over by the time Daddy found a safe way for us to climb out of the hole in the roof that the tree had made.

When Mama and the kids started making their way through the hole, my brain and my heart got in a scuffle. Surviving the nightmare meant getting out of the attic, but I didn't wanna leave Memaw behind. She didn't like being by herself   always making sure one of us was close by for company. How could we just up and leave her so—alone?

Me and Daddy were the last ones left in the attic. I wanted to tell him it was wrong to leave Memaw, and that I was sorry for being hateful, but I wasn't ready to talk to him just yet. So I kept quiet, letting myself be pushed through the jagged hole and onto the roof.

The sky was midnight blue, with tiny white stars blinking everywhere. I took a deep breath and sucked in a huge gulp of the fresh night air. It was the first real breath I'd taken since Memaw had died. A new batch of tears filled my eyes. I squeezed the compass-locket between my hands.

I tore my eyes from the star-filled sky and seen the silhouette of Mama keeping watch over her babies. They were sleeping at her feet. She was holding herself and swaying from side to side. She stared up at the dark sky, the moonlight shining off the soft curves of her face.

Mama had lost her mama. I took in another long breath of the sweet nighttime air.

It was like the house knew we were gonna be needing to come stay on the roof, so it turned itself just so, giving us a tiny, almost flat spot to be on. Even still, I was nervous walking in the dark on the slippery roof, shuffling along in the bulky rubber boots.

Mama never took her eyes off Heaven. I slipped my hand into hers. She squeezed it with all her might. I leaned into her and cried. The starlight caught hold of a tear sliding down her cheek.

We stood there for a time, letting the sadness take over while heaven looked on.

———

"No way!" Georgie shouted. His voice cut through the night air. "Daddy, look at this!"

Not again.

Georgie was shining the flashlight back and forth in front of him, looking at something over the side of the roof.

The sound of sloshing, dogs barking, people hollerin', Cricket whining—the noise filled my head all at once.

I inched closer so I could see what he was fussin' about.

"We've floated out into the middle of the Gulf, Daddy!" Georgie had Cricket up under his arm. I didn't care. My arms were too heavy for holding.

"Armani," Mama said, touching my arm. "Stay here with the twins. Don't let them move."

I nodded. Mama baby-stepped her way on shaky legs over to Daddy. He held her tight when she stared over the side. I held my breath wondering what it was that she might've been seeing down there. Her hand flew up to her mouth. She buried her head into Daddy's shoulder.

"What's going on?" Sealy asked.

"I don't know," I answered.

Daddy walked Mama all careful-like back over to where I was with the little ones.

Mama looked at me with mournful eyes. "There's water *everywhere*," she said in a heavy, tired voice. She all but fell into my arms—all the weight of her sadness was on me.

Daddy cupped the side of my face in his big, shaky hand. I wanted to hug him more than ever, and for him to hug me back. But I couldn't look at him. I didn't want him to see the wanting in my eyes. I turned my eyes away and found a star to stare at.

"You shouldn't make promises you can't keep," I said.

Daddy's hand slowly fell away from my face.

Mama went to crying softly again.

Daddy picked up Khayla and dragged hisself back over near the edge of the roof and sat down. Georgie and Sealy sat down on either side of him. Georgie's glasses kept sliding off his sweaty nose, so Sealy stuck them down inside her book sack, since he couldn't hold onto them and the puppy too. Cricket looked snug and safe up on my brother's lap.

Somewhere close by, something loud splashed into water. Somewhere close by, someone screamed. Chill bumps ran down my back.

"Where did all the water come from, Daddy?" Sealy asked, with her head resting on Daddy's arm.

Kheelin was fussin' and Khayla whined nonstop about being hungry. I did my best to help poor Mama keep them settled. But mostly I concentrated on my ears and whatever Daddy was fixin' to say.

"Well, the levees must've breached and flooded the city. For years people have been saying this could happen. I just never imagined . . ."

"So what's gonna happen to us?" Georgie asked. Him and Daddy looked so much alike in the shine of the moon—both of them without their glasses. "How are we gonna get down from here, Daddy?"

"I don't know, son. I don't know."

———

Cricket was harder to handle than Khayla and Kheelin put together. None of us wanted to let her walk around on account of us being up on a rooftop and all, but she couldn't handle being held another minute.

Daddy told Georgie to let Cricket loose so she could move a little, but to watch her close. Georgie set the puppy down, and right away

Cricket went to sniffing—walking with her little nose stuck to the rooftop.

It wasn't like Hurricane Katrina had blown any good sense in for Georgie, so I kept a close eye on the situation.

When the twins weren't sleeping, they were fussin'. Poor Mama had her hands full trying to soothe them with nothing more than the sweetness of her voice.

Sealy had took to mothering Khayla. I hadn't seen Sealy with a book of any kind in a good while. Maybe she was feeling about reading and writing the way I was feeling about talking and helping.

I watched the stars disappear as the sky turned to a softer blue with the promise of light right behind it.

Daddy'd been sitting over by hisself for a long while. It tugged on my heart to go talk to him. I needed him to know that I was sorry and still loved him.

I stood up, fixin' to go make my apology, when Cricket went into a spin. She was spinning and yapping and chasing the stub of a tail connected to her backside. Kheelin started to giggle.

Georgie walked in circles around the spinning puppy. He started laughing too.

"Be careful, son," Daddy warned.

"I will, Daddy."

Even though it was a relief to hear something besides the constant sound of the water rushing, and the far-off shouts echoing in the early morning air, it still seemed wrong that anyone could laugh with Memaw lying dead right up under us.

Like someone flipped a switch, the sun showed itself—pouring a creepy, beautiful orangey glow over everything. I didn't have to go look over the edge of the roof no more to see the water. It was *everywhere*, just like Mama said. Water for miles and miles. The sun reflecting off the gasoline-smelling water made it look like we were surrounded by liquid fire. It felt like the end of the world.

I clomped in Memaw's boots, heading over by Daddy. No matter what, I needed him to know I was sorry. But I never made it that far.

CHAPTER 20

A huge telephone pole floated by and slammed into the side of our house. Every one of us gasped. It was a wonder it didn't split the house right in half. I almost got shook clean out of the dang boots.

But Cricket—she kept right on going with her performance, spinning faster than ever, looking like a cute little circus dog entertaining an audience. The kids clapped along and went back to their laughing.

Mama didn't think it was funny. Neither did Georgie or Daddy—or me. The sight of that puppy circling out of control gave me a heavy feeling of dread.

The dog was spinning and yapping herself closer and closer to the edge of the roof. Daddy was on his feet, looking every bit as nervous as me. My heart pounded harder—faster.

"Georgie! Grab her!" I yelled. *How stupid could he be? All he had to do was reach down and pick her up!*

"I'm trying!" he said in a high, squeaky voice. He was walking with his legs spread, hunched over right behind her, with his hands held out. But the puppy was fast.

"Cricket," he kept saying all nervous-like. "Come here, Cricket." He pushed his glasses that weren't there back up on his nose.

Cricket was spinning herself silly.

"Georgie! Just pick her up!" I stomped my foot. I was scared to move too fast, but I knew I had to get over there and grab the dog. I took a few clumsy steps.

"Armani, stop!" Daddy hollered.

At the exact same time Georgie yelled, "Cricket!"

And Mama yelled, "Nooo!"

I froze, with my mouth hanging wide open, and watched sweet little Cricket spin herself right off the edge of the roof.

A split second later, a very small *plop* sound came from the water flowing no more than twelve inches from the top of our house.

My hands flew up to my mouth.

Georgie twisted his head around and looked at me. Our eyes locked in on each other. I was fixin' to tear into him regarding how incredibly stupid he was, when he blurted out, "It's okay, Armani! I'll get her!"

Before any of us could scream *No!*, that crazy boy jumped right off the roof.

CHAPTER 21

Mama was wailing at the top of her lungs.

I could barely see the tiny black speck of Cricket bobbing in and out of the disgusting water. It was flowing like an orange river, and my puppy had already floated far away.

But it was my big brother who made the world stop spinning. The second Georgie landed in the gross water, he went completely under. His head popped up to the surface and he swung his arms every which way. He was in trouble.

The water was taking him away from us so fast! He kept taking huge gulps of water into his mouth every time his head disappeared under the orangey-black foamy water.

Someone was screaming, "Georgie!" Then I realized it was me.

Daddy stood on the edge of the roof, his chest heaving in and out so fast it looked like he'd been running. He turned and looked at Mama.

"Katherine," Daddy said softly.

Mama slowly pulled her stare away from the water. She closed her eyes. Tears were streaming down her face. Then she silently nodded her head *yes*, just one time.

She opened her eyes and looked at Daddy. With a sob, she whispered, "I love you, George." It was the first time I ever heard her call him by his first name.

Daddy's eyes met mine, just for the tiniest second. He never said a word.

And then Daddy jumped into the water.

CHAPTER 22

Mama crumbled to her knees and a long, deep cry poured from her heart out into the world. It was a sound that came from the place where all the deepest sadness gets stored up. There was no one in the entire world who was feeling more grief right then than Mama. The sound of her heart breaking must've reached Heaven, 'cause just then, it started to rain. Not hard—a soft rain, like tears sprinkling down on us. There was so much sadness coming from our rooftop it had reached the angels. They were crying too.

———

The drizzling rain had stopped. The sun was shining. The sky was perfectly blue. The hurricane had come out of nowhere, changed everything, and then it was gone.

I couldn't see a single living soul in any direction, but I could hear them. It felt like we were alone in the new upside-down world, left—just the five of us—alone with the sounds of suffering. Dog barks echoed all around us. People screamed and wailed—the shrieking kind that makes the top of your head tingle with fear. I'd close my eyes and listen careful, hoping it might be Daddy or Georgie hollerin' for help. But it wasn't.

The mesmerizing orange of the water was gone—the dark ugliness of it was plain to see. The water was thick. Black. Alive. And the smell—the smell got laid down in me and brought a shiver that ran along my bones.

I sat on the roof in the clump of what was left of my family—me and Mama with our backs against each other. I held Khayla on my lap, Mama held Kheelin, and Sealy lay by our side.

The buzz of motorboats filled the air, and with that came more screams and shouts from people we couldn't see.

We sat there—sat and did nothing but swat flies. We sat with Memaw lying dead beneath us in a disgusting attic. We sat without Daddy and Georgie and my birthday puppy 'cause they were gone—sucked away by the water monster.

So we just sat.

———

Sealy jumped to her feet and pointed at the sky. "Armani, do you see it?"

I really didn't feel like playing one of Sealy's immature guessing games, and I definitely wasn't in no mood to be bothered. So I just said, "Um-hmm," and kept staring at the way Memaw's boots caught the sun when I moved them just so.

Mama had a grip on Sealy's wrist, but the girl started waving at the sky with her free arm.

"Armani, look! It's a helicopter!"

Whop, whop, whop, whop, whop . . .

I tore my eyes away from the boots and put my hand up over my eyes to block the glaring sun. That's when I seen it. It *was* a helicopter!

I practically tossed Khayla onto Mama's crowded lap and jumped to my feet.

Please stop, please stop, help us, please stop . . .

My heart was racing. I went to bouncing on my tippy-toes up inside the boots. I almost smiled. But I didn't. I was full of nervous and excited at the same time.

"Mama! It's going to be all right!" Sealy hollered. "We're gonna be rescued!"

Me and Sealy jumped up and down, shouting and waving our arms at the approaching metal bird.

Mama stood with the twins sitting between her spread legs. She waved and hollered louder than I've ever heard before. "Over here! Over here! I have children! Over here!" She stifled a whimper with her hand over her mouth.

All of us, even the twins, were yelling and flapping our arms as it got closer.

The wind coming off that thing made waves that slapped up against our house so hard it shook. The helicopter was right above us.

Sealy was hollerin' about something, but I couldn't hear her on account of the loud *whop, whop, whop* of the helicopter blades twirling two thousand miles an hour. It flew so low, I thought it was gonna take off the tops of our heads.

A man hanging out of the side of the helicopter waved at us. We waved back, smiling and jumping for joy!

And then, just like that, the helicopter was gone. The pilot flying that thing flew right past us, like he sees families jumping and shouting on rooftops every day.

I felt like I'd been punched in the belly.

Sealy whipped around with big ol' puppy eyes. "They're coming back, aren't they, Mama?"

Mama stood there with her sorrowful eyes locked on the empty sky. Her whole face sagged.

I fiddled with Memaw's locket and took a big breath. With an award-winning smile, I said, "Well, of course they're comin' back. They can't just go landin' helicopters on people's roofs without permission. Right, Mama?"

Mama looked at me, her eyes telling me I'd found the right words, so I kept going. "They're most likely flyin' back to their headquarters right this very minute, so they can get the go-ahead to fly on back here an' rescue the Curtis family. Watch. You'll see."

Sealy looked sideways at me. "Are you sure they saw us?"

Mama took a step away from the twins and stepped closer to me. She put an arm around my shoulder and kissed me lightly on my cheek.

"Of course they saw us, sweetheart," Mama said. "Armani's right. There are procedures for things like this. They saw for themselves that we're fine, and they'll be back before you know it." Mama gave an award-winning smile too.

Sealy let out a sigh. "Well, that makes sense." Then she gave us one of her sunshiny smiles and said, all bubbly, "I can't wait to be rescued!" She all but skipped back to her spot on the roof and pulled the journal out of her book sack.

Mama hugged me and whispered in my ear, "Thank you."

She went back to sitting with the kids, making sure no one moved from their spots. I stood for a good bit staring into the murky water, wondering how long it takes for a person on a roof to die from no food and no water.

I was fixin' to sit back down with my family when a big ol' speckled dog came floating by. He was standing on top of one of them red and white coolers, just a-wagging his tail, letting out happy barks, like he was having a good ol' time. He sailed right on up to the side of our house, bounced off, then kept right on gliding by, taking the same exact path that Daddy and Georgie had.

————

Mama and Sealy decided that since we were about to be rescued, we should try to clean ourselves up. We took turns fixin' each other's hair. Mama tore the hem off her dress and tied lime-green headbands on Khayla and Kheelin to keep the sweat from running in their eyes. It almost felt—normal. But then, I'd hear a far-off shout, or sirens, or a *whop, whop, whop* and my brain would snap right back to the nightmare we were living. I wished more than anything that Memaw would've been there to hum us through our horrible time on the roof.

Sealy had her hands all up in Mama's hair and I was looking out across the nasty water trying to count rooftops when a yellow butterfly came and landed right on the toe of my rubber boot. Khayla took a swat at it but it stayed there, opening and closing its bright, perfect wings.

I was fixin' to ask how it was that a little butterfly could survive a storm that had ruined everything else when I felt a bump up against our house.

"Excuse me, ma'am?" The man's voice came out of nowhere. Me, Mama, and Sealy almost rolled right off the roof at the same time.

Sitting right there, so close I could touch him with a stick, was a big, burly white man in a teeny-tiny boat.

CHAPTER 23

We must've looked a sight to that man. All of us sat there for the longest time staring at him, like we wasn't expecting company.

Then Mama started to shake. The quivers traveled from Mama's head up Sealy's arms, where she still had her hands lost in Mama's hair.

Mama pulled loose from Sealy's fingers and stood on shaky legs. She pointed at the water in the direction where Daddy and Georgie had floated away. Her hand was trembling so bad, I had to keep myself from reaching up to hold it still.

"My . . . my . . . my husband and son . . ." Mama managed to say, but then she shuddered with upset.

The man looked in the direction that Mama had pointed. He pulled off his black and gold ball cap and hooked one of his thumbs in the tattered strap of his blue jean overalls. He wiped the top of his almost bald head with the back of his arm, and put the hat back on.

"Yes, ma'am. I been gettin' a lot of that from folks." He hung his head and shook it back and forth a couple times too many.

When he looked back up at us, he squinted at the twins. "You got babies up there." He said it like maybe he was telling us something we didn't know.

Before he introduced hisself, he tossed up bottles of water. It was the most delicious water I'd ever had. It was clean, and sweet, and cold.

Mama cried grateful tears. She kept saying thank you while we took long gulps of the water.

When he threw the fried Hubig's pies to us, Mama reacted like she'd been thrown a bag of gold. Khayla tore into hers before I could even get the wrapper all the way off. She had the whole thing gone before we had a chance to thank the generous man.

I ate about half of mine, chewing every sugary bite real slow, while my taste buds popped and grabbed hold of all the crusty, creamy lemony flavors.

Khayla stared at me with her mouth hanging open, eyes glued to my food, globs of lemon filling from her forehead to her elbows. I was starving. I could've ate at least a hundred of them flaky fried pies right there on the spot. But when I seen the hunger showing on my baby sister's face, I took one more small bite, then gave the rest to Khayla. She didn't say thanks, but her smile let me know I'd done the right thing.

Sealy unwrapped hers all gentle-like. She took one bite, and moaned, "Mmm . . . ," chewing at the same time. Then, like in slow motion, she folded the edges of the wrapper back over the top of what was left and tucked it down inside her book sack. She took a careful step closer to the edge. Mama grabbed her arm. "Are you here to rescue us, Mister?"

"Well, I reckon y'all need rescuin', that's for sure." He had a smile that I liked.

"I—I can't leave," Mama said in a panic.

"But Mama," Sealy said, "we *have* to leave. We can't stay here."

Mama looked at Sealy with eyes full of worry and confusion.

"Ma'am?" the man said directly to Mama.

Mama tore her eyes from Sealy and planted them on me. "I don't know what to do, Armani."

Tears were flowing. I didn't know what to say. My own eyes were blurry.

Sealy stared at me with her face all hopeful. The sweaty, sleepy-looking twins sat there on the hot roof, too pitiful to even fuss.

I looked down at the plump white man in the tiny boat, with the smile I'd taken a liking to. I caught a glimpse of something yellow on his cap. I rubbed my eyes with my fists to get rid of the blurriness. There right on top of the wore-out ball cap was the yellow butterfly that had been resting its wings on my boot a few minutes earlier.

I couldn't take my eyes off of it. "We would sure appreciate it, sir, if you could get us off this roof." As soon as I said the words, the butterfly fluttered away. Chill bumps raced down my arms.

Mama moaned.

I took her hand. "Mama, we have to get the twins somewhere safe."

Her eyes were closed and she wouldn't stop crying.

"I promise, Mama," I said, like I was the mama and she was the child, "we'll tell the police or someone about Daddy and Georgie." A cry got caught in my throat. "But we *have* to go with this nice man."

Sealy was crying quiet. I kept my teary eyes on Mama. I took hold of Sealy's hand and walked her to the edge of the roof.

I sat down, my legs hanging over the side. Sealy climbed up on me, and I whispered in her ear, "I'm gonna slide you down. You'll be okay." A tear rolled down my face.

"I trust you, Armani," Sealy said in a whisper-cry.

The man in the tiny silver boat reached up, and I slid my little sister off my lap and into the arms of the stranger.

———

His name was Mr. Oscar Dupree. He's the man who saved us from wasting away on that roof.

After Sealy, I slid Khayla down. As soon as that baby thunked into the bottom of the boat, she grabbed hold of Mr. Oscar's leg and made it clear she wasn't letting go for nothing.

When I asked Mama to give me Kheelin so she could get on the boat next, she turned from me and started to cry all over again.

"You—you go on without me," she sputtered.

"Mama, you have to come with us." I swiped at a useless tear, wishing she would stop being so hardheaded. I real careful got to my feet.

There was a fear and a sadness carved into my mama's beautiful face that filled me with a knowin' that I figure I'll always have.

"Armani," she said, nodding her head, talking like she was begging me to keep a secret. "Take the girls and go." She looked past my shoulder and down at the little boat.

"Mama, we ain't leaving without you." I looked her straight in the eyes, my words coming from my heart.

"I can't leave without your Daddy." She took in a big breath. "And Georgie . . . and Mama Jean." Her world caving in was the most horrible thing I've ever seen in my life. I didn't know how to make it better for her.

"But Mama." I finally found my voice. "Please, Mama. I can't do this. I can't leave you."

Sealy was crying loud down in the boat.

"Excuse me, ma'am," Mr. Oscar said, clearing his throat. "I know it ain't none of my business, but—"

"Mama, I can't do this without you. I *need* you." I was near a full-blown panic. Mama closed her eyes and shook her head back and forth.

I leaned up on her chest and wrapped my arms around her and Kheelin. I whispered, "Mama, Sealy and Khayla need you. I can't take care of them proper without you. *Please*, Mama."

She opened her eyes and looked at me, her face wet with tears. As plain as Mama has ever said anything, she said, "I'm sorry, Armani, but I can't. I can't leave them." She stood tall and sniffed. Her tears stopped flowing. "Now, you do what I say, and you get on that boat."

"But Mama . . ."

"You can do this, Armani. I have faith in you. You're special, my darling. You're strong. I know the children will be fine with you." She wrapped herself around me and squeezed for a quick, long second. I didn't want that hug to end. Not ever. When I looked up at her, she smiled sweet and said, "Your daddy's going to be so proud of you, Armani."

I looked down at my sisters sitting in the boat. They were both crying, looking so pitiful and small. Somewhere deep inside, I knew I had to get on that stupid boat.

I never paid no attention to where my heart sits up inside my chest, but it wasn't ever gonna be a mystery to me again. The breaking of it was a feeling like a hundred thousand cinder blocks piled on top of me, making it so I couldn't breathe.

I kissed Kheelin and gave Mama a kiss on her cheek. I reached behind my neck and unhooked the locket that Memaw had gave me right before she died. I stayed fixed on Mama's watery eyes till I had the compass-locket sitting pretty around her neck. Then I made my way over to the edge of the roof in Memaw's clunky boots. I sat down all wobbly, almost falling headfirst into the smelly, murky water.

Mr. Oscar reached up and helped bring me aboard his dinky boat. He wiped his tears away. I was glad to see that his heart matched his smile. He told us to sit and stay still. I didn't take his advice. If I was leaving Mama and my baby brother on a roof, I was at least gonna stand, so I could watch her for as long as possible.

"Ma'am, I'll send word regardin' you and the baby. I'll try to come 'round an' check on ya if I can," Mr. Oscar Dupree said, looking at Mama.

"Take care of them," Mama blubbered, crying wide open.

"Yes, ma'am," Mr. Oscar said. Then his foot pushed up against the side of our lopsided house, shoving us out into the rolling water.

"Mama!" Sealy wailed.

"Maaaamaaa!" Khayla hollered over and over. She reached her short, thick arms up and out, like Mama could stretch across water and nab her right out of the boat. Sealy held tight to her the best she could, till Khayla took to kicking and squirming. Khayla plopped out of Sealy's arms and landed with a tiny thud back onto the bottom of the boat. She screamed. I looked down, knowing I should pick her up, but I couldn't move.

Mr. Oscar scooped Khayla up and went straight into a bouncy, singsongin', "Shhshh, *bébé*, shhshh."

All I could do was stare at Mama holding tight to Memaw's compass-locket and Kheelin, wondering why God was taking away my family.

CHAPTER 24

I had my eyes fixed on Mama still standing on the roof with Kheelin when Mr. Oscar Dupree's boat made a *clunk* sound. We'd run into something.

I turned just in time to see a big ol' tire, like the kind that goes on a school bus or eighteen-wheeler, bouncing off the front of Mr. Oscar's boat.

"Will ya look at that," Mr. Oscar mumbled under his breath.

"Armani, look!" Sealy said, pointing at the sight.

The Boman kids . . . clinging for dear life up inside a tire boat.

All four of the kids stared at us. They didn't say hey or nothing. They just slowly drifted past us. They wore pajamas and were even filthier than usual. I tore my eyes away from them and stole a look at Sealy and Khayla.

Right then I knew the only difference between them Boman kids and us was the color of our skin. I couldn't help but wonder if their daddy was floating somewhere, or if their mama was standing stubborn on a roof.

The littlest Boman kid lifted his arm like it weighed a ton and tried to wave a tired wave. Tears fell from his droopy blue eyes, running streaks right through the grime on his face. Sealy waved back all slow, and started a new flood of tears all her own before burying her face in the top of her book sack.

"You know them?" Mr. Oscar asked.

Without taking my eyes off the tire full of kids, I answered, "No, sir, not really. They just ride our bus." I ain't sure why, but right then, maybe 'cause of the look in the oldest boy's eyes, I felt like maybe I *did* know them.

"Armani!" Mama hollered off in the distance, jumping up and down and waving one arm in the air.

"Sealy! Armani! Come back! Hurry!" Mama screamed. Something had Mama in hysterics.

"Go back!" I yelled at Mr. Oscar.

"We can't go back," the man said. "I promised your mama I'd get you kids somewhere safe."

Sealy stood up and the little boat tilted to one side. "Please, Mr. Oscar," she said in that sweet way of hers.

Without another word, Mr. Oscar Dupree turned his boat around. He zigzagged around floating trees, knocked-down telephone poles, chunks of people's houses, and lots of things I couldn't or didn't wanna recognize—and we headed back to Mama.

Wheezing. Loud wheezing, a sound I never thought I'd be grateful to hear. It's on account of that terrible sound that Mama was forced to come to her senses.

No one had to talk her into getting in the boat. Mama all but jumped right off that roof when we came up alongside the house.

"What's going on with that boy?" Poor Mr. Oscar looked like he was about to kick all of us off his boat, just for being too much trouble.

Mama's voice was loud and strong. "He's having an asthma attack and the inhaler's empty. I have to get to a hospital." I liked the sound of Mama being strong.

"I can't take ya to a hospital." Mr. Oscar looked nervous and wore out like the rest of us. "I hear they got some Red Cross folks scattered about," he said while steering the boat in the direction of safety.

"Yes! Take us there," Mama said. "But, Mr. Dupree, please hurry."

The man looked at Kheelin struggling to breathe in Mama's arms. He turned his dirty ball cap around backward and stood up tall and straight, poking his extra-round belly out. "Yes, ma'am," he said, and nodded at Mama. He handed her an ice-cold water from his Styrofoam cooler. "Don't y'all worry. That young boy's gonna be fine once we get him cooled down." The man was right, 'cause after Mama rubbed water bottles from the cooler along Kheelin's back and face, the wheezing all but stopped.

"Now y'all sit down and let's see how fast we can get ol' Nessie goin'."

"Who's Nessie?" Sealy asked. She pulled out her stashed Hubig's pie, took the tiniest nibble, then slid it back into her book sack.

Mr. Oscar tapped his hand on the outside of the boat. "This here's Nessie, darlin'. She might not look like much, but she gets me up and down the bayou just fine."

Sealy giggled. "That's funny. You named your boat Nessie."

"Yup," Mr. Oscar said. Then he looked down at my sister and gave her that smile of his that reminded me of Santa Claus. "Ol' Nessie outrunned four gators in one day, yeah she did."

"Really?" *Sealy believed everything.*

While they went on talking, my eyes met Mama's. Neither one of us said anything. It was like we were talking to each other without words. Something had changed between us. I could feel it as much as I could feel the weight of Khayla putting my legs to sleep.

CHAPTER 25

We drifted past the first dead body when the sun was bright and high in the sky. The body was floating upside down and bonked right into the side of the boat. Mama shoved Sealy and the twins' heads into her bosom, hiding their eyes from the sickening sight.

I couldn't stop staring.

"Close your eyes," Mama said. But I couldn't. My eyes were wide open.

I tried to push the ugly thoughts away of Daddy or Georgie floating out there somewhere. I felt sick.

———

Nothing looked familiar. I knew we were in the Ninth Ward, where I'd been living my whole life. But I was lost.

We drifted along in Mr. Oscar Dupree's boat. I only counted three houses that weren't completely under the water, or outright destroyed, or sitting cockeyed crazy like our house was.

"Hey, over here!" a man standing on a roof yelled at us.

"That man's hollering at you, Mr. Oscar," Sealy said.

"Umhum," he mumbled. I seen him look up at the man without moving his head.

The man on the roof wasn't alone. There were about ten people up there with him—some of them were kids, like Sealy and the twins. A large, heavyset woman walked to the edge of the roof and threw something. The empty Coke can landed in the boat, barely missing the side of Kheelin's head resting in Mama's lap.

I jumped up, rocking the boat, and hollered, "Are you crazy? You almost hit my baby brother!"

"Crazy?" The round woman screamed and threw a string of cuss-words down at us. "I'll show ya crazy if y'all don't get us off this hot roof!" When that woman started flapping her fat sausage-looking arms around, I knew right away who it was.

"Mrs. Louell! Hey, it's me, Armani Curtis!"

"I don't give a rat's behind who ya are. All's I'm sayin' is y'all best get that white man over here and get me an' mine off this roof!" With every word, that woman's voice got louder and squeakier.

Mr. Oscar never took his eyes off the water in front of the boat. He said real quiet, so Mrs. Louell and her family couldn't hear, "There's no room on this here boat. I'm sorry, darlin'."

I stole a quick look over at Mama, and knew that Mr. Oscar was right. There wasn't no room, especially for the likes of Mrs. Louell. But I still felt terrible just leaving them there like that.

"Mrs. Louell, there ain't enough room. We'll send someone for you." I had to turn around to shout at her 'cause we'd already drifted past their house.

That woman and half her family threw anything and everything they could get their hands on at us. Luckily, none of them was quarterback for the Saints.

From then on, it was mostly a quiet, bumpy, roundabout ride. I hung my head, trying to breathe in the fading lavender smells buried deep down in Khayla's hair. I had to do something to cover up the gassy, rotten smell coming off the nasty water.

Mama all but came up out of the boat when somewhere close by gunshots rang out and the sound of dogs barking blasted through the air.

Mr. Oscar Dupree kept saying under his breath, "We're almost there." Never, one time, responding to the sights and sounds around us. I was beginning to wonder if there really was a place called "there."

The air in my lungs stopped moving altogether when I seen the steeple of our church sticking up out of the water. And the Bibles. There were floating Bibles *everywhere*.

Sealy reached over the side of the boat and scooped one of the books out of the putrid water. It smacked with a wet *thunk* on the floor of the boat. None of us said nothing. But we all knew she'd done the right thing.

The flash of hope I got from seeing something I knew and recognized got swallowed up quick by the rush of nausea that filled my whole body.

Uncle T-Bone's house was gone. If the steeple was poking up out of the Bible-filled water, my good sense told me that Uncle T-Bone's house should've been right there. Even if it was under the water, it should've been right where I was looking. But it wasn't.

Mama let out a gasp.

"Y'all all right, ma'am?" Mr. Oscar asked.

Mama squeezed her eyes shut and shook her head no.

"We're almost there," he said again in that same calm voice.

I was fixin' to ask him once and for all if he knew where the heck he was going when my mouth snapped shut.

Something in the water caught my eye. A wave of familiar swept through me, bringing tingles to the back of my neck. I stared and stared, trying with all my might to remember what the floating thing was, and where I'd seen it before. The thought crossed my mind to ask Sealy when out of nowhere, the answer slammed into my head.

Floating there in the water, right along with all them waterlogged Bibles, was a big, floppy tangerine hat—the exact hat that Miss Shug, Lorraine, wore so proud on her head at my birthday party.

I leaned over the side of the tiny metal boat named Nessie and vomited fried lemon pie and bottled water.

CHAPTER 26

My head was pounding and the sour taste still lingered when I seen Mr. Frank's ol' beat-down school bus sitting upside down on top of the building next to the doughnut shop. It was lying up there like a dead animal off to the side of the road, with its legs stuck straight up in the air, except it was the Goodyear tires pointing to the sky instead of stiff armadillo legs.

The bright red shingles of the doughnut shop roof were poking out of the murky water. The shop my Daddy got doughnuts from at the end of every month was the only one in the whole Ninth Ward with a roof the color of snakeberry red.

A new batch of tears went to building up when, all of a sudden, Mr. Oscar brought the little boat to a stop. "This is gonna be as far as I can take y'all," he said.

Mama made herself busy gathering up babies.

"But Mr. Oscar, there ain't nothing here." I swooped my arm, trying to show the nice man that he'd made a mistake.

Mr. Oscar was fiddling with his boat engine and was obviously too busy to notice that he'd stopped his boat in the middle of nowhere, surrounded by water.

"Water's shallow here," Mr. Oscar said, to no one in particular. He wasn't making no eye contact.

"Shallow?" The familiar feeling of panic was creeping in. "What are you trying to say, Mr. Oscar?"

"He's saying the water's not very deep here," Sealy said.

I glared at my sister. "I know what shallow means, Sealy."

I was surprised when Mr. Oscar was the first one to get out of the boat, mostly 'cause he didn't have to get out at all. When he stood in the disgusting, murky water, it came up to somewhere between his kneecaps and his belly.

Sealy picked up the damp Bible from the bottom of the boat and brushed it off with her hand.

"Let me see, darlin'," Mr. Oscar said, and took hold of the used-to-be-waterlogged book. He pulled a red bandanna out from his back pocket. He wrapped the Bible up in the cloth and handed it to my sister.

Sealy just beamed. "Thank you, Mr. Oscar."

"Yup," is all he said.

Sealy put the wrapped-up book down in her book sack and nodded like she was good to go. I closed my mouth and rolled my eyes. I couldn't believe she'd stick anything that'd been in that water inside her book sack.

"Ground's slippery," Mr. Oscar Dupree said, still keeping his eyes busy not looking at any of us. "Y'all be careful ya don't slip."

Whatever. It was obvious he didn't really care, or he wouldn't dump us like a batch of unwanted kittens on the side of the road.

Mr. Oscar offered his hand to Mama, and she took it. She didn't move, though. She held Kheelin with her other arm and stood there for the longest time, staring at the man whose hand she was holding.

A feeling of relief swept over me. Mama wasn't gonna get off the boat. She had too much good sense for that. I wondered how she was gonna inform the man that he had to take us somewhere with land. Dry land.

Mr. Oscar gave his head a little nod, and Mama nodded back at him. "I've got ya, ma'am," he said. "I ain't gonna let ya fall."

Mama turned and handed Kheelin to me without saying a word. A pounding started in my head. I reached for Memaw's locket, forgetting that Mama was still wearing it.

Mama grabbed hold of the corner of her dress and held it up all ladylike. I hoped she wasn't thinking that was gonna prevent it from getting wet. The boat rocked back and forth till Mama was finally up and over the side of the boat and down in the water.

As soon as she was standing, Mama's lime-green party dress took to floating and puffed up like a parachute all around her. The big air bubble caught up under her dress was the problem. Mama started doing her best to push the silly giant bubble down without making a fuss.

Khayla was the first one to start laughing. "Funny, Mama!" she said, pointing at the ridiculous sight.

Sealy's giggle made Mama smile, and before I knew what was happening, Mr. Oscar started to chuckle. His big ol' stomach took to bobbing up and down, causing the water to make laugh ripples.

I'd seen enough. I set Kheelin down in the bottom of the boat and jumped over the side, not even pausing for a second to consider what I was jumping into.

I made a terrible splash. Memaw's boots filled with water, making my efforts to get to Mama clumsy and slow. I slapped at Mama's dress with my hands flying every which way. I didn't care that my splashing was getting Mama and Mr. Oscar's faces wet. I didn't care that I was scaring my brother and sisters to death.

I kept on slapping till I'd shoved all of Mama's poofed-up dress down into the water where it belonged and looked normal.

"There," I said, satisfied and out of breath. I looked at Mama for the first time since I'd jumped off the dry boat. The look on her face stopped me cold. Her eyes were huge, but droopy in the corners. Her mouth was turned as far down as it could've gone without the whole thing just slipping right off her face.

Mr. Oscar had his head down, staring at his own big belly.

"What?" I said, turning toward the boat. Sealy was clutching the twins. Tears streamed down her baby-looking face. Kheelin looked at me like he didn't know who I was.

Mama touched my arm. "Armani, are you all right?"

"Sure, Mama. I'm just fine. Fine as pie." My voice was extra high and disrespectful. "We're all just fine, ain't we, Mama?" I glared at her, sliding my head—crying.

Mr. Oscar Dupree had his arms around me. "Hush, hush . . ." he shushed in my ear.

I wiped my teary face into the man's shirtsleeve.

"You gonna be fine, *bébé*."

I nodded. I couldn't look at him. I wiped my nose on the back of my hand. I reached into the boat and took Kheelin from Sealy. It was plain that he didn't wanna come to me by the way he pulled away and tried to latch onto Sealy for his dear little life. I didn't care. I gave an extra firm tug and took him anyway.

I tried to stomp my way over to Mama, but the dang boots made it feel like I had melons tied to my feet. Kheelin sat up high on my hip, and his legs dragged through the water.

I plopped my baby brother into Mama's arms. I turned back to get another kid before Mama or anybody else had a chance to say a word.

CHAPTER 27

We slogged through the soupy water—one foot in front of the other—not even knowing if we were walking in a straight line. Every time I took a step, I'd scrunch up my toes to keep Memaw's boots from sliding off my achy, wet feet. I tried to concentrate on counting my steps to keep from thinking about what might've been lurking up in that thick, nasty water with us.

Then I started to see all the people. At first it was two or three walking together, making their way through the muck, then I seen more and more. Survivors—like us. It was strange. Never in my whole life had I seen people coming together in the same place, at the same time, and not one of them saying a word. There wasn't no, "Hey, what's up?" or "Hi, how ya doing?" Helicopter buzz filled the air, but it couldn't hide the sounds of the sloshing water, babies crying, dogs barking, and Mama's sniffling.

The heaviness up inside my own self was growing bigger and harder to carry every time another soggy, sad somebody joined our growing group. It was like all the sorrows coming together was turning into its own somebody. Everyone had the same look—scared, confused, hungry, and wore down.

Mr. Oscar Dupree had gave us the foam cooler for one of the twins to ride in. Sealy was so scared her book sack was gonna get wet, she took it off and laid it down under Khayla in the Styrofoam boat. Sealy's only job, besides staying upright on her own two feet, was to help push the cooler holding our little sister while I pulled.

Every time I looked down at Khayla, I was about a hop-skip from losing it. The girl was all smiling and happy, like she was having a good ol' time. She even said, "Go faster," a couple times, like she was on a ride at the church carnival.

I'd be lyin' if I didn't admit that I had more than one thought of wishing I were small enough to ride in the cooler and let someone else worry about hauling my butt through the water while I sat all dry and happy. The thoughts didn't stick around long 'cause I was too busy pulling the dumb Styrofoam boat, switching from my right arm to my left every few minutes.

I dragged my stupid heavy feet through the slime. Heavy on account of the ridiculous, ugly boots. Memaw's boots. Heavy 'cause they didn't fit. Didn't fit 'cause Memaw didn't have enough sense to find shoes that fit. I wiped my idiot tears and snot on my shoulder. Memaw should've known they'd fill up with water. She shouldn't have died in the attic. Everything was so heavy.

Sealy did the best she could pushing the boat-cooler, but the ground up under the water was uneven and slick. We looked like we were drunk the way we kept swaying this way and that.

I was fixin' to ask Mama how much further when my foot slid into a hole in the ground and went sideways. I stumbled. My face was headed for the nasty water!

I grabbed hold of the side of the cheap boat-cooler with both hands to keep from falling. A chunk of white Styrofoam broke off and sent the boat-thing into a rocking wobble.

Khayla squealed and clapped.

Sealy froze.

Mama reached for Khayla's arm too slow.

Khayla tipped right out into the water, making a *plop* sound, just like my birthday puppy did when she spun herself off the roof. She went face first into the goo-water-stew. Me, Mama, and Sealy all scrambled at the same time, all but knocking each other down trying to rescue her.

"Khayla!" Mama shrieked.

I grabbed hold of one of her flailing arms and yanked fast and hard.

Lord have mercy. Memaw sighed in my head. Her voice was so clear and real, I turned my head, expecting to see her standing right there next to me. But she wasn't there. There was no Memaw, no Daddy, and no Georgie, just us—me, Mama, Sealy, forever-wheezin' Kheelin, and soaked-to-the-bone, lucky-to-be-alive Khayla.

It was like the cooler had a mind of its own. It dumped my baby sister out, then went right back to sitting as nice as it could be, with Sealy's book sack tucked all neat and snug at the bottom.

Khayla coughed and made gagging sounds. The disgusting water spewed from her mouth. A tiny bit even dripped out of her nose. She was flapping her arms like a baby bird fixin' to fly. I went to remembering the broken bird family in the nest on top of Daddy's truck. A cold, fast shiver ran from the top of my head to my toes.

"Khayla, are you okay?" Mama cried. Behind the river of tears and trembling lips, I seen something I thought I'd never see in my mama's facc—the soft around her eyes was gone. Her face was all squished into the side of Khayla's plump, wet cheek. She was staring at me and not looking at me at the same time. The sight of her fright had me too scared to speak.

My insides jumped when she took in a big gulp of air and said, "First Georgie, now *Khayla?*" She squeezed her eyes shut. "This is Henry and Shelton all over again. . . ." Her voice drifted off into a whimper.

I was nauseous. Whatever was happening, it was *nothing* like what happened to my dead uncles. Tears fell. I opened my mouth to say sorry, but Mama spoke first.

"What is *wrong* with you?" She whispered the hateful words that cut through me like no kind of hurt I'd felt before. Mama ain't never spit words out at me like she did just then. She glared at me with teary eyes, then just like that, she turned away.

I stood there blinking with my mouth half open in a "Sorry" that Mama never heard.

It *was* my fault that Khayla got dumped in the disease-filled water. I knew *all* of it was my fault.

CHAPTER 28

I struggled to hold on to Kheelin and watched what was left of my family walk on ahead of me while I stood there missing Daddy and Memaw and Georgie. My brother would've found some way or other to make me smile. Memaw would've understood—she always understood me. And Daddy would've known what to do. He'd carry the little ones and take the weight away.

"Armani, it's dry!" Sealy happy-hollered.

Sure enough, I watched Mama set Khayla down on dry concrete. Not a speck of water that I could see. Sealy was staring after me, waving her hand for me to come on.

I walked to dry land and emptied my boots.

———

We walked at least a block before we came around the corner. "Sweet Jesus," Mama mumbled when she seen the sight waiting there for us. Her words were a perfect way of saying exactly what flew through my mind.

There were people *everywhere*. It was like the Super Dome was a giant fire ant hill and all them people around it were the ants. Busy ants, climbing over each other, moving every which way, carrying whatever they could, without leaving their hill—the Dome.

Me and my brother and sisters all scooched up real close to Mama, barely giving her enough room for her legs to move. Khayla was so tucked up under the back of Mama that sometimes when she took a step, her chubby head would disappear altogether up the bottom of Mama's dress.

My mind was reeling. All I could think was that Daddy and Georgie and TayTay *had* to be in that sea of people somewhere. Thumps of excitement tapped up in my chest. *I know I can find you, Daddy.* I was determined to find him. *Where are you, Daddy?* I looked in every direction at the same time. He'd be easy to find—he was tall and handsome and . . .

There were too many people. My mouth got so dry it made a *smack* sound every time I opened it. Sweat ran down from the top of my head and got in my eyes. Panic knocked with loud beats up in my head. It was gonna be impossible to find Daddy and Georgie without standing on a fireman's ladder and shouting at the top of my lungs for the two George Curtises to please raise their hands.

Mama had the look of understanding too, but she kept on searching every which way but up.

"Step aside. Coming through," barked two huge Army guys brushing past us. They were wearing National Guard uniforms like Uncle T-Bone had on when he first got back from Afghanistan, but I don't remember my uncle carrying around a big ol' gun like them soldiers.

They stopped smack-dab in front of us and set a large cardboard box down. I couldn't stop staring at the gigantic, *real* guns.

"Ma'am?" one of the Army guys said, handing Mama bottles of water. She took them and gave one to each of us kids, keeping one for herself.

"Thank you," Mama said, wiping at her dry, puffy eyes. "I need first aid. My son—"

A woman shoved Mama out of her way. The soldier wasn't even paying attention to us no more. Him and the other soldier were yelling at all the thirsty people who came running up, crying, pushing, cussing, begging—*begging* for a bottle of water.

Sealy took a step toward the stirred-up crowd with her bottle held out like she was fixin' to give it to someone.

I yanked her back by her arm.

"Armani—"

"Shut up, Sealy" is all I said.

Mama gathered us up in her arms the best she could and steered us away from the crazies.

Babies were laid out all over the place. Some sound asleep, some lying on the mushy ground, rolled into little dirty, sweaty balls. Most of them didn't have on nothing but a diaper. Every time I sucked in even a tiny bit of stale air, it smelled thick with sweat, stinking canal water, and dirty diapers.

Mamas cradled their children, crying and mumbling. Men walked around with mad looks one minute and holding their own heads in their hands the next.

I twitched with fright every time someone wailed or hollered out. My whole self was a bundle of nerves. Even my eyes were jumpy.

We slogged along with Mama, stuck to her like white on rice—never more than an inch from her side.

Daddy. Georgie. TayTay. Where are y'all? I was so fixed on trying to find them, I didn't notice the dead woman till I'd already gone and tripped over her.

She was lying there shoved up to the side of a brick wall like yesterday's trash. My heart took to racing. The shaking of my body moved the rattle in my head down my arms and settled in my fingers. I tried to reach for my dang boot that had fell off during the act of tripping, but my brain wouldn't let my wobbly hand reach no further toward the boot on account of the fact that Memaw's ol' ugly flowered clodhopper was resting right up in the dead woman's armpit.

"Don't look, Armani! Don't look!" Sealy slammed into my chest, burying her face and squeezing the life out of me at the same time.

I patted her on the back. "It's okay, Sealy. I ain't lookin'."

But the truth is, I couldn't stop looking. I knew who the person was laying there with flies on her eyes. I knew as soon as I seen that filthy, long, gypsy-looking dress. It was that woman outside Pete's with the messed-up dogs.

I couldn't move. I think I might've stood there like a dummy staring all day long if Mama hadn't gone and reached up in front of me and snatched the boot, slapping it firm in my hand all in one quick move.

Mama had the look of nothing on her face. She didn't look mad, or sad, or scared. She didn't even look grossed out by having to remove her child's rubber boot from the armpit of a dead woman. A boot that a few days prior had belonged to her mama, who was now lying up in a hot, wet attic. That's the only way I know how to describe what I'd seen just then on Mama's face—the look of nothing.

I slipped the boot back on and took to walking with my head down, stealing looks into the crowd every couple of steps so that I wouldn't accidentally pass by Daddy and Georgie or TayTay.

CHAPTER 29

I didn't even hear the whistle-wheeze. But when Mama spun around clutching Kheelin to her chest with *that* look on her face, I knew it could only mean one thing.

Mama found us a tiny square of soggy ground and went to arranging us kids like we were lawn furniture.

She hugged wide-eyed Sealy and gave her a forced smile. She wet her thumb with spit and wiped the corners of Khayla's mouth. She kissed her on the top of her frizzy head and laid her down on the ground. She went and balled right up like a scared roly-poly. As quick as a lick, she was as snuggled up as a kid can get lying in dirty grass.

I should've been breaking into a panic, 'cause it was clear that something like a good-bye was coming. But instead, I blinked a couple times, trying to keep my eyes from burning, and sucked in gulps of air.

"Armani," Mama said, "I'm going to go find help for Kheelin."

"But Mama," Sealy whimpered from somewhere behind me.

"You all will be fine." Mama still hadn't looked me in the eye. "I won't be long. Khayla needs to rest. I can move faster without . . . and I won't . . ." Mama cleared her throat. "I won't be long." She was talking fast.

"Please, Mama," Sealy cried, "please let us come with you."

Mama looked at me. "Armani, I need to find help fast. If anything happens to this baby . . ." She squeezed her eyes shut and shook her head from side to side, biting into her bottom lip.

I put an arm around Sealy's shoulder. Right away she went to leaning into me, making it hard for me to keep my balance.

I followed Mama's gaze when she opened her eyes and looked at the craziness all around us. Her head dropped.

Kheelin's wheeze was loud and rumbly. He was having the kind of attack that would've meant calling the ambulance if we'd been at home—before the water came.

"Mama," I said, having a hard time breathing myself.

Mama slowly brought her head up so I could see her face. It was like looking straight into the face of my sweet Memaw. My poor mama's face had gone and turned into an ol' lady face. I wanted to reach out and hold her. I wanted her to hold me too.

The wheezing turned to choking whimpers.

"I have to go, baby girl," she said. A tear slid down her cheek.

"I know, Mama."

Part of growing up meant not crying and fussin' over every little thing. So I sniffed good and strong and let my blurry eyes settle on a smudge on the shoulder of Mama's dress.

"Armani," Mama said, reaching behind her neck to unhook the compass-locket.

I laid my hand on one of her arms and shook my head. "It's all right, Mama. Keep it so you can find your way." I tried to force a smile. A tear found its way into the corner of my mouth. "You can put it on me when y'all get back." I kissed Kheelin's pasty forehead. The salt from his skin laid thick on my lips.

Mama let go of the locket clasp and pulled me in close. She squeezed me as tight as she's ever done. "I'll be right back, I promise." She said the soft words straight into my ear. A burning stabbed at my heart when she said "promise."

She turned and took off, zigzagging fast through the people. The crowd swallowed Mama up, and just like that, she was gone.

CHAPTER 30

There was no telling how much time had gone by since Mama had left. Didn't matter one way or the other nohow, 'cause just one minute sitting there in the middle of nowhere like that was one minute too long.

The smell coming off the earth was rotten. I turned so my nose was close to my shoulder and took in a whiff. A shudder went through me. I smelled like the earth.

Scaly's head rested in my lap and I stared out at the sight I still couldn't believe I was seeing.

I locked eyes with a kid about my age who was sitting off in the madness by hisself. He had that look I'd seen earlier on Mama's face— that look of nothing. I was fixin' to turn away when I seen a girl, a familiar girl.

TayTay?

A bolt of energy shot through me.

"TayTay!" I hollered. I jumped to my feet. Sealy's head hit the ground and her eyes popped open.

The girl kept walking, walking like my cousin with that certain bounce that's all her.

"TayTay!" I hollered and waved my arms.

The girl stopped and looked around, but never in my direction. A cry started building in my belly. The girl went to walking again.

"Is that TayTay?" Sealy asked.

"I think so!" My heart was racing, my head pounding.

"TayTay!" me and Sealy hollered at the same time.

The girl disappeared in the crowd.

"No!" I cried.

"Go after her, Armani!"

I couldn't stop the tears. "I can't."

Khayla looked up with them big sleepy eyes of hers. She smiled at me.

"But you *have* to go after her!" Sealy didn't understand. If I went after TayTay, I'd have to leave *them*.

I rubbed my hand across Khayla's forehead. She closed her eyes and went back to sleep. *Please watch over TayTay*, I prayed for my cousin. *Let her find Daddy and Georgie.*

I sat back down and let my head flop back so I could stare straight up into the bluest sky I'd ever seen. I realized just then that the only thing the storm hadn't ruined was that sky—that buttermilk frosting blue sky. A cry got strangled in my throat. How the sky could be so beautiful, shining all its blueness down on so much ugly, wasn't making a bit of sense to me.

Something large and dark stepped smack-dab in front of me, instantly blocking out the whole promising clean sky.

"Hey, aren't you T-Bone Curtis's niece?" Hearing my uncle's name got me to standing.

The voice belonged to a soldier girl. I recognized the pretty brown face, but I couldn't remember why or how I knew her. Or why or how she knew *me*.

She patted her open hand against her own chest and said "Specialist Salazar" in a voice that reminded me of J.Lo. She seen my eyes fixed on the long gun she had cradled like a baby with her right arm. Real quick she stopped standing stiff as starch and lowered the gun so it was pointing down at the ground. She tilted her head, her eyebrows all but getting lost up under her Army hat. "Stella Salazar. I was with your uncle in Afghanistan."

Her eyes shifted from me to wide-eyed Sealy, then to Khayla laid out in the mud-grass, then down to my feet. She frowned. I wanted to explain that they weren't my boots, but her eyebrows sank over her heavy-hearted eyes, and just then, the boots didn't much matter.

"I was at your house a few months ago for the crawfish boil when our unit first got back from overseas." While she talked, I remembered that day.

It seemed like the whole Lower Ninth turned out for that Welcome Home crawfish boil. Memaw and Mrs. Tilly had sung praises right over the top of Mr. Jasper Junior Sr.'s jazzy saxophone playing in the middle of our road. That had been a great day. The day the soldiers came home. The day Uncle T-Bone came back in one piece.

"Hey." Stella Salazar's voice snapped me back from remembering. "Your name's Armani, right?" She smiled when she said my name. I liked the way she said it, she made it sound pretty. I nodded, wishing I could smile back.

"I remember your name," she said, "because that's the name of my favorite perfume." I liked her.

Sealy threw herself into the girl and wrapped her arms around her. "I remember you!" Sealy squealed. "You're Stella!" They hugged good and tight so long a stranger would've thought they was family. Even after the hug ended, my sister kept right on hanging on poor Stella. My arms were too heavy for hugging.

From somewhere in the belly of the crowd, ear-splitting screams tore through the thick air. Quick *pop-pop-pop* firecracker-like sounds made my insides twitch.

Stella's smile fell right off her face. "Where are your parents?"

Sealy's eyes filled with tears. I swallowed hard and tried to open my mouth to speak, but my lips wouldn't separate. I wondered if Stella could feel Sealy wiping her nose on her Army shirt.

Stella reached down and unbuttoned a long pocket on her pants. She pulled out a bottle of Coke and handed it to me. I forgot all about the times Mama had drilled it into my head about not sharing on account of not knowing exactly where another person's mouth has been.

After me and Sealy took some sips, I offered the bottle back to Stella. She waved her hand in a way that told me she didn't want the bottle back, most likely 'cause her mama taught her the same rule about germs.

Stella was fidgety. "Tell me where your ma—"

Somehow I got all folded up in Stella's strong arms where I cried harder than I thought possible, and blubbered on and on about my missing family. Stella kept saying, "Shh, shh, it's okay, I know, I know," and then some words in Spanish I didn't understand. She sniffled a couple times before she bent down on one knee in front of me. She tipped my chin up with her finger. My eyelids were heavy and tired.

"How long has your mama been gone, Armani?" She said the words soft and quiet, like we were sharing a secret.

I shrugged and looked back up at the sky. I grabbed the sleeve of my shirt so I could clean the tears off my face.

"She's been gone a long time," Sealy said, staring down at the ground.

Khayla started to stir and Sealy went over to her. I was grateful 'cause I couldn't move. I felt like I was up to my knees in cement and it wasn't 'cause of Memaw's boots. It was 'cause all them cinder blocks piling up on each other in my chest had somehow settled in my feet, making it so I couldn't move from the spot I was in. I didn't know if I was *ever* gonna be able to move—anywhere—ever.

Khayla woke up and went straight to fussin' about her tummy aching. Stella picked her up and rubbed on her back. Muffled voices, talking mostly in numbers, came pouring out of the walkie-talkie she had strapped to her shoulder. Deep creases spread across her forehead. She turned her back to me and talked gibberish into the walkie-talkie. She whipped around and looked at me and Sealy again, then took a deep breath.

"Come on," Stella said, with a nod of her head.

"What? Come where?" I asked. I stood there like a dummy, watching her shift Khayla in her arms. Sealy looked at me with her saucer eyes and I could tell her bottom lip was fixin' to pout out.

"You can't stay here, Armani. It's not safe. There are buses." She looked around, lowering her voice to a firm whisper. "They brought in buses to get people out of here, especially kids and women."

This was the best news I'd heard in days. I think I might've even smiled. I could tell Sealy was feeling the same as me, 'cause when I caught a glimpse of her out of the corner of my eye, she was smiling real big and bouncing on her tippy-toes, all excited. She still had them weird, unblinking saucer eyes, though.

"We goin'?" Khayla asked.

"Yep." I smiled all sweet at my baby sister, then smiled just as sweet at our new friend Stella. "That's right, Khayla-girl, we're gonna go all right." I was just a-nodding my head up and down the way Georgie was famous for doing. "We're gonna go find Mama, then get on a nice bus and get right on outta here." I was a rambling, smiling fool. "Ain't that right, Miss Stella?" I nodded at Stella, confirming our plan.

I didn't like the way she tipped her head to the side and her eyebrows went and got all lost again in her pulled-back hair.

"What?" I said. I was ready to go.

"Armani, we can't go find your mama—there's no time. Besides, it's impossible. There's too many people and it's going to be dark soon. The last bus is leaving in fifteen minutes. We have to go *now*."

"What are you sayin'?"

"She's saying we have . . . to go with . . . out Ma . . . ma." Sealy had crying hiccups.

"Well, we can't," I said.

Stella let Khayla slide down her leg till the girl was standing on her own feet. Then she put her arm around my shoulder and led me away from my sisters. "Sealy, I just need to talk to Armani for one sec, okay?"

Sealy sniffed and nodded.

Stella stopped walking after we'd gone a good ways from my sisters. She rested one hand on each of my shoulders. "How old are you, Armani?"

I blinked a tired blink. "What day is it?"

"It's Tuesday. August thirtieth."

"Tuesday?" A whooshing sound filled my head, like the wind moving our world upside down when we was stuck up in the attic and my birthday cake went floating. . . .

"Armani."

I looked at her and the sounds of the chaos around us came rushing back into my ears. "I'm ten."

"Oh, man. Ten?" Stella looked up at the sky and closed her eyes.

"Well, ten an' two days." I sounded pitiful even to my own self.

She took a deep breath and looked at me with a familiar softness around her eyes that made me wonder if Stella had a kid of her own. "Okay, look, I'm only telling you this because you need to understand." Another deep breath. "Bad things are happening here. You and your sisters can't stay here. Not tonight. Do you understand?"

"But what about Mama? We can't just leave her." That stupid shaking that starts in my toes was already making its way up the back of my wobbly legs.

She put her hand up under my chin and squeezed just enough to where it felt like a chin-hug. "You know what I think?" she asked with a little smile.

I shook my head.

"I think I know why your mama left you with the younger kids while she went to get your baby brother the help he needs. She did it because she trusts you and she knew that you could handle it."

The wobble in my legs was going away. "I bet you're a real responsible girl, right?" I shrugged but nodded in a "yeah, sort of" way. I stood a little taller. "Your mama and daddy would want you to leave here on the bus." Stella paused, and stopped smiling. "I'm serious when I tell you that you *can't* stay here tonight." Her smile was completely gone and she had that hard, soldier-like look in her eyes again.

I cleared my throat and looked past her shoulder at Sealy, who was watching me real close. "Well, where's the bus going? How will Mama an' Daddy find us?"

"I don't want you to worry about that right now. You just get to a safe place away from here, and I'll do my best to find your parents and tell them where you are." Loud mumbled voices came pouring out of the walkie-talkie again. "We have to go, Armani. They're about to start loading the last bus."

"Well, maybe we can just wait for Mama in there." I pointed at the huge Super Dome lurking up behind my sisters and a million other people.

"You can't go in there!" Stella all but bit my head off. "First of all, it's about a hundred and six degrees inside the Dome. And besides that, it's no place for little kids."

I forced my shoulders back, trying to stand a little taller. "I'm not a little kid."

"Look, I don't have time to argue with you, Armani. I'm trying to help you because T-Bone's like a brother to me." Stella took a deep breath and turned her head, before looking back at me with them big, round brown eyes. "You have to trust me. Do it for them."

I looked over at my sisters. Sealy was just staring. She was so small, standing there like that.

"Hey," Stella said. "You okay?"

No, I'm sure NOT OKAY. Can't you see that my family is disappearing right before my eyes? I'm NOT OKAY. Nobody's ever gonna be OKAY again. EVER. I screamed in my head.

"I guess," I said in a shaky voice too soft to be coming from me.

Where was Mama?

CHAPTER 31

Specialist Stella Salazar held Khayla with one arm and her rifle in the other. Sealy had hold of a loop attached to Stella's Army pants and was all but running alongside of her to keep up. People stopped pushing and shoving and got out of the way when they seen the soldier with the kids stuck like Velcro coming.

I walked fast and stiff as a board, thinking my chest would burst from the scream I was holding in. I forgot again and tried to grab hold of the locket that wasn't there.

There it was. The bus. I don't know exactly what I was expecting, but I know for sure it wasn't no school bus. There must've been about a hundred thousand people all up in there around that bus.

My heart stopped when the door snapped shut and it started rolling inch by inch away from the crowd of people. I seen ladies smacking the sides of the bus and even throwing perfectly good full water bottles at it. Seemed like everyone was yelling and cussing and acting a fool.

My insides twisted into a knot. I sucked in a gulp of bus fumes when I seen that there was another bus hiding behind the one that just left.

The doors to the bus flew open. A soldier stepped out onto the steps with his legs spread and his rifle up in plain sight for everyone to see. People shoved and pushed and hollered. Two more Army guys came.

"Stay with me," Stella shouted.

I grabbed hold of one of the loops on Stella's other pant leg and put my head down, letting her lead the way. All I could see was feet, lots of feet.

We were at the door to the bus. Stella was talking fast to one of the soldiers as he came down off the bus steps. He nodded at her and she turned to me. She didn't even waste time trying to put on a smile. "Okay, this is it."

My eyes were jumpy, looking every which way, hoping that Mama was up in the crowd somewhere.

Sealy was looking at me all puppy-eyed and sniffling. She wiped her snotty nose across her shoulder.

Khayla wouldn't let go of Stella. I tried my best to peel the girl's fat fingers away from Stella's neck, but my legs went to wobbling and Khayla wasn't budging. I felt like throwing up. *What am I supposed to do?*

Get on the bus, NeeNee. It's gonna be all right. Get on the bus.

Memaw's voice was as loud and clear as ever. I could even hear the hum and smile behind her words.

My head cleared. I knew Memaw was standing beside me. I could *feel* her. A calm fell over me.

"What are we going to do, Armani?" Sealy tugged on my arm.

"We're gettin' on the bus," I said, as sure as I'd been about anything since leaving my other life behind. And just like that, Khayla slid into my arms like it was exactly where she wanted to be.

A loud crackle of noise poured out of Stella's walkie-talkie. "I need to go," she said. She bent down and hugged Sealy. She straightened Khayla's lime-green headband and cupped her hand around one of her cheeks and kissed her there. Khayla never lifted her head off my shoulder or said a word.

Stella held her arm out to me and I fell into her with my whole body. I buried my face in the rough camouflage shirt and she kissed my forehead. "Please find Mama and tell her where we're goin'."

"And Daddy too," Sealy added.

"I'll do my best," Stella said. She started walking away. Me and Sealy stood there watching her go. She stopped and half-turned. She tapped her closed-up fist against her chest two times, pointed straight at me, and hollered, "Stay strong!" My breath got caught. I nodded before she turned to go.

"I will," I whispered.

Specialist Stella Salazar marched off into the sea of crazies.

With Khayla in her usual spot up on my hip and Sealy hanging on to the back of me, we slowly made our way up the bus steps. My nerves were wearing down fast. People were shoving and hollerin', not one bit happy that we'd skipped to the front of the line. Sweat was pouring in my eyes and my arms were trembling from the weight of my baby sister. I kept telling myself, *Stay strong.*

When we finally made it to the top step, I all but stopped breathing when my eyes adjusted to the dark of the bus and I seen all the people. There's a certain way a school bus looks all jam-packed with kids going to school, but it takes on a whole different look when you stuff grown, wore-down people up in there like that.

I barely took two steps into the aisle, when the stupid bus driver stuck her arm out in front of Sealy and said, "Nope, that's it. I can't take no more."

"Armani!" Sealy hollered.

I tried to lift the lady's arm, "Oh, she's with me. She's my sister."

"I don't care who she is. I take seventy-five. Not seventy-four—not seventy-six. Seventy-*five*. Period." The lady had one blue eye that was looking at me and one that was floating off on its own. I didn't like looking at her.

"But she's my *sister*." I thought maybe the driver just didn't understand.

Sealy was whimpering and trying to wiggle her way over to me when that triflin' lady stuck her leg out and blocked the whole dang aisle so Sealy couldn't get to me.

"Armani!" Sealy yelled again.

Khayla felt like ten sacks of sweet potatoes weighing on my arm, and it didn't help when she went to crying about her belly aching. I was drenched in sweat. Somehow I kept from plowing my fist into the ugly woman's fat head and knocking her good eye loose. "But, ma'am," I said as sugary-sweet as I possibly could and pointed at Khayla hanging off the right side of my body. "This one here is gonna sit on my lap. You can't really count her, right?"

"I don't care if she sits up on your nappy head. She counts." The lady wasn't no lady at all. She was a low-down simple mess. Other people on the bus went to fussin' and hollerin'.

"Either you two go sit down and that one there catches the next bus, or all three of you can just get off," she said. "It don't make no difference to me."

I opened my mouth to say something I most likely would've regretted when someone came walking up the aisle from the back of the dark, sour-smelling bus. There was something familiar about the shape of the person who was all but taking up the whole narrow aisle, but I couldn't figure out why.

The driver looked up in her mirror and told the person in the aisle, "Go sit back down."

"No. They can have my seat."

Danisha?

CHAPTER 32

She stepped out of the dark of the bus's belly, and sure enough, it was Danisha. My eyes filled with tears. "Danisha . . . what . . . where . . ."

"I know, Cuz." She wrapped her thick arms around me and Khayla.

"That's it," the stupid bus driver said. "I want all of y'all off my bus. Go on. Get off."

Danisha took hold of my hand. Tears sprung to her eyes. "I lost Bugger. I don't know what happened. Charlie brought us here." She glanced out a window toward the Dome. "Something happened, Armani. Something *really* bad."

"Thirty seconds," the triflin' bus driver said.

A fat tear slowly made its way down Danisha's cheek and dropped to the floor. "My mama was attacked last night. They beat down Charlie, and Bugger took off runnin'." She rubbed up under her nose. "Next thing I know, he's just gone, Cuz. I been looking for him ever since. He was standing *right* next to me."

"Maybe he's with your mama or Charlie." I wanted to tell her about Daddy and Georgie, but I didn't have no energy for it. The driver tapped her watch with one finger.

"Look, I don't wanna leave without Bugger and my mama anyhow." She sniffed loud. "Take my seat, then y'all will have three." Danisha's swelled-up bottom lip started to quiver.

"But, Danisha, you can't stay here. It's dangerous. You have to come with us." I turned to the driver. "*Please* let us all stay on. This is my cousin an' these are my sisters and . . ."

"Yeah, and I'm your long-lost mama." The evil driver snickered at her own bad joke. "Time's up. Someone, I don't care who, but someone gets off *now*." People outside the bus were screaming and shouting almost as much as the ones inside the bus. "I'm gonna count to three and then I'm gonna throw *all* of you out on your butts. One, two . . ."

Danisha smiled a lopsided smile and hugged me again. She squeezed past me and glared at the driver until the mean woman's good sense told her to move her leg before my second cousin moved it for her.

Danisha walked backward toward the steps to the door. "Keep your eye out for Bugger, hear?"

"I will."

Sealy wrapped herself around one of Danisha's legs so tight I thought she was gonna knock her down. Then my little sister looked up at my cousin with tears running like a river down her face. "Find Mama and tell her where we are. And Daddy and Georgie."

Danisha took one more backward step down and the stupid driver slapped the folding doors shut right in her face. Sealy scooched past me and flung herself across the laps of three old ladies sitting in a seat. She stuck her head out the open bus window and shouted, "Find Mama! She'll take care of you. Thank you, Danisha!"

As the bus rolled away from that awful place, all I could see was the long, dark walk lying out in front of me. Another cinder block took up space up inside my crowded chest. I slowly started making my way down that long, narrow aisle, putting one clumpy boot in front of the other, searching, praying for an empty seat through blurry eyes. A heavy feeling of dread spread through my body like a fever as I headed further and further to the back of the stinky, hot, shadowy bus with all that was left of my family clinging to me, making it so I could hardly breathe.

CHAPTER 33

The bus rolled along as slow as molasses. My head rested up against the cool glass of the window. Sealy pulled out her swirly green and white journal and the matted-looking feather pen. She stared for the longest time at the blank pages in front of her with her pen froze between her dirty fingers. All I could think just then was how mad Mama would be that Sealy had dirt up under her nails. She'd have me leaning over the tub scrubbing those nails with the little blue nailbrush when Sealy took her bath, the smell of lavender soap floating up my nose.

"Armani," Sealy said, still staring at the blank pages. "What's a refugee?"

A lady fanning herself, holding two snotty, sick-looking babies on her lap in the seat across the aisle from us, said without even turning her head or glancing in our direction, "We are, baby. You. Me. All of us. We are the refugees. Cast from our homes."

Sealy looked at me and said, in a quivery, quiet voice, "Armani?"

I just sat quiet. I pressed my nose into the top of Khayla's head and took a deep sniff. The lavender smells were gone for good.

Sealy closed her journal and put it back in her book sack.

"Ain't ya gonna write in there?"

"No, I don't feel like it." Sealy sighed. She zipped up the sack and let it sit in a blob between us on the seat.

I ain't never in my life rode on a school bus that was so spooky quiet, except for the sniffling and coughs and mumbles. One old lady up front wailed and prayed. She was crying for all of us.

We rode like that for a long while, zigzagging down the chunks of tore-up interstate with police cars—one in front and one in back of the bus—flashing their lights and all. Creeping along, slower than a slug, dragging me further and further away from my home, while I seen outside my window how New Orleans was all but worn away from being touched by that storm.

I sat with my head bouncing up against the window and watched the sky turn from bluey-orange to patches of shadowy gray and snake-berry red. Hurricanes must not reach all the way to the sun, 'cause it was moving across the sky just like it always did, like nothing had happened at all.

My eyelids were puffed up and wouldn't stay open. When most of the orange was gone from the sky and it was almost completely chalk-board black, I seen the reflection of a girl I didn't recognize in the glass of the window. I turned my head to see if she was sitting behind me. But I only seen Sealy, who sat with her face turned away with Khayla's head rested on her shoulder.

I looked back at the window. There she was again, the girl with the frizzy lopsided head and the swelled-up eyes. My heart thumped in the sides of my head. I was fixin' to check behind me one more time when I noticed the girl in the window-mirror turning her head too.

I froze solid. The girl I didn't recognize was *me*?

I rubbed my eyes and forced them wide open. I moved in closer to the window till me and the reflection in the glass were all but touching noses.

A tear inched down the face of the girl in the glass, a tear holding the color of orange from the sky outside. With every little bit the tear moved down the face in the window, I could feel all the blocks sitting up inside my chest crumbling. Every single one of them.

All at the same time, they turned to dust. The dust pile they made settled down into the very bottom part of my belly. The heavy feeling I'd been carrying around up in my chest was gone. It felt empty. When the teardrop finally slid from the face in the glass, wetness fell onto the top of my hand.

I slowly tore my droopy eyes from the window-mirror and stared down for the longest time at the way the tear just sat there. I wondered if my hands would ever get a chance to be as old and soft as Memaw's.

Sealy's eyes were on me. I didn't care.

I picked up her book sack and unzipped it. My sister didn't say a word.

I found the fat, crinkled-up Bible Sealy had fished out of the black nasty water, still wrapped in Mr. Oscar Dupree's bandanna. I pulled it out. I zipped the bag back up and put it in a nice pile between me and my sister.

I slowly lifted my head and looked up at Sealy. She was staring with her mouth half-open and her lips quivering something terrible.

"Wanna sit next to the window?" My voice sounded groggy, like I'd just woke up. I blinked one long, slow blink.

Sealy shrugged, never taking her eyes off my face.

I stood up with my back against the seat in front of us and looked down at her and my half-awake baby sister.

"Are you sure, Armani? You always like sitting by the window."

"Not no more." It was impossible to keep my heavy eyelids open.

She scooted over, dragging Khayla with her. I sat down in my new spot and gently pushed Khayla's head down on my leg and went to rubbing her sticky forehead. I ain't sure how long Sealy sat looking at me.

I tucked the smelly, used-to-be-waterlogged book all wrapped in red up under my arm. I closed my eyes, and went to sleep.

CHAPTER 34

The shelter. Soldiers stood guard outside the bus and in front of the doors of the building we were being told to go into—long guns in their arms just waiting to be used.

I ain't sure if the soldiers were there to keep bad people from going in, or to keep people from going out. I kept my head down and my mouth shut, trying my best to ignore the screaming blisters up inside my muddy boots.

As soon as everyone piled off the bus, people in red vests shuffled all of us into lines with signs overhead reading INTAKE. We got in the line that didn't move. We stepped maybe one whole inch forward every hour. I wanted to sit on the floor like bellyaching Khayla, who scooted forward on her butt whenever the line decided to move.

The smell of sweat and boiled beans was thick in the air. My empty stomach went sour. Noise. Hollerin'. Loudspeakers. Crying babies. The scraping sound of metal cots dragging across the hard, shiny floor. Every sound in that place echoed off the concrete walls with no windows and the sky-high ceilings. Bright yellowy fluorescents flickered and lit up everything, shining too much light on the confusion everywhere. It was like the hurricane had brought its chaos up inside the building to shake us up some more, just in case we hadn't had enough already.

There was commotion at the front of our line. Two kids holding hands caught my eye. The smaller kid was fussin' and the older one with a huge flat Afro was arguing with a tall, mean-looking man in a red vest with hair the same tacky color as his carrot-orange shoes.

"I'm going to ask you one more time," the orange-haired man said to the older kid. "Are you with an adult or not?"

I held my breath waiting for the older kid to answer.

"Armani." Sealy tugged on my arm.

"Shhh. Not now, Sealy." I never took my eyes off the Afro kid and the orange-haired man.

"Ummm." The kid turned and looked at the fussy little boy standing next to him. I knew the answer to the man's question.

People in our line were hollerin' for the kid to hurry up and answer. I slipped my hands over Khayla's ears on account of all the cussing up in there.

The orange-haired man was speaking into a walkie-talkie. He finally looked at the older kid again. "Step over here, please," he waved, showing the boys where to stand.

My heart was beating faster and my head was starting to buzz like the overhead lights. I'd been watching people for hours get to the front of that stupid line. They'd jabber for a bit with the man in his ugly red vest, get handed a trash bag and a paper with the word RULES printed all big across the top, and then walk on over to one of the other hundreds of lines in the overcrowded crazy place. Every single one of them went somewhere, except them two kids.

My insides took to shaking.

The two kids stepped off to the side like the man told them to. The little kid was hanging tight to the older one. The older kid turned, and for a long second we seen each other. He looked right at me with his scrunched-up mad self. He lifted his chin in a nod just enough so that I could tell he did it. I nodded a "hey" back.

The line moved an inch. Khayla scooched forward.

While my eyes were still locked on the kid, out of nowhere came a lady who didn't look like she belonged in that dreadful place at all. She was wearing a red vest, but it looked like part of her outfit the way she wore it. Her long, dangly, apple-red earrings were the same exact color as the dang vest. She even had red accessories stuck up in her praline-tinted wig that was piled on top of her pointy head.

I wasn't the only one staring at her. Truth is, a person couldn't help but stare. She was shiny and *clean*—all done up, looking like a brown Marge Simpson on her way to a Mardi Gras parade. I could all but smell the soap on her even from where I was standing. She was just a-smiling and went right up to the two scared-looking boys.

"Armani." Sealy tugged again.

"Hang on, girl." I shrugged her hand off my arm. I squinted my eyes and put all my focus on my ears, tilting my right ear in the direction of the kids and the shiny lady.

"My, my," the shiny lady said in one of them high-pitched, sugary-sweet voices set aside for what Memaw calls the highfalutin' types. "What do we have here?" Her smile was plastered on in a way that reminded me of the kind a nurse wears right before she shoves a long needle in your arm.

The older kid took to staring at the floor, and the little one went and hid behind him. The orange-haired man barely looked at the shiny lady when he said into his walkie-talkie, "Two unchaperoned minors. Child Protective Services dispatched."

My legs felt like they were full of muscadine jelly.

"Well, all righty then," the shiny lady said. I don't know how words rolled out of her smiling mouth when it didn't even look like her lips budged.

The line moved an inch. Khayla scooched forward.

The shiny lady reached out like she was gonna touch the older boy's Afro, but he took a quick step back and said, "You need to let us be. I'm fifteen years old, man. We don't need anybody. We can take care of ourselves!"

"Oh, darlin', it's gonna be just fine," the shiny, highfalutin' lady said. She tipped her head and kept right on smiling with her extra-large white teeth flashing this way and that. "Come on, now. We're gonna find us a nice place to rest, and get y'all fresh water and somethin' to eat. How's that sound?"

The little kid poked his head out from behind the older one right when the older kid glanced over at me. I had to remind myself to breathe. His nostrils opened and closed real big. His chest moved up and down *fast*. The boy looked like a bull getting ready to charge. "We're not goin' *anywhere*."

CHAPTER 35

The orange-haired man in the tacky red vest looked at the kid with the lopsided Afro. "You don't have a choice. You either go with this nice lady or I call security." The man got all up in the kid's face. The kid finally looked away, rolling his eyes.

This time when the shiny lady reached out, the kid curled up his lip and let her put her arm around his shoulder. "Well now, see? I told y'all it was gonna be all right." She took hold of the little one's hand. "Let's see if we can find you a nice cookie, darlin'."

The older kid turned his head and looked back at me one more time before the three of them got lost in the crowd. I could still hear that highfalutin' voice way after they were out of sight.

Khayla scooched forward.

I knew what I needed to do.

"Armani," Sealy said for the umpteenth time.

"What?"

"That man over there wants us to come here." She pointed at a very tall white man standing off by hisself. His long gray hair almost reached the pockets of his dirty PawPaw pants that were pulled clear up by his armpits. He seen Sealy pointing and he waved back with a heavy, wrinkled hand and a great big happy smile. She waved some more and let out a giggle.

I pushed her waving hand down. "Are you crazy, girl? Don't be wavin' at strangers."

"But he's nice, Armani. He has Dumbledore eyes." She wouldn't stop staring and smiling.

"Dummy sounds about right." I stood in front of her to block her view of the homeless-looking man.

"Not *dummy*, silly, Dumbledore. Look." Sealy pointed again, still grinning from ear to ear, and leaned to the side so she could see past me. The girl had lost her mind.

The line moved again. The knot in my stomach twitched.

Khayla whimpered, "I haffa go potty."

I ain't never been so happy to hear them four words.

"Sealy." I snapped my fingers in her face, trying to get her attention on me and off the white man with the high pockets. I grabbed Khayla by the hand and pulled her to her feet. "Follow me," I told Sealy over my shoulder.

"Where are we going?"

"Just hush up and do what I tell ya. And stay close."

"But we'll lose our place in line, Armani."

"What part of hush don't you understand, girl?" I'd done lost my patience. "Just follow me and don't talk to nobody."

Khayla was holding herself and bouncing around like fire ants were crawling up her legs. Mama would've made her stop jumping around, acting a fool, but I was glad she was doing it, 'cause it made it easier for me to get us out of line, and quick.

My rubber boots squeak-squeaked every time I took a step across the hard shiny floor. Heat filled my cheeks. I needed to get us as far away as possible from the orange-haired man and his meddlin' self.

Loud enough, but not so loud that it sounded suspicious, I said, "Hang on, Khayla, there has to be a bathroom around here somewhere."

"I haffa go, *now*." Khayla was playing her part perfect.

"Armani—"

"What?" I said, taking another squeaky step away from the line.

"The bathroom's over there." Sealy had stopped behind me.

"How do you know?"

"Because *he* told me." She pointed and smiled at that ol' mister so-and-so with his pockets all high and his grin too big. *He was following us?*

He seen me looking at him with my lip curled up, and he went on smiling big with one of them *follow me* nods of his gray-covered head.

"See?" Sealy said, all happy.

I let out an annoyed poof of air. "*Whatever.*"

We fell into the back of the line for the bathroom. The bellyaching pouring out of Khayla was so loud, about a thousand eyes fell on us. We were finally away from the worry of mister orange hair pulling us off to the side so Miss Highfalutin' could come haul us off to who knows where, and now Khayla's fit had everyone in the world looking at us. The baby girl needed a toilet, and she needed it *fast*. She wasn't holding her front side no more—now she had both hands planted firm on her backside. It had become a serious emergency.

Out of nowhere, a teenage girl wearing a red vest came up beside us and wanted to know why Khayla was hollerin'. She wanted to know if the baby needed a doctor. She seen for herself the way Khayla was clinging for dear life to her booty. The girl hurried up and told us to follow her.

Sealy and Mr. High Pockets man gave each other a thumbs-up. I didn't have the want-to or the time to try and figure out what was going on with Sealy and that strange ol' man.

I followed the red-vested girl all the way to the front of the line. I swear Sealy skipped up behind me the whole way.

———

The tangy smell of pee flew up my nose. Walking into the bathroom was a whole new kind of fool-headed crazy filled with blabbering, bickering women and girls and babies all shoved in there like crawfish in a boiling pot. I ain't never seen Sealy's mouth so wide open as it was when she went to staring at them nasty ol' women standing around in nothing but their bras and pantics, just a-jabbering and doing their laundry in the tiny gray-white sinks like they did it that way all the time. Soon as they seen Khayla up on her tippy-toes grabbing hold of her backside, they all but opened a stall and shoved all three of us inside.

"Oh, my gosh. This feels so good!" Sealy said, splashing water from the sink up on her face. I watched the water drip off the round part of her chin. She looked into the cracked mirror and went to smoothing down her flyaway hairs with her wet hand.

After cleaning my sisters the best I could with the rough brown paper towels, I pulled a wad of towels down out of the dispenser and ran them up under the water to get them good and wet. I closed my eyes and tried to scrub hurricane muck from my skin. A shirtless woman pushed me out from in front of the sink and started scrubbing her hairy armpits with the lunch-bag-colored towels. She messed with herself in the mirror, not even taking the time to look my way. *Whatever*. It was fine by me. I didn't wanna look in no mirror nohow.

Before we left the bathroom, I pulled Sealy over to a corner. I tried to whisper so no one would hear. "Listen, Sealy, we can't tell no one that Mama an' Daddy ain't with us. You understand that, right?"

"But why?"

"Why what?" I was trying to get Khayla up off the floor where she'd gone and plopped her sleepy, fussy self.

"Why can't we tell anyone that we're by ourselves?"

"Because we just can't, that's why. Didn't you see what happened to them boys?" Sweat was pouring off me. "Khayla, stand up." I nudged her with my foot.

"How come, why, Ah-mani?" Khayla said, with her eyes half closed. Sealy wasn't even *trying* to help me with our baby sister.

"We need to ask someone to help us," Sealy said.

"No, we don't!" I said louder than I meant to. Khayla weighed a ton. I couldn't get her up.

"But if we don't get someone to help us, what will we do? How will we find—"

"Did you forget that I just made ten?" I yelled in a whisper. "Mama left *me* in charge of y'all, remember?" My head hurt when I tried to slide it.

Sealy wasn't backing down. She flipped her watery eyes up at me and about knocked me over backward when she put both her hands where her hips should be and did a perfect head roll. "Well," she sniffed, "you can be in charge, but we still need to tell *someone* about Daddy and Georgie so we can send help." She wiped the back of her hand across her soggy face, not even caring about the snot she left there. Her beady little eyes never left mine. Hot stabs poked the inside of my chest.

I grabbed her by both shoulders and pulled her close to me. I tried to press my nose up against hers, but she did a good job of pulling her head back as far her little neck would go. "You better listen good, Sealy Jean Curtis! Mama ain't here, now, *is* she?" My fingers started to dig into her shoulders. "And I sure don't see Daddy." The shaking in my legs moved fast up to my middle. "You better do what I say, or I swear, I'll just leave your butt right here." Me and Jesus knew that I'd never leave my sister nowhere, nohow, but right then, I shut the door on babyfyin' lil' Miss Sealy.

Big ol' alligator tears rolled down her cheeks. I pushed back on her shoulders when I let go, and she stumbled backward. I didn't care. I was tired. I looked away and took a step back. I took a couple fast, deep breaths. Without thinking twice, I whipped around and got back in her wet baby face. Her hands flew up like she thought I was gonna hit her or something. "And if Georgie was stupid enough to go an' jump off the roof into the water like an idiot, why should I care?" My eyes burned. My whole entire self was shaking.

A snot bubble came halfway out of Sealy's nose and popped. I grabbed Khayla by one arm and slung her up onto my hip. I didn't hear one sound out of her for a long while. I didn't have a clue what Sealy was or wasn't doing, mostly 'cause I didn't care. I didn't care right then if my sister was mad or not. All I knew was that I had to do what Mama and Daddy expected me to do—keep Sealy and Khayla and me together—and safe.

I marched as best I could with Khayla melted into me, and whiny-baby Sealy and her snot bubbles trailing behind, the whole while making loud squeaky noises with my dumb boots on the super-shiny marble-looking floors. Finally, we made it out of the stinking bathroom.

"Excuse me." A lady tapped my arm.

I looked quick to see if she had on a red vest. She didn't. The only red she was wearing was up in her cheeks. I turned and glared at her.

"I'm sorry, but I couldn't help but overhear you in the ladies' room," she said. My heart started beating up in my head. "Are you children alone?" She tried to look at me like she cared.

"That ain't none of your business." I looked away and took a step. She touched my arm again.

"I'd like to help, if you—"

"Oh, look, Sealy," I sniffed and pointed. "There's Daddy." I thought my heart would stop when Sealy looked at me with that look of Christmas morning on her face.

"*Daddy?*" Sealy whispered.

I did the *come here* wave and that mister high-pockets man smiled and walked toward us. I switched squirmy Khayla to my other hip.

I wanted to hug Sealy and tell her I was sorry for fooling her into thinking that our own daddy was right there, but I was more worried about that meddlin' woman.

I stepped away from the busybody woman for the last time. She looked confused. Her eyes turned to teeny slits, looking from us to the old white man and back again. "Oh, I must have misunderstood. This man's your father?"

"Uh-huh, my father," is all I said. Sealy's eyes weighed down on me.

The woman kept right on staring at us while she slowly walked away.

"You should've just told her the truth, Armani." There was a look in my sister's eyes that made me sad. Her eyes were just plain ol' brown. The twinkle was gone.

I opened my mouth to say something, but went on and closed it when I couldn't think of what else to say.

The man with pockets up by his armpits stood close enough to where I could smell the peppermint coming from him. The sweet, fresh smell didn't match the look of him—all dirty and most likely homeless.

He reached his arms out to Khayla and nodded his head, staring at me the whole time. Khayla reached her arms up to the tall man.

"What?" I asked him, still feeling uneasy.

The man nodded at Khayla again, but this time he moved his arms up and down.

"You want to hold my sister?" It was bugging me that the man wouldn't just open his mouth and speak.

He nodded his head and smiled so big it took up most of his face. Sealy was right: There was *something* about his eyes.

"Yes, sir, you can hold her," Sealy said, all polite.

As soon as the man took my baby sister from me, she went and snuggled her head into the soft-looking spot where long, silvery hair bunched into a pillow up on the man's shoulder. My empty arms felt like stretched-out rubber bands just hanging off my body.

Sealy took hold of Mr. High Pockets's hand. My breath got caught somewhere up in my chest and settled like a chunk of dry cornbread. They took about two or three steps, then the man turned with that smile of his and motioned with his head for me to follow.

Sealy never looked back. Not one time.

CHAPTER 36

"You're being rude again, Armani," Sealy said. If you asked me, my sister took the prize for rude right then.

"How am I being rude? I'm just standing here." And that's exactly what I was doing—just standing there.

Good ol' Mr. High Pockets managed to scoot us right on by the long INTAKE line and took us to a corner clear on the other side of the huge people-packed room, stopping in front of what looked like the only two empty cots in the whole entire place.

Someone must've hit a switch, 'cause the overhead lights went from blinding bright yellow-white to flickering gray. A loud buzz filled the room. The kind of buzz them lightbulbs at school make right before it's time for Daddy or one of the other maintenance men to change them.

As far as I could tell, the shelter was at least ten times bigger than our school gym, and smelled ten times worse. Thinking about our gym made me think of our table. The scuffed-up table made me think of Mama, and suppertime, and Memaw with nut dust, and the attic.

"Hello." The little voice belonged to a very old Chinese lady not much bigger than me.

"Hello," I mumbled. I sure didn't want Sealy thinking I was rude.

"You are very pretty girl," the little lady said, smiling so big her eyes all but disappeared. She nodded, admiring my sisters.

"My name is MawMaw Sun." She offered me her hand.

I shook her small, soft hand. The lady called MawMaw Sun smiled and nodded some more.

"You kids need anything, we right there." She pointed where two more MawMaws—one black and one white—sat on a cot side by side just a-waving at us.

I gave a little wave back. Sealy tipped up on her toes and waved, all excited.

"You kids in right place. You bring good energy." She nodded at the man who brought us to the corner, then she patted Khayla on the head. "You be okay," she said to my sister.

We stared after her while she made her way back to the other two smiling MawMaws. I didn't know what they had to be so dang sappy-happy about.

The man laid Khayla down slow and careful on one of the cots. It had one itty-bitty paper-looking pillow and a thin brown blanket. I couldn't see why anyone would want a blanket with it being so stiflin' hot and sticky. Khayla stayed rolled in a ball and didn't move an inch when Sealy lay down and curled up with our sleeping baby sister.

"Armani," she said in a sleepy voice, "you said that you'd leave me. Would you really do that?" Her eyes were barely open. She blinked slow and heavy.

I stood there feeling stupid for even saying the hurtful words to her. "No, I'd never leave you, Sealy." I stopped staring at the floor and looked at my sister. She wasn't much bigger than Khayla. "Just go to sleep."

"I'm sorry for making you mad," she said with her eyes closed.

A heavy wanting came over me. A wanting for everyone and everything that used to be.

Mr. High Pockets was tapping on the back of his head. I glanced over at Sealy. She was already sound asleep. I looked back at the man and there he was just a-tap-tap-tapping with one hand on the back of his head. He looked at me for just a second with twinkly eyes. He smiled, looked up at the ceiling, and then he turned his freckled face back at me with a startled look. The whole while, he was tapping away on the back of his gray-haired head. My mouth hung as wide open as my bugged-out eyes.

I ain't lying when I say that all of a sudden, that man, with his pants the color of old and pockets all but buried in his armpits, pulled a shiny quarter right out of his nose. He looked at it this way and that, like he was admiring some long-lost treasure. Then he flipped it way up high in the air, caught it, and stuck it down in one of his too-high pockets. He looked at me just then, and I seen the warmth of Daddy in his old man eyes. He walked over, keeping his eyes on me, and picked up the scratchy-looking blanket from the empty cot. He held it up against hisself and nodded. I nodded back at him. He smiled real big, tilted his head to the side, and silently thanked me with the grin in his soft copper-colored eyes.

I watched him walk over by the concrete wall. He shook out his blanket, letting it float down to the hard floor. He stretched both arms up over his head, like he was reaching for the ceiling. He yawned and gave me a little wave. Then that tall, skinny ol' white man laid hisself down, flat out on his blanket-bed.

I seen the empty cot beside me, and was fixin' to holler at him to get up off that dirty floor, but just then he folded his hands up under his head, let out a sigh, and smiled, closing his eyes.

———

The cot was so comfortable. I laid there on my own cot, all by myself, wondering if maybe someday I could get one of them things for my bedroom. If I had a bedroom. If I had a house. If I could just be nine again.

I couldn't stand it for another second. I scooped Khayla up into my arms and brought her to bed with me. I pulled her in close and forced my eyes shut.

———

I sat straight up on my cot. The room was filled with a buzzing and a spooky gray. But *not* quiet. Tramping feet and songs and screams echoed through the air. My ears felt like they were stuffed with Mississippi mud, making the sounds muffled and loud at the same time. I stuck a finger into each of my ears and gave them a wiggle. It didn't do no good, so I sat there wide awake with clogged-up ears and gray lights flickering down on me.

I got up as quiet as I could from the cot. The paper pillow crinkled and Khayla flopped from her tummy to her back. I tippy-toed in the dumb boots till I was standing right over sleeping Sealy. "Hey, Sealy, you awake?" I whispered. Nothing. She didn't move a speck.

I unzipped her book sack enough to let my hand slip inside. I found the pad of pink Hello Kitty paper and went back in for something to write with. I was feeling around when my hand stumbled up on something that made me stop. I didn't have to see them to know what they were.

Georgie's glasses. "What are these doing in here?" I said out loud to nobody. I touched the little part that holds the glasses up on a person's nose. Georgie's nose. *He won't be able to see. Mama always says that boy can't see his own hand in front of his face without his glasses on.*

Real slow and careful, I put the glasses back where I'd found them. Right there in plain sight was a pen. I grabbed it and headed over to the man lying up by the wall.

I bent down and nudged him with one finger. He didn't move. "Hey, mister."

One eye popped open.

I about fell out of my boots. "Sorry for wakin' you up."

He sat up and yawned big, stretching his long arms about a mile. He smiled and tapped the floor next to him. I sat down. He made it easy to ask.

"You can't talk, can you?"

He shook his head slow from side to side, never breaking the look between us. He had wrinkles running every which way across his face deep enough to hold that quarter that fell from his nose. I wanted to reach out and touch one of the creases, but I didn't.

"Can you write your name so we know what to call you?" I offered him the paper and pen.

He scrunched his shoulders up and held them there.

"You can't write." I didn't ask, I just came right out and said it. I wasn't surprised. I ain't trying to be hurtful, but he had that look about him—the look of someone who can't read.

The man shook his head one more time and smiled.

"Do you mind if I give you a name?"

His whole face lit up.

"Well, I think your name should be Mr. High Pockets."

He took his chin between his pointer finger and thumb. He scrunched his eyes and lips like he was thinking real hard. I was fixin' to tell him to never mind, that I knew it was a dumb name, when he popped in his seat and burst into an even bigger smile. He was on his feet so fast, I forgot he was old. He pointed at his own high pants pockets and slapped his knee. The man was belly laughing with no sound coming out. I couldn't help it, I laughed too.

I swear I seen Sealy stealing a look our way, but when I turned my head to look at her, her eyes snapped shut. Her eyelids fluttered like butterfly wings. I could tell she wasn't for-real sleeping.

Mr. High Pockets had me on my feet with his arms around me quicker than a lizard lick. He gave me a good squeeze, and I squeezed back.

I stood over Sealy for a long minute, her eyelids fluttering the whole time. It must've been hard for her to keep from opening her eyes and letting me know she was really awake. I slipped her stuff back into her book sack. I leaned over and kissed her on the back of her head and wondered if she understood how far we'd drifted from home.

I cozied back up beside Khayla. I wrapped one arm around my baby sister and one arm around me.

CHAPTER 37

It was strange the way quiet came with the morning. Used to be that the dark of the night turned everything to a whisper. Not no more. It was morning, and mostly quiet, except for the sound of the big push broom lazy-sweeping back and forth across the cold floor and the drowsy motor sounds vibrating off Khayla's lips. The girl had been lying belly-down on the cot pushing an empty water bottle from one side to the other since before they'd turned the daytime lights on. I'd already done taken her to the toilet twice. Every time we passed by the MawMaws, all three of them would holler "Good mornin'" like they hadn't already said it twenty thousand times.

Sealy was busy writing in her journal. I slid on up behind her and kept myself busy foolin' with her braids and trying to get them cute again.

Mr. High Pockets had woke up and stretched his long arms higher than the heads of people shuffling about. When he stood up, he seen me looking and gave a nod my way. I was fixin' to holler "Hey" when a highfalutin' voice came out of nowhere.

"Well, hello, dears! Ain't y'all just the purdiest things?" If it wasn't the squeaky-clean-shiny lady herself, with that big ol' triflin' grin on her face, staring down at me and my family. The temperature in my face went up by at least one hundred degrees.

"Hello," I mumbled, trying my best not to actually look at the woman, hoping the whole while that she couldn't see the fear oozing out of my skin.

"Is your mama here, precious?" The woman's body smelled like a flower garden and her breath smelled like Juicy Fruit gum.

Sealy tried to turn her head. I swear I felt her mouth fixin' to speak just by the way the hair on her head moved. I gave one of her braids a quick tug like a person riding a horse does to get the animal to stop.

"Ouch," Sealy said, and rubbed her head.

"No, ma'am. Mama ain't here right now." My good manners were surprising, even to me. Especially considering the way my insides were twisted in a knot like I'd gone and caught Khayla's bellyache.

"What about your daddy?"

My heart thumped in an unnatural way on both sides of my head. If Miss Highfalutin' didn't stop trying to get all up in my business, I was gonna shove one of Memaw's boots down her Juicy Fruit throat. She needed to go on and bother someone else.

"No, ma'am. Daddy ain't here, neither," I said, just as nice as pie. My eyes scanned every which way searching for our stand-in daddy, Mr. High Pockets.

Sealy went back to writing in her journal.

"Oh my, you're keepin' a journal!" the woman said, looking down at Sealy like she was gonna eat her up. "I always keep mine close by, 'cause I never know when I'm gonna need it."

Sealy whipped around, all but tearing my fingers loose from her hair. I seen the tiniest twinkle come back in her eyes. "Me too! My teacher says the only way people can stay sharp is if they read and write *every* day."

"Well, it sure sounds like you've got a fine teacher." She winked at Sealy, and Sealy beamed. "It's so nice to see you writin' away with your pretty little feather pen. I've got a flamingo-pink one at home just like it."

Sealy giggled, but it didn't do one thing to settle my nerves.

Khayla scooted up close to me. She stared at the loud lady and rubbed her eyes with her fat little fists. The lady tilted her head and smiled at my baby sister all sweet-like, the same way she looked at that little kid she hauled off to Child Protective Services the night before. I was seeing straight through her pretending-to-be-nice act.

I stood up. "Well," I said, letting my eyes drill holes into the meddlin' woman, "we best be gettin' back to what we was doin'. Thanks for stoppin' by to say hey." I took a clumsy step closer to the confused, sweet-smelling woman. "Y'all say bye to the nice lady. She's leavin' now." I gave her one of my famous *you-best-be-leaving-now* looks and a good head slide.

Instead of saying bye, Khayla stood up and took Miss Highfalutin's hand in hers and looked up at the woman with her belly and lip poked out bigger than ever. She said in her cute little voice, "I wanna see Mama now."

Me and Sealy shot each other a look. I hurried up and wrapped my arm around Khayla's shoulder, planting a quick smile on my face. My lips stuck to my dry teeth. Whatever I was fixin' to say flew right out of my head.

That woman looked straight into me. I wanted to pull my eyes away, but they were fixed on her, just staring. I couldn't even blink. I could *feel* her looking around up inside my head.

I tried to swallow, but there wasn't nothing in my mouth to swallow. The outside corners of the woman's eyes drooped and I seen a tear growing in one of them. There was a look of lonesome sitting in her pretty green-brown eyes that forced me to blink. She smiled a small, soft smile that made my arms ache for one of Mama's morning hugs. My own eyes got blurry.

She nodded at me, then kneeled down next to Khayla. She folded her free hand over the top of the one she had holding Khayla's. As soon as she let loose of my eyes, I pulled the sleeve of my shirt up to wipe across my face.

"What's your name, sweetheart?" she asked my sister.

"Khayla."

"Khayla." She said the name and put her hand on the side of my sister's chubby face. Khayla leaned into the woman's hand. "I'm not here to take you to your mama, sweetie. I'm here to see if there's anything I can do to help y'all." She glanced up at me.

"Are y'all thirsty? What if I get ya somethin' yummy to drink?" Her Juicy Fruit breath floated up and got in my nose. I noticed her name tag for the first time. Priscilla Nash. I was surprised it didn't say Miss Highfalutin'.

Khayla stuck one pudgy finger in her mouth and said, "I want Mama." Her bottom lip went to quivering and I could see the ugly cry building up on her face.

"Actually," Sealy said, "she hasn't been feeling very well. She has a tummy ache and dia—"

"Oh, she's just fine. She's just got a little gas. Ain't that right, Khayla?" I faked a loud laugh. Too loud. Not *Priscilla Nash* or nobody else needed to know our business. Sweat ran into my eyes.

When I threw a look at Sealy to let her know her mouth was the size of the entire Gulf of Mexico, Khayla wandered away from us. I tried to point with my head and shifty eyes, but Sealy was too dim-witted to figure out what I was trying to tell her. She just kept staring at me like she was born yesterday.

"Sealy," I said with my teeth all clenched together. But just then, Khayla got swallowed up by the crowd of people shuffling from every corner of the stupid shelter to get up in the growing food lines. A stab of panic shot through me like it was tied to a rocket.

"Khayla!" I screamed. But the second my fear hit the air, I seen my baby sister rise up over the tops of everybody's heads, smiling all big with her hands wrapped around the top of good ol' Mr. High Pockets' silvery head. He had her up on his shoulders and by the looks of it, he was enjoying the ride as much as Khayla.

Mr. High Pockets' smile went from stretched across his freckly face to a smile that wasn't so sure when he got a good look at me. He brought Khayla down off his shoulders and held her in one arm up against his side, situating her lime-green headband back into place on her frizzy head.

There was an honest-to-goodness ache in my face trying to keep the stupid smile on there. But I had to, on account of Miss up-in-your-business Priscilla Nash watching *everything*.

"My, oh my," the woman said with both her hands folded up across her chest like it was her sister who almost got lost. "Thank goodness your daddy was right there!" She turned to look at me. "This man *is* your daddy, right?" I couldn't look at her for more than a second, so I found a spot on the top of Khayla's head to stare at instead.

"Yep," is all I said. I took Khayla from the man and set her down beside me, careful to keep a hand on her shoulder.

Miss Priscilla Nash walked over to Mr. High Pockets. My brain was screaming: *Why can't this woman just leave us alone?*

"Hello," she said, "My name's Priscilla Nash." She held out her hand and Mr. High Pockets shook it. "I've been chattin' with your delightful children."

Lord have mercy. If Memaw didn't say the words in my ear right then, I don't know who did. Miss Priscilla Nash looked at each one of us, sprinkling her sweetness on us with her eyes. It was making me half sick.

"I haffa use it, Ah-mani." Khayla hopped from one foot to the next.

"Okay, well, I hate to be rude," I said, "but she really needs to go to the bathroom."

Miss Priscilla Nash looked slanty-eyed from me to Mr. High Pockets, who stood there with a lopsided grin on his face. The lady was most likely wondering why our *white* "daddy" wasn't saying a single word.

"Get your book sack, Sealy," I said, avoiding the eyes of Miss Priscilla Nash.

"My book sack's on my back, silly."

I stopped all the fiddling I was doing and shot another look at Sealy. It was obvious by the sound of her voice that she didn't have a clue that we were in big trouble if we didn't hurry up and get away from that nosy woman in the red vest.

Eyes poured down on me. I took a deep breath and tried to count to ten the way I'd seen Mama do a thousand times. Fake smiling and trying my best to sound *not* annoyed, I said, "Okay, well, let's take Khayla to the bathroom then." I rolled my eyes and my head went to sliding from one shoulder to the next. My head just did it, despite my good intentions.

Miss Priscilla Nash and Mr. High Pockets were looking at me like I was crazy. I didn't care. Right then, I *felt* crazy.

I grabbed Khayla by the hand that she wasn't using to hold herself and I walked right over and slipped my other hand into Mr. High Pockets' leathery hand. I clomped off, heading to the stupid mile-long line for the bathroom. I never looked back at the lady I'd left standing there. Sealy scuttled up behind me and hollered, "It was very nice meeting you, Miss Priscilla Nash!"

"Likewise!" the woman hollered back.

"Whatever," I said under my breath, walking as fast and meaning-ful as I could in the ugly boots.

"What?" Sealy asked when she came up alongside of me.

"We'll see how *nice it was to meet her* when she hauls your babyfied butt to juvenile court or some foster home." How could I explain to Sealy that I knew Miss Priscilla Nash was a nice lady? I'd seen it in her eyes. But nice people trying to *do the right thing* can be the most dangerous kinds of people. Memaw said so all the time. "Messy do-gooders like that can't be trusted, Sealy."

Sealy stopped walking. I took a bunch more steps, then turned back to see her just standing there. "Come on, girl, Khayla needs to use it." She did too. She was doing the potty dance, hopping from one foot to the other.

"Why are you so mean, Armani? She's a nice lady. She could help us."

A family carrying a stack of Styrofoam food containers walked right between me and Sealy, making it so I lost sight of her. I didn't like the feeling that swept through me for that one second. The hungry family finally moved out of the way, and there she was, looking more pitiful than ever.

"I ain't mean, Sealy Jean Curtis. I'm tryin' to look out for you, but you're too young an' dumb to understand that." I turned and headed for the bathroom. Mr. High Pockets' head looked heavy on his shoulders. He was shaking it with a huge frown scrunched up on his face.

"I wish you weren't my sister." Sealy's words boomed through the air for the whole world to hear and slammed into my chest. I didn't hear nothing else except those hateful six words. No other people. No lights buzzing. No footsteps. No babies wailing. No noise at all. Just Sealy's words, *I wish you weren't my sister.*

CHAPTER 38

Me and Sealy went the whole day without speaking to each other unless we had to. I felt more alone than ever. It was fixin' to be lights out again. The end of another long, frustrating day spent wasting away lying on them cots and walking in circles counting tiles, trying to figure out up in my head how I was gonna go about finding Mama and Daddy.

Khayla still had the runs. Right after we ate disgusting tuna and crackers for lunch, she couldn't make it to the toilet in time. But don't you know, Miss Priscilla Nash showed up, like some kind of fairy godmother, with a new set of clean clothes for her.

I helped little Khayla get into her pretty, new dandelion-yellow shorts set. The stretched-out lime-green headband didn't match, but it was from Mama's dress, so it stayed right where it was. Everything fit perfect. Mama would've been happy that Miss Nash had got the size right, especially on her first try.

As soon as Miss Meddlin' seen with her own two eyes how cute Khayla looked in her new clothes, she asked if we all wanted some. Sealy jumped up and down so crazy, it was embarrassing. If we would've been on speaking terms, I would've told my sister she'd made a begging fool out of herself. Memaw would've explained to

Sealy that our daddy provides us with everything we need on account of his hard work, and the Curtis family sure didn't need no handouts from nobody. But me and Sealy *wasn't* on speaking terms just yet.

I'd been seeing folks grabbing and taking whatever was being handed out, whether they needed it or not. I even seen one lady snatching up waters and shoving them into her shirt. I don't know why—there was red-vested people handing out waters all day long like we were fish and couldn't survive without it. Daddy would be making sure that we took only what we needed, leaving the rest for people less fortunate.

When she came back with the bundles of new clothes for me and Sealy, I was grateful Miss Priscilla Nash didn't ask *why* when I set my stupid pile up under my cot. I thanked the lady and admired how nice my sisters looked in their fresh new outfits. It was amazing how just by changing what they were wearing made such a difference.

"Y'all are so welcome. Ain't that somethin' how I got the sizes right and everything?" It was obvious that Miss Priscilla Nash was just as pleased as punch with her own do-gooding.

"Yes, ma'am," Sealy gushed. "I love my clothes. Thank you so much." She ran over and wrapped her arms around the woman's waist. I had to admit, my sister *did* look cute in her khaki shorts and lavender tank top. Miss Nash had even brought a little sandwich baggie filled with new barrettes and hair ties.

"Oh, sweetheart, it's my pleasure." She squeezed Sealy good and tight. She looked over at me and I remembered to smile. "Oh!" Miss Nash said with such a start that she all but pushed Sealy to the side. "I almost forgot the most important thing!" She looked at the floor from side to side till she found the white plastic bag. "I would lose my head if it wasn't attached."

Sealy giggled. I watched, somehow dreading whatever it was that the woman had up inside that bag.

Miss Priscilla Nash hurried up and swiped the bag to the backside of her, like she was hiding it. She cleared her throat and looked at me, big smile and all. I felt sick. "Armani, honey, I picked these out special for you. I sure hope you like 'em." Out came the *surprise* from behind her back.

"What is it, Armani?"

I opened the bag and knew before I looked inside what it was.

"Well, what is it?" Sealy could barely keep hold of herself.

I closed the bag and held it out for Miss Meddlin' to take back.

The color of Tabasco red crawled up her ripe-banana-brown neck and spread into her cheeks, turning her whole face purple. "I . . . I don't understand," she stuttered. I could see the strain it was for her to keep the ridiculous smile in place. She never took the bag. I wanted to get right up in her face and scream, *You don't even know me! And you sure don't know nothin' about my boots!*

"What's wrong? What's in the bag, Armani?" Sealy said all nervous, looking from me to the busybody woman.

"You wanna know what's in the bag, Sealy?" I snapped, never taking my eyes off Miss Nash. I flung the bag at my sister. She caught it and right away looked inside.

She held up the new white sneakers with sky-blue stripes and the bag floated to the floor. "Armani, it's just shoes," she said like she was giving me some new piece of information.

"I don't *need* shoes. In case y'all haven't noticed, I've *got* shoes." I held one foot up, to make sure they could see, and shook my foot in the air. The boot slid back and forth and almost fell off. I put my foot back down, knowing I'd made my point. I tore my eyes from the confused-looking woman and shifted my mad at simple-minded Sealy, who didn't wanna be my sister no more. "Put the shoes back in the bag an' give it back to Miss Nash so she can give them to someone who needs them."

Sealy just stood there staring.

"Armani," Miss Nash said slow and direct, "I'm here to help you." A cry got stifled in her throat. "But I can't help you if you won't trust me."

"But *why* do you wanna help us? We didn't ask for no help. You don't even know us!" My eyes stung and I wished that she'd stop looking at me with them eyes of hers.

She took a step toward me and I took a half step back. She stopped and gave me a tiny soft smile with her head leaning to one shoulder.

I couldn't look at her no more. "Fine. Whatever." I snatched the shoes out of Sealy's hands. I shoved them back in the bag and tied the bag shut. I put the bag up under my cot next to the pile of clothes I had no intention of wearing. Without taking my eyes off the floor, I said, "Okay, well, thank you."

Miss Priscilla Nash kissed her own hand and touched my cheek with it. "Things are gonna get better, child," she whispered.

The lights faded away, spreading the gray everywhere. It was aggravating the way the huge lights hugging the ceiling buzzed even louder at night than they did during the day when they were on full blast. But every night at nine o'clock, somebody hit a switch somewhere and turned our new sit-and-wait world the color of nightmares. Up in my head, when I talked with myself, I'd started using the word *hell*. I didn't think Jesus would hold it against me on account of I wasn't letting the word leave my mouth. Besides, I figured He already knew the truth about where we were anyhow.

I was lying there on the rock-cot missing my life when I was nine when Sealy's voice came floating over my way. She was telling droopy-eyed Khayla a story, but the part that made my ears perk up and pay attention was when she said, "It must have looked like this to Pinocchio when he found himself up inside the whale's belly."

I pushed up on one elbow so I could look over to where Sealy was stroking Khayla's forehead, staring up at the gray-soaked ceiling. A *whale's belly*. That was exactly what it looked and felt like—and smelled like too—all musky and poopy and stinking like someone burned the red beans.

I wondered what them sneakers felt like on the inside. I pushed all the air out from my lungs, then breathed in big and deep. I rolled over, said good-night in my head to Daddy, and Mama, and Georgie, and TayTay, and Memaw up in heaven, and forced myself to go to sleep . . . again.

CHAPTER 39
Thursday, September 1, 2005 - 6:28 A.M.

"You must have prior approval to board the transport unit departing for Houston at eleven A.M. *If you do not have your authorization code, please report to one of the transfer counselors immediately. Repeating: The first bus bound for Houston, Texas, will depart promptly at eleven* A.M. *You must have prior approval . . ."*

The voice boomed through the stuffy morning shelter air. I flipped onto my belly and tried to fold the stupid paper pillow over my head to cover my ears. I opened one eye. Sealy was standing over me, holding her journal, looking down with a look of worry spread across her face. I flopped over and sat straight up. "What? What's wrong?"

"You were crying and kicking in your sleep again."

"No, I wasn't."

"Yes, you were. You can ask them." I didn't have to look to know she was pointing at the three MawMaws. They were always staring, and whispering, and shaking their heads like it was their job to watch over us.

Khayla's head popped up off the cot like it was on springs. I moaned. I wasn't ready to get up. Even though my stomach was growling, begging for food, I wasn't ready to start another long day of lugging fussy Khayla back and forth to the stinking bathroom, knowin' good and well that something was wrong with her, and knowin' at the same time there wasn't nothing I could do about it without exposing the truth about my family. I reached over and pushed Khayla's head back down on her cot and tried to shush her back to sleep.

"I think Khayla needs to use the bathroom," Sealy said in a tired voice and sat down next to Khayla. The girl didn't have no good reason for being anything but rested.

I squeezed my eyes shut and said, "Well, then, go on an' take her." It would've been nice to see her do *something* to help me out with our sister.

"Never mind," Sealy said. "I don't think she has to go anymore." She never took her face out from between the swirly green and white cover of her dumb journal. I stared at her wishing I was still a little kid so I could sit and scribble in a book all day.

"Khayla, do you need to use it?" I'd only been up a few minutes and I was already aggravated.

"No."

"Good," I mumbled to the air, "then I'm gonna go." I scooted and huffed and puffed, and slapped at the crinkly, useless pillow—fussin' the whole time, trying to get up off my idiotic cot.

"You can't leave us here," Sealy said in her Sealy way. "I'm too young, remember?"

I wasted one of the best crusty looks I've ever made when I threw it over at Sealy. She didn't see it 'cause the girl never looked up once, as far as I could tell. Whatever.

Khayla came walking up behind me.

I turned around, pointing my finger. "No, Khayla."

From behind her journal, Sealy said all sweet-like, "Come see, Khayla. Come see Sissy." Khayla turned around and headed back to Sealy. I was fixin' to tell her to put the journal away and pay attention to her baby sister, but right then she set the book down and planted them sad puppy eyes of hers on me. "Are you really going to leave us by ourselves, Armani?"

I turned away and started walking. "I'm so sick of doin' *everything*. Can't I just go to the bathroom one time by myself?" I was so wore down. "Y'all will be fine. You got them to watch ya."

I let out a tired sigh and waved at the three happy MawMaws.

———

I hated being on that side of the shelter. There were too many red vests and too many sets of eyes and ears. I wiped beads of sweat off my forehead. I was thankful for the short line. I got in and out of the bathroom quick so I could hurry up and get back to our corner, where I felt safe.

"*Attention: The first bus bound for Houston, Texas, will depart promptly at eleven . . .*" I don't know why they kept making the same announcement over and over. It didn't do nothing but add to the noise.

I was trying to make my way through the people and fuss when a big ol' woman pushed past me. Based on the size of her rear end, it was a good thing she didn't find no part of me with her feet, or I would've been crushed to death for sure.

"Hey!" I hollered. But by the time the words left my mouth, all I could see was the woman waddling away as fast as her short legs could go with a crying kid on her shoulder. A kid with a daffodil-yellow shorts set.

My heart knock-knock-knocked up inside my chest.

"Hey, are you okay?" Someone touched my shoulder.

I never took my eyes off the huge backside shifting from side to side as the crazy woman zigzagged through the room of cots and people. My head went to thumping. I tried to take off running, but tripped over my own boot-covered foot and fell to the floor.

"Whoa, girl. Slow down," the person said, grabbing hold of my arm.

"I—I can't. I think that woman has my baby sister." Panic filled my whole body when I said the words out loud.

"What?"

I finally looked the annoying stranger straight in the face. I blinked, trying not to get lost in the ocean blue of the boy's big eyes. I searched my brain for the kid's name. "Wh-what are you doin' here?"

CHAPTER 40

The Boman kids. I couldn't believe my eyes. The last time I'd seen them kids they were all tucked up inside a tire drifting off to who knows where. Now, here they were, all four of them lined up like stairsteps from the tallest one down to the shortest. The name of the boy who'd grabbed hold of my arm didn't come to me, 'cause I never knew it to begin with.

"What's wrong? Are you okay?" the oldest Boman boy asked.

I pointed into the muck of people. "I don't know." I started thinking maybe all I'd seen was a rude fat woman trying to run with a girl who happened to be dressed in yellow. Maybe the red-vested folks were handing out daffodil-yellow shorts sets to all the little girls. I stopped pointing and adjusted my shirt that was stuck to me like I was made of flypaper. *Khayla is safe with Sealy,* I started chanting up in my head.

"You sure looked scared." The Boman boy's voice had a nice even tone that Memaw would've compared to butter.

"I'm not scared." I tried to keep my lip from curling up like it sometimes liked to do. "It was just a case of mistaken identity." I reached up with my free hand and made an attempt to smooth the hair bumps all over the top of my head. I wished I would've took half a second to check myself in the bathroom mirror when I'd had the chance.

The Boman boy smiled a gap-toothed smile. "Well, who was it that you mistakenly identified?" The other three Boman kids were making me uncomfortable just standing there watching and not minding their own business. I had half a mind to shoo them away.

"Oh, it was nothin'." The feel of my smile was strange. I went to swaying side to side. "Well, see, what happened was, I was just walkin' along when some huge, rude woman flew by an' about knocked me down. I thought she was runnin' off with my baby sister Khayla in her arms." I let out a nervous giggle that sounded more like Sealy than me. "But it couldn't have been her 'cause she wears a lime-green headband made from the hem of Mama's dress, and that baby girl didn't have one." I wished more than anything right then that I could stop rambling. *Please let Khayla be with Sealy.*

"Man, that must've been scary." The boy had a dimple that played hide-n-seek right alongside of his mouth. "I know how ya feel," he said, and looked over at his brothers and sister. "If anyone ever tried to mess with one of mine, I don't know what I'd do." His voice had a calming effect on me.

I closed my eyes and concentrated on just my nose. I took in a real good, long whiff. I moved my head back and forth to try and stir up any smells that might be trying to hide. All I smelled was shelter— pure and simple mildewy shelter. What I *didn't* smell was onion water.

I smiled, and the happiness of knowin' the smell wasn't there spread all the way across my face.

I opened my eyes and there were four sets of blue eyes watching me like I was a mime on Bourbon Street.

"Hey, are you sure you're okay, Armani?" He knew my name.

"How do you know my name?" I hoped I didn't look like Miss Priscilla Nash and her plastered-smiley self.

He shrugged his shoulders. "I don't know. Just do, I guess."

The only Boman girl stepped up. She was wearing a lavender tank top just like Sealy's new one. That shirt filled me with relief. If there was more than one lavender-colored tank top, it made sense that there'd be more than one daffodil-yellow shorts set.

The girl tugged on her big brother's sleeve. "Matthew, can we go now? I'm hungry." His name was Matthew.

"*Attention, residents: You must have prior approval to board the transport unit departing for Houston at eleven* A.M. *If you do not have your authorization code . . .*"

The stupid recorded voice echoing through the air set my nerves in motion again. *What if that fat lady with the kid dressed in yellow was running to catch a bus?*

"Well, I best be gettin' back." I nodded and started to take a step.

Matthew took a step with me. He laid his hand on my arm. "Armani," he said in a hushed voice. He looked around. I knew that look. He didn't want anyone to overhear whatever he was fixin' to say. "Are y'all alone? I mean, where's your mama and daddy?" Truth potion must've been pouring out of his blue eyes, 'cause without even considering my answer, I shrugged.

"Yeah, us too." He swung his head to the side, moving the hair out of his eyes. "Our foster Auntie Mama got crushed by a tree." He said it like he was telling me what he'd had for supper. The other three Boman kids had their heads hanging—all that blond hair swooping down toward the floor. "She couldn't get outta the way fast enough in her wheelchair." *Crushed like poor Mrs. Tilly.*

I couldn't think of one thing to say right then.

"So, anyway," Matthew said, "this is my sister, Martha, and my brothers Lukey and little John." One of the mini-Matthews looked up from under his wavy hair. I could tell by the way he looked at them that Matthew had special feelings for each one. "Lukey won't talk. He ain't said one word since the tree fell." The boy named Lukey stared at the floor. Even with all that hair covering half his face I could still see the cute in him showing through.

"How old are you?" I asked Martha.

She twirled long honey-colored hair around her finger. I was thinking about how much I'd love to braid that hair. The braid would come clear to the middle of her back. "I'm seven," she said all proud. "I like your boots."

"Oh, thanks, they're my Memaw's. My Sealy's seven years old too. You'll like her—everybody does." Sealy was gonna be so excited to have someone her own age to talk to. I wondered if Martha liked books. I was fixin' to ask her when Matthew spoke.

"Is Georgie with y'all?" My whole body stung when he said my brother's name. The heat ran out of my face. "Me an' him have math class together. He's funny."

"Umm—"

"Did a tree fall on him?" little John piped up. His eyes were so sad.

I blinked the sting from my eye. All I wanted to do was get back to my sisters.

Matthew leaned in and whispered, "What happened to Georgie?" Our faces were so close I could feel the air coming out of his nose.

"I don't know where Georgie or my daddy is." I swiped at the tear that ran down my cheek. I knew when I seen the look on Matthew's face that I'd tell him everything, but not in front of them sad little boys.

My arms felt empty for the first time in a long while. I was grateful when Lukey, the boy who didn't talk, came over and took my hand in the two of his. Martha smiled a sweet smile at me. Matthew grinned. "He must like you, 'cause he don't take to many people."

I squeezed the little boy's hand. "Well, I like him too, and I don't take to many people neither." Lukey didn't smile, but when he looked up at me, I seen the possibility of happy sneak up into his eyes.

Matthew sniffed, shook the bangs out of his face, and cleared his throat. "So it's just you and your sisters?"

"Well, we have Mr. High Pockets. Do y'all wanna meet him?"

CHAPTER 41

The Boman kids followed me, except for Lukey, who was latched onto my hand.

"Oh, look." I pointed to where ol' Mr. High Pockets was lying on his side, facing the wall with his back to us. "Y'all are gonna love him. He does tricks."

"You mean like magic tricks?" asked Martha.

"Yeah," I said. I stopped walking. Something was wrong. A tiny thump started in the back of my head. Our cots were empty.

My heart was about to pound right out of my chest.

I just stood there.

"What's up?" Matthew asked.

I let go of Lukey's hand. I couldn't take my eyes off the empty space where Sealy and Khayla should've been, waiting on me. The shaking started in my knees and spread every which way so fast there was no stopping it. My breathing came in huffs.

"My sisters. The cots. The cots are empty!" I felt like I was gonna throw up.

"Ain't that Sealy over there?" Matthew said all calm.

I looked, and there they were. Sealy was standing up in the middle of the three MawMaws, and Khayla was all snug as a bug on Maw-Maw Sun's lap. Sealy seen me and gave a little "hey" wave.

I sat down on one of the cots and buried my head in my hands. I rocked back and forth for a good while, knowin' I'd crumble up and die if I ever lost Sealy or my baby sister.

Sealy never knew about me thinking I'd lost her and Khayla. She must've thought I'd lost my mind, though, when I came walking up behind her while she was telling the three MawMaws one of her I-read-this-in-a-book-one-time stories and I all but tackled her with a big ol' hug. I couldn't stop myself. Sealy was my sister, and right then it didn't matter one way or the other if she liked me or not.

"Hello! Hello!" MawMaw Sun said, waving us in closer like she was having us into her house for supper.

"Where have you been, Armani? I was getting worried about you." Sealy wiggled out of my hug. "Khayla was crying for you."

Khayla scooched off MawMaw Sun's lap and buried her face in my belly. I hugged her head.

I introduced the Boman kids to Sealy. Her and Martha came together like a pea and a pod.

Sealy was giggling, the Bomans and the MawMaws were saying their "Hey"s, and I was thanking Jesus up in my head.

I sat there a good long while hugging my knees when I spotted Mr. High Pockets sitting up against his wall. I stared at Khayla sleeping restless up between Sealy and Martha, and then I glanced over to where Matthew had slid two cots in for him and the boys. Everyone was knocked out napping except for me and Mr. High Pockets.

I slipped my boots on and got up. There was no way I was gonna be able to sleep ever again until I told someone what was sitting heavy on my mind.

CHAPTER 42

I pressed my back against the wall and let myself slide down into a sit the way I'd seen Mr. High Pockets do a thousand times. For a good while we just sat there, sharing space. Somehow he knew it wasn't magic I was needing right then.

"Khayla's sick." My voice was barely more than a whisper. "Sealy don't know it yet, but in the morning I'm taking Khayla to the clinic so she can see a doctor." Out of the corner of my eye I could see Mr. High Pockets nodding away at my words. "She hasn't had but maybe one cracker to eat since yesterday. And I don't know why she won't drink for me no more."

Without lifting my head from the wall, I turned and looked at my friend. His sadful, watery eyes tugged on me.

"I'm gonna miss you." I choked on a sob.

He scrunched up his shoulders and tilted his head in a *whatcha-talkin'-about* way.

I didn't have the energy to explain to him that when I went marching into that clinic to get help for my sister, we'd be turned over to the authorities for sure.

My head found the man's shoulder. It was hard and lumpy—not comfortable like Memaw's.

Khayla had to get better, and if that meant us all going to foster care or something, oh, well. I swallowed the cry trying to find its way out.

Mama and Daddy weren't coming, and I could barely breathe.

CHAPTER 43

A soft voice floated into my ear and the smell of Juicy Fruit gum made its way to my nose. "Hush, hush, honeybee, it's gonna be all right." I shivered with cold. Soft mama-like arms wrapped around me and took me in. Miss Priscilla Nash sat flat on the floor with her back up against the hard wall and stroked my head resting in her lap. I wanted to stay there forever.

I looked up and there was Mr. High Pockets looking down, keeping watch over me. He smiled a smile of worry leaving and then he turned and walked away.

"Do ya feel like talkin'?" she said quiet-like into my ear.

"I can't."

"I know." She purred the words like a mama cat. "I know, child. Everything's gonna be all right."

"It's my fault. All of it." My head did a teeny hop every time I hiccupped between messy sobs and sniffs.

"You'll see, honeybee, it's all gonna get better." She stroked my lumpy, frizzed-out hair.

I pulled my heavy head up. She right away caught my face with a wad of tissue. My own mama hadn't wiped my nose for me since I was six or seven, but I didn't care. I let the lady wipe whatever she thought needed wiping. My face was swelled up. Even my lips poofed out. "Miss Nash—"

"Please, call me Priscilla." Her soft, round, made-up face matched her mama-like arms.

"Miss Priscilla, you don't understand. Everything that's happened to my family is my fault."

Miss Priscilla stuck some tissue in my hand. "Nothing that's happened is anybody's fault. It was a terrible, spiteful storm." She let out a long sweet-smelling sigh.

"I know." I picked at the tissue. "But you don't understand." My eyes got heavier by the second.

Miss Priscilla leaned in and laid her cheek up on the side of my wet, gooey face. Her nutshell-brown cheek felt warm, and the flower garden smell on her was strong.

"All I wanted for my birthday was a puppy." The words came out of my mouth in a calm whisper. I turned my head up and let my heavy eyes fall on the sad eyes of Miss Priscilla. I wasn't crying no more, but the tears kept coming. "I broke my promise to Cricket. I told her I'd always take care of her an' keep her safe."

Miss Priscilla dabbed at her own eyes with a tissue. "Oh child, I don't know what in the world you're talkin' about, but I *do* know that whatever it is that's got you so upset"—she blew her nose hard into her tissue—"I'm here to help any way I can." She shoved the used-up tissue into the pocket of her red vest.

She didn't understand.

"I'm sorry," I mumbled.

"Hush now and rest," she said. "You don't have a thing to be sorry about."

Yes I did. I had plenty to be sorry about.

I sat there all snug and sad with my eyes stuck shut. She just kept on with her hushing.

"Khayla's sick," I said. "She needs a doctor."

"I know. I've been wantin' to talk to you about that," Miss Priscilla said. "My oh my, would you look at that?" She sounded like Memaw when she said them words.

Walking toward us was all the kids. Matthew Boman had poor little Khayla in his arms, where she was resting her head on his shoulder. Lukey and little John stood behind their brother, playing shy with me and Miss Priscilla.

I held my arms out and Khayla leaned down, wanting to be with me. Sealy and Martha took seats on the floor with me and Miss Priscilla.

Sealy was so young. I wondered if she was gonna forgive me for ruining her life when I confessed to the people in charge at the clinic that we were kids without parents.

"What's goin' on?" Matthew said, looking from me to Miss Priscilla.

"Oh, Matthew, it's . . . ," Miss Priscilla said.

"You know Matthew?" I interrupted.

They looked at each other and nodded. "Sure, Miss P.'s been lookin' out for us ever since we got off the bus."

I was as shocked as collard greens in ice water.

Matthew smiled all dimply at Miss Priscilla. "She's been helpin' me sort out some stuff, you know—with CPS, 'cause of what happened to Auntie Mama and us bein' foster kids an' all." He walked over and offered his hand to Miss Priscilla, and she took it. She stood up with a grunt.

"I don't understand," I said to Matthew. "You *talked* to CPS?" My tired heart went to racing again.

"Well, yeah." Matthew shrugged his shoulders. His smile looked more like a smirk.

"Did you report us to CPS? Tell me the truth."

Miss Priscilla raised her eyebrows and looked at Matthew. He shrugged again.

"What? Tell me. I wanna know if them people from CPS are comin'!" It felt like I was sucking all my oxygen through a straw.

Sealy looked fast from one of us to the other—panic showing plain as day in her eyes.

"Honeybee, you're breakin' my heart. I *am* CPS."

Sealy gasped.

"No, you're not," I said.

"Sure she is, Armani," Matthew said. "How did you *not* know that?"

"I . . . I . . . I don't—"

"So are you taking us to jail now?" Sealy whimpered.

"Good heavens, no! Why on earth would I do that, darlin'? I'm just here to help y'all. I was assigned the task of lookin' after the unattended children—like all of y'all." She swooped her hand at the group of us.

"But I seen you," I said. "I seen you the night we got here and you took them two boys! I thought you were takin' 'em to CPS so they could haul 'em off to jail or foster care or somethin'." Lukey and little John's heads popped up when I said the F word.

"Oh, sweetie, I don't know which boys you're talkin' about. Unless you mean Tyrone and Trevor," she said, and pointed. About four rows over, as sure as my mama can make a pie, a tall kid with a huge Afro nodded a "hey" and went back to doing whatever he'd been doing.

Me and Sealy just stared at each other.

CHAPTER 44

It took a whole lot of sweet-talking for Miss Priscilla Nash to convince me that she was still the same ol' caring friend she'd been before I learned the truth about her real identity. But the reason I didn't go on and on about the CPS thing was on account of the way it seemed Khayla couldn't even hold her own head up for more than a second or two.

"Khayla needs a doctor," I said, noticing for the first time how much lighter she felt in my arms. "I know I should've asked for help sooner, but—"

"We do the best we can with what we know, honeybee. The important thing is that you're askin' now. It takes a lot of courage to ask for help."

"What do you think is wrong with her?" Matthew asked.

"My guess is our little Khayla has the water bug. They've been treating folks in here left and right for a gastrointestinal virus." She gave a little shiver. "It's a nasty ol' bug."

"Gas . . . row . . . what?" Sealy asked. "What's that?"

"It's an ugly tummy sickness, sweetheart. They say it's from drinking tainted water." Right away I remembered Khayla's head slipping under the poisoned water when she fell out of the cooler-boat.

"But don't you worry," Miss Priscilla said to Sealy and straightened herself up tall. "I'm not gonna let some ol' bug mess with any of my kids." She winked at the group of us.

Khayla's belly rumbled up against me. I knew the way she shivered wasn't from being cold, 'cause the heat coming off her little body had me in a full-blown sweat.

"Why don't y'all go get something to eat?" I said to all the kids. "I need to talk to Miss Priscilla alone."

"No problem. Take your time, Armani," Matthew said, and stepped away with Sealy and his brothers and sister.

I fixed my attention on Miss Priscilla. "I want you to take my sister to the clinic. She needs to see a doctor, and maybe you can get her in quicker than me."

Miss Priscilla looked at me and raised her eyebrows just the teeniest bit.

I passed the sleepy, bellyaching lump that was Khayla to the lady in the red vest, knowin' for the first time in a long time that I was doing the right thing.

"Well then," she said, and dabbed at her eyes with what looked like a piece of used-up tissue, "let's not waste another second of this precious day."

———

I left the plastic bag under my cot while I laid the clothes out—one piece at a time, thankful that nothing there was foo-foo or frilly.

Sealy and Martha were playing a clapping game like happy fools. The sound of their giggles floated through the sticky-thick air like an after-supper breeze. Lukey and little John colored in the coloring books they'd stood in line almost an hour for. And Matthew was plopped on a cot, eating another cold cheese sandwich.

"Hey," I said to Matthew, "do you mind watchin' Sealy while I go change?" I held up the clothes for him to see.

"Naw, go ahead." He looked over at the girls slapping each other's hands. His eyes fell on my boots. "They have shoes at the clothes station, y'know. Just go up in there and tell 'em what size ya need."

Heat filled my face.

"Yeah, I know. We got some new ones from Miss Priscilla." I tried to smile and tuck flyaway hairs behind my ear, but they wouldn't stay. "So anyway, you don't mind watchin' her? I won't be long."

"It don't matter. But I don't get it. If you got new shoes, how come you're wearin' them fishin' boots?" Matthew smiled and shoved more sandwich in his already full mouth.

I stuck out my hip and planted a hand there. "Look, it ain't none of your business what kinda shoes I do or don't wear. Why do you care anyways?"

The boy smiled that annoying gap-toothed smile of his. I wanted to slap him. "Well, I *don't* care. But why do *you* care so much about whether or not I do?"

"Whatever. For your information, I don't care one dang bit if you care or not."

"So," Matthew said. He stood up, yawned and stretched his arms above his head. "If you don't care, then why don't you take them old boots off and get some decent shoes that fit?"

My eyes stung. I forced my idiot feet to move. I took two or three steps away from Matthew. I stopped with my back facing him.

"They were my Memaw's." The words were barely more than a whisper. "She gave them to me. She wanted me to have them. She's dead. She died in our attic and I have to wear her boots."

"Aww, man. I'm so sorry. I didn't know."

I wiped my face with the pile of clean clothes.

"Ya know," he rambled on, "now that I'm gettin' a closer look at 'em, I kinda like those boots. They ain't all that bad."

I half-turned and looked at him. He swiped the bangs out of his eyes and I could see the sorry sitting there.

"I understand why you don't wanna be takin' 'em off just yet. If my—"

"It's okay," I said. "You didn't know."

Me and Memaw's ugly garden boots clomped off to change into my new clothes.

CHAPTER 45

Miss Priscilla looked like a proud and fancy mama duck with the six of us kids following up behind her through the huge shelter like a row of light and dark baby ducks off on a walk. I could've followed that woman with my eyes closed just by letting my nose track her scent.

The cots left behind by the people on their way to Houston were gathered up and stacked out of the way, making more space for groups of little kids to have races from one side to the other. They ignored the tired-looking orange-haired man every time he hollered for them to stop running inside. I knew he was just doing his job, but if they couldn't run inside, where were they supposed to run?

Sealy and Martha walked in front of me holding hands—swinging their arms—giggling and whispering secrets. Watching them and thinking about seeing Khayla added a bounce to my own step.

"All right, y'all," Miss Priscilla said and turned to face us. "C'mon now, scooch yourselves on up here."

We bunched around her in a huddle, standing by the opening of a huge indoor tent.

Miss Priscilla stood up straight and smiled big, fluffing her teased-out wig with both hands. "All righty then. Now, I'm gonna check and make sure it's a good time for visiting. Y'all stay right here and don't move a speck. I'll be right back."

We stood all smushed up on each other by the flapping canvas door. People walked past us going in and out of the tent-clinic. Every time the flap went this way or that, a whoosh of Lysol disinfectant flew up my nose. I kept my eyes on the black-and-white-checkered floor and tried to keep my breaths coming. Miss Priscilla had made it clear I didn't need to worry about no one asking me questions in the clinic, but I sure couldn't turn down the worry going on up in my head.

"Hey, you okay?" Matthew asked in my ear.

"Yeah, I just want Miss Priscilla to hurry up. What's takin' her so long?"

"She's only been gone a minute," Matthew said. "She'll be back soon."

As soon as the words came out of his mouth, Miss Priscilla popped her happy head out through the tent-clinic door. "Y'all follow me now, and stay close. No wanderin'." She used her pinched-together finger and thumb to pretend she was zipping her mouth shut. Sealy and Martha copied her. I even seen Sealy pretend to throw away the invisible key.

We walked a good ways in when Miss Priscilla stopped and said, "The doctor's in with Khayla, so we'll wait here for him to finish his exam. By the way, I asked y'all's friend, Mr. High Pockets, to sit with your sister till we got here. The nurses say he hasn't left her side."

"That's cool," Matthew said.

"It sure is," Miss Priscilla beamed, "and helpful too. It's nice to have someone makin' sure Khayla-girl doesn't pull out her IV."

IV? My stomach tightened up.

"What's the matter, honeybee?"

"Nothin'." I shrugged. "Why don't y'all go on ahead without me? I can wait here." I looked around and there was no place for me to stand or sit—or wait. We were in the middle of a teeny hallway made out of tent walls.

"Khayla will want to see you, Armani." Sealy looked at me with Mama's eyes.

I looked down and traced the outline of a square with my boot toe. "I'll see her soon as she's feelin' better."

"Well, if Armani's not going, then I'm not going," Sealy said, and folded her arms up tight across her chest.

A lady with a crying, coughing baby scooched by and shot a crusty look at the group of us clogging up the skinny hallway.

"Yeah, I agree with Sealy," Matthew said. "If Armani ain't goin', I ain't goin' neither." I might've grown one full inch right then.

"Get over here! All of y'all. *Right now.* C'mon." Miss Priscilla looked as aggravated as a mama who's lost control of her bratty kids in the grocery store. We squished in for another huddle.

Miss Priscilla's mouth tried to look mad, but her eyes were still soft. "Now y'all listen here." She started pointing at each of us, but mostly me. "I had to pull a lot of strings to get y'all back here. So listen up and listen good." She paused, staring at me. "There's a baby girl on the other side of this wall"—the wall flapped—"who is very excited to see y'all. Especially you, Miss Armani. So, I expect y'all to put on a happy face and stop all this fussin'."

Miss Priscilla unwrapped a fresh piece of gum and stuck it in her mouth. She smacked her lips and the juicy smell filled the air, temporarily covering up the odor of Band-Aids and diarrhea.

"Can I tell y'all a secret about your Mr. High Pockets friend?"

"Yes, ma'am."

She grinned. "I can tell by the twinkle in his eye that he sure does like my gum." She winked, and Sealy and Martha and the little Boman boys giggled.

Miss Priscilla reached into her pocket and pulled out a new pack of gum. Lukey and little John squeezed to the front, instead of hiding behind Matthew like usual. Miss Priscilla pulled the wrapper string, and the fresh smell of Juicy Fruit snapped into the air and made my mouth water. She gave each of us our own piece. It was more refreshing than a glass of iced-down sweet tea.

The Boman kids went to smacking their gum, not chewing polite with their mouths closed like Mama taught me and Sealy.

Something about chewing that gum brought out the sweet in me and changed my mind from wanting to run the opposite way like a frightful dumb scuttlebug.

CHAPTER 46

A soft hum came from somewhere in the room. Not the annoying kind of hum that came from the gray lights at night. This was a nice, soothing hum.

Mr. High Pockets was his usual slap-happy self, sitting up in a big ol' rocking chair next to Khayla's bed. When he seen us, his grin went so big and real, I knew we'd made his day just by walking in. Mr. High Pockets pulled me in for a hug with a strength I didn't know he had.

While the kids were saying all their heys to Mr. High Pockets, I stood over Khayla, who was lying on her back in the oversized metal crib. I couldn't take my eyes off the tube hanging out of her arm.

"Go on, honeybee," Miss Priscilla said. "You can pick her up."

Khayla's arms went straight up into the air, begging me to hold her.

Miss Priscilla must've known that I was nervous about touching my own sister, 'cause without saying one word, she lowered the side of the bed and scooped up Khayla. She plopped her up against me and had the IV tube tucked somewhere so I wouldn't accidentally yank it out of her little arm.

"Are you feeling better, Sissy?" Sealy asked.

Khayla nodded, then grabbed me with both hands and hugged my head.

We stood there taking up space around the crib, filling the curtained room with the smell of Miss Priscilla's gum. Mr. High Pockets closed his eyes and pulled in a long breath through his nose. He smiled and opened his twinkly happy eyes. It was impossible not to smile with him.

The hum got louder—more familiar—causing an uneasy feeling to come over me. The look on Sealy's face let me know she heard it too.

Khayla was fidgeting so much it took everything I had to keep from dropping her. The girl wouldn't leave my lip alone. It must've been the smell of my gum that had her wanting to pull my mouth right off my face. I took hold of her little hand as careful as I could, on account of the tubing and all, and moved it away from my face at least ten times. But, as sure as muscadine grapes turn purple in August, that girl reached right on up and had at it some more with my sore lip, stretching it out like she was gonna pull it right up over my head.

"Stop it, Khayla!" My lip was gonna be as fat as a truck tire if she didn't leave it alone.

The humming stopped.

"Do you want me to take her?" Matthew asked.

"No. I just want her to stop pullin' on my dang lip." The girl was getting on my last nerve with all her aggravating pulling and not listening. I could tell she was feeling better.

The curtain moved behind me. Someone on the other side was trying to open it. Khayla reached over my shoulder and slapped at the sheet-curtain.

The curtain slid across the metal bar till it got stuck and came to a stop. The person on the other side yanked and tugged, but the curtain wasn't budging.

I turned to set Khayla back down in her crib when my baby sister grabbed a fist full of that curtain-wall and pulled hard. The whole stupid thing came tumbling down! The curtain fell like a suffocating parachute over the top of me.

I heard Sealy gasp.

A loud *clink* rang out when the metal curtain rod hit the floor.

I swung my arm, trying to get the germ-filled ugly sheet-curtain off me before I smothered to death.

"Somebody get this nasty thing off me!" I was sweating and headed to a panic.

Then Matthew's white hands came up and under, grabbing hold of the curtain, and with one big whoosh the thing floated up and off my head. I reached up to smooth my hair when I seen her.

"What the . . ."

I stopped breathing.

I couldn't move. I couldn't believe my eyes. Standing there, with her face smeared in tears and her hands folded up by her heart, was Mama.

CHAPTER 47

The caved-in look of Mama's face all but did me in. I crumbled into a ball of mush hugging my knees so fast, I ain't even sure how I got there. Mama slid to the floor and gathered me into her. Sealy squeezed herself up in, and we sat like that for a good long while—rocking and swaying back and forth. Miss Priscilla helped Khayla out of the crib so she could get into that big sobbing, mother-daughter happy pile too. I ain't no doctor, but I swear Khayla looked better just from seeing Mama's face and getting washed in her kisses.

To be in Mama's arms again just felt *right*. It was like Christmas and my birthday all at once. I ain't sure how she held us all at the same time like that, but she did. We could've stayed like that—like we was one person instead of four—for the rest of time, and it would've been fine by me.

"I knew you would find us, Mama! I just knew it," Sealy said from up inside our mama-hug.

It wasn't till right then that I realized I'd been thinking I might not never see my mama again.

I looked up from under all of Mama's lovin'. Miss Priscilla was beaming from ear to ear with tears streaming down her face. Matthew went to Martha and put his arm around her shoulders. She reached up and patted the top of his hand. Matthew's eyes filled with happiness and he nodded at me. The feeling coming from him drifted across that itty-bitty space and found my heart. A mix of laughs and cries filled the air.

Mama stood up on wobbly legs with Khayla clinging to her. She grabbed hold of the matching metal crib holding Kheelin. I helped Mama steady herself while she adjusted to the sight of finding her lost children.

"Khayla. What's happened to Khayla?" Mama's words were as shaky as her legs.

"She's sick, Mama," I said.

Sealy flew into a long story about how Khayla had the runs and wasn't eating right. I didn't mind her doing the explaining. How was I supposed to tell Mama that it was on account of me and my stupid clumsy feet that her sweet baby girl was sick from sucking in putrid water—water *I* dumped her into?

Mama put Khayla into Kheelin's bed. The two of them slipped into twin-talk and giggles. I leaned over the rail, kissed my baby brother on his cheek, and untangled the twisted oxygen tube from around his ankle. I warned them both not to be yanking on each other's tubes.

"Well, for goodness' sakes. Will y'all look at that?" Miss Priscilla said, soaking up the sight of my twin brother and sister lovin' on each other. "I don't think I've ever seen a sweeter sight in all my days." She pulled an old wad of tissue from her pocket and found a spot on it to wipe under her nose.

For the first time, Mama took in the sight of the freckled man rocking away with the lopsided grin.

"This is our friend, Mama," I said. "His name is Mr. High Pockets."

He stood up fast, almost knocking over the wooden chair. He swooped his arm, inviting Mama to please take his comfortable seat.

"He has nice eyes, doesn't he, Mama?" Sealy giggled.

Mama and Mr. High Pockets nodded at each other. Mama barely got out a "Hello" before Sealy took off rambling again. The girl was wide-open.

It was easy to see that Mama and Miss Priscilla had a secret understanding and a liking for one another. The two of them close together like that made me realize how much Mama could use some of Miss Priscilla's mothering. A tear for Memaw rolled down my cheek—a wish that she was there sharing in our celebration of finding each other.

Khayla and Kheelin were lost in being with each other, and Sealy was talking a mile a minute, not even pausing between words to take a breath. "A soldier girl named Stella made us get on a bus. She knows Uncle T-Bone from the Army, and then—"

The little wanna-be room was as noisy as the French Quarter in February, and I was more happy right then than I'd been since the day I made ten.

I looked over and seen Matthew slowly inching his way out of the room with his family out in front of him.

"Wait!" I said.

They stopped. Matthew turned and looked at me. "It's cool. I'm happy y'all found your mama, but we best be gettin' back to the cots."

"Mama, this is my friend, Matthew," I said, never taking my eyes off him. I took hold of the stubborn boy's hand and pulled him over by Mama.

"It's nice meetin' you, Mrs. Curtis," Matthew said. "This here's my sister, Martha, and my brothers Lukey and little John." Mama looked past the boy and straight into Miss Priscilla.

"No family . . . ," the woman whispered to Mama.

Watermelon red filled Matthew's cheeks.

Mama held out her arms and Matthew stepped closer to her. She pulled him in and squeezed him good and tight, planting a long kiss into the top of his thick blond head. She let him loose, and he wiped a tear from his cheek with the back of his hand.

Mama studied him, sad and happy showing up at the same time on her pretty face. "You remind me of my Georgie." She looked over at the other three Boman kids with sad love pouring from her eyes. Martha wandered over and let Mama hug her too. Lukey and little John stayed smushed up against Miss Priscilla.

"Look, Mama! Remember this?" Sealy broke the awkward quiet spell that had laid itself down over the room. Her book sack fell to the floor when she pulled out the swelled-up Bible that she'd fished out of the floodwaters.

"I've been reading to Mr. High Pockets every day. Now we can take turns reading to him like we did for Memaw, right, Mama?" Sealy scooched up onto Mama's lap the best she could—being too big for laps and all.

"When Memaw sat with her Bible, she said she could draw strength from knowing the word of God was resting in her lap. Remember,

Mama?" Sealy took a big breath. I don't think the girl was in control of her own mouth right then.

"Well," I mumbled, "I never heard Memaw say nothin' about God sittin' in her lap."

"Not God, silly. The *word* of God. She said it a lot."

"She sure did," Mama said in a far-off voice. "I'm not sure what your Memaw enjoyed more—sitting on that old porch swing with you, Armani, or listening to you read, Sealy." Mama sniffed.

A blanket of quiet fell over us.

"I like to read to Lukey and Little John," Martha piped up.

"Shhh . . . not now," Miss Priscilla said, and patted the side of the girl's leg.

CHAPTER 48

It turned out to be the kind of morning that would've made Memaw linger in the kitchen till way past breakfast time. When I closed my eyes, I could almost smell Mama's pies baking in the oven and warm chicory brewing in the coffeepot. We spent most of the day lovin' on Mama, and Mama lovin' on us—*all* of us. It was clear as the blue in Matthew's eyes that Mama had already made space up in her heart for the Boman kids. I sat cross-legged on the floor, watching my mama spread her goodness to every single soul in that cramped dinky room.

Miss Priscilla surprised us all when she came gliding in sometime after noon with a huge bag full of cheeseburgers and fries from McDonald's. I ain't lyin' when I say it was the best burger I've ever had in my whole life. Miss Priscilla even brought shakes for Mr. High Pockets and the twins.

There we were—the eleven of us—gathered wherever we could squeeze in around the beds, eating juicy burgers and gulping down Cokes on ice. The room was filled with "Mmms" and "Thank yous," but I couldn't help but feel the empty space from Daddy and Georgie not being there growing bigger by the minute as the day wore on.

Sealy and Martha sat together on the floor up against Mama's legs. The two of them chomped on fries, happy-bobbing their knobby knees and heads. Not one time did Mama say a word about all the smacking going on or the talking with mouths full.

Matthew and his brothers ate in a huddle watching Mr. High Pockets put on a magic show. The man kept making loud slurping sounds even long after it was obvious his shake was gone.

I might've been the only one who noticed Miss Priscilla grinning from here to Mississippi. Then, like she couldn't hold it no more, she blurted out, "It's all settled, y'all!"

"What is, Miss P.?" Matthew asked, handing the quarter back to Mr. High Pockets. The boy had been trying forever to figure out how to get that shiny coin to fall out of his nostril. I ain't trying to be hurtful, but you couldn't pay me a million dollars to touch that nasty quarter, especially if I was eating at the same time.

"Okay, y'all, listen up. Here's what we're gonna do." She looked at each one of us, but her eyes settled on me. "We're gonna shift the furniture around in here so y'all can stay with your mama tonight. That is, of course, if y'all *want* to." She winked.

"And the Boman children?" Mama asked. "I know we can squeeze everyone in."

We all stared at Miss Priscilla.

"Y'all are so silly sometimes, I swear." She smacked a time or two. "When I said 'y'all,' I meant *all* of y'all. It's gonna be a tight squeeze, but if the twins don't mind sharin'—and it sure don't seem they do— we'll get rid of this other crib and bring in a roll-away. Y'all can decide who sleeps where."

Mama let out a big sigh and whispered, "Thank you, Jesus."

Matthew swiped at his eyes with the back of his hand and I real quick looked somewhere else, pretending I didn't see him do it.

"Now," Miss Priscilla said, "First thing in the mornin'—I mean *early*, y'all, most likely even before the first breakfast call—they're gonna move Khayla and Kheelin to the Pediatric Unit over at Baton Rouge General. It's a good hospital with fine doctors."

"But how?" Mama asked.

"All the arrangements have been made, Mrs. Curtis. Your babies are gonna get the care they need. You have my word on it."

Mama closed her eyes tight and the tears came streaming down.

"Well, now look what you've gone and done," Miss Priscilla said in a shaky voice. She cleared her throat and reached into her pocket, pulling out a tissue. "Now you've got me cryin' and my face is gonna run right off. Trust me now, y'all don't wanna see me without my face on."

Mama's smile shined through her tears. "Miss Priscilla, you're a beautiful person, with or without your face on."

"And now I see why your children are so special."

Lukey was stretching out the bottom of Matthew's T-shirt, making it clear that he needed to use the bathroom.

"The hospital's settin' up a private room for y'all, Mrs. Curtis."

"Please, call me Katherine."

Miss Priscilla took a long breath and looked at Mama with the look of someone fixin' to ask for a favor. "Katherine, would you be willin' to take temporary guardianship of the Boman children?"

Mama didn't take but half a second to say, "Oh, yes, whatever I can do to help."

Matthew looked at Mama like he was laying eyes on an angel.

Miss Priscilla snuck a peek over at Mr. High Pockets, who had his eyes closed. She lowered her voice to where I could barely hear her. "The hospital's agreed to make an exception and bring in a bed for Mr. High Pockets, since it appears he's adopted y'all. But that's up to you, Katherine."

I glanced over at pretend-sleeping Mr. High Pockets, and the man had the tiniest smile sitting in the corner of his mouth. I covered my own smile with my hand and waited to see what Mama was gonna say.

"Yes, of course he can stay with us." Mama stood and reached her hands out to Miss Priscilla. "I don't know how to thank you."

Just then a bald, busy nurse squeezed her oversized self into the room. We all squished backward as far as we could, trying to make room for the nurse and her overflowing backside and big, shiny white head so she could get up close by her patients. The woman filled the room the same way Mrs. Louell filled the doughnut shop.

"Good afternoon," she said to nobody. She right away went to fussin' with the tank that pumped oxygen into the tube going up my brother's nose. "Do we have to go tee-tee?"

"I do," said Lukey.

Everyone in the room looked at the boy who hadn't said one word since his foster mama had got crushed—everyone except the nurse.

"Pardon?" she asked, still not looking at anyone.

"Oh, it's nothin'," I said, putting my arm around the little boy's shoulder. "Lukey here just needs to use the bathroom."

She finally looked up like she was noticing the room full of us for the first time.

"Are you all family?" she asked.

Matthew came and stood beside me. "Yes, ma'am, we're family."

The nurse locked eyes with Mr. High Pockets. He smiled with his twinkly copper-colored eyes and gave a thumbs-up.

The nurse looked at me, then Matthew, then around the room at each one of us. "I'm sorry for interrupting, but I need to check vitals."

"You do whatever you need to, sugar," Miss Priscilla said.

She fiddled with Khayla's IV bag. Then she reached up under my sister's head and pulled out her little pillow. She held Khayla's head careful with one hand and gave the pillow a couple of good shakes with the other. Quicker than Daddy could give a raspberry, the nurse had the fluffed pillow back under her patient's head. After foolin' with my sister, she checked Kheelin's temperature. I liked the way she tickled his belly before she did her exam.

I spotted her name tag—Bitty Pinkerton, R.N. I wondered if her mama had known that her daughter was gonna grow to such a large size when she chose the name Bitty.

After the nurse named Bitty finally finished doing all of her nurse stuff, she stood in the center of our room and slowly turned herself in a circle, pointing at each one of us, and counted. One . . . two . . . three. . . . By the time she got to eight she was saying the numbers like it was one hundred and eight instead of just eight.

"Eleven," she said like she wouldn't have believed it if she hadn't seen us with her own two eyes.

My heart sank. I just knew that woman with her big bald head was fixin' to tell us we were gonna have to go back to our cots in the corner. I was already feeling the burn in my eyes coming on and the woman hadn't even spoke yet. I inched my way closer to Mama.

"Y'all are blessed," she said, still shuffling herself around in a circle, looking at the bunch of us. "There's folks up in here that've lost more than half their families. There's some . . ." She got choked up on her words. Water pooled up in her eyes. ". . . lost *everything*. I haven't even heard from my own people. Some in New Orleans and my daddy's people who stay in Bogalusa." The nurse buried her face in her hands, but it couldn't stifle the tiny cry that came from her.

I took a couple steps toward Miss Nurse Bitty. I wrapped my arms the best I could around the middle of the lady and shushed into her ear. "It's okay, it's gonna get better."

The nurse placed one of her wet hands over the top of mine. "I know you're right. I know you are."

The lady blew her nose softly, then she stood up good and straight. She cleared her throat. "Like I was saying, y'all are blessed. Don't any of you forget that."

No one said nothin'.

"I best get back to work," she said with a soft smile. Miss Nurse Bitty looked at me, with wetness still under her eyes, and said, "Let me know if you need anything, you hear?"

"Yes, ma'am," I said.

I never saw Miss Nurse Bitty Pinkerton, R.N., or her beautiful bald head again.

Miss Priscilla blew kisses into the air for all of us, then she said we needed to be good and keep the noise down so the sick folk could get their rest.

"I'll walk with you, Miss P.," Matthew said. "I need to take Lukey to the bathroom and check to see if we left anything at the cots."

"Well, I sure would enjoy the company. . . ." Miss Priscilla stopped and turned to face us like she just remembered something.

Her mouth opened, then closed, then opened again. "Oh, never mind, don't mind me. I best be goin'." She turned and started walking away, giving us a little wave over her shoulder. Matthew looked at me and shrugged. But after about two steps, Miss Priscilla whipped herself around and said, "Well, I'm just gonna come out with it."

CHAPTER 49

Every single one of us stared at Miss Priscilla, waiting to hear what she was fixin' to say.

"What is it, Miss Priscilla?" Mama asked.

"Well," she said, and sat down in a folding chair. "Shortly after y'all get transported in the mornin' to the hospital, I'll be leavin' myself."

I think every single one of us let out a gasp.

"What are you talkin' about, Miss P.?" Matthew said.

Sealy's eyes went all big and she looked over at me, shaking her head.

"The authorities have opened the spillway bridge to people with special clearance." She was talking to the floor. I don't know about Matthew and the rest of them, but me and Mama looked at each other 'cause we knew the road home to New Orleans went over the spillway bridge. The road *home*.

"But," Mama said, "I was told just yesterday that no one's allowed back into the city."

Miss Priscilla tore her eyes from the floor. "Well, technically, that's true, unless you have one of these." She pulled out a badge hanging at the end of a necklace from inside her blouse and showed it to us before putting it back where she kept it. "With my clearance as a CPS representative, I've been granted a permit to enter the city. Of course they've implemented a strict curfew, so we're only gonna have a few hours. I sure hope it gives us enough time."

My mind was going a million miles a minute.

"There's a nice gentleman who'll be ridin' with me. Poor thing is just as distraught as he can be with worry about his family. Since I don't know my way around the city, he's comin' along as my guide."

"But you're comin' back though, right?" Matthew asked, flinging his bangs out from in front of his face. His breathing was faster than normal.

Miss Priscilla placed her hand on the side of his face. "Of course I'll be back, sweet boy. Even if Brad Pitt himself asked me to marry him tomorrow and move me to a palace in Rome, Italy, I'd still choose to come back here to be with y'all." She grabbed hold of his chin and gave it a squeeze before letting go. Matthew smiled and put his head down, but not before I seen the pink spread into his cheeks.

Mama started to say something, but before she could get her first word out, my own words exploded into the air. "I'm goin' with you."

"No, Armani!" Sealy threw herself into me so hard it knocked the air out of me. I had to pry the girl's arms from around my middle.

"Armani, I can't let you—" Mama was on her feet.

"But Mama, I can try to find Daddy and Georgie!" My heart was about to pop out of my chest. So many things were flying into my head all at the same time. I couldn't decide what to say first.

"No," Mama said firm with her eyes closed. "I just got you back. I can't let you go."

"Please, Mama, *please*. I can do this." I looked at Miss Priscilla. "Will they let me ride with you?"

Miss Priscilla looked from me to Mama with her lips moving but no words coming out. Finally she managed to say, "Well, I . . . I sure don't see why they wouldn't."

"See, Mama?"

"But of course, it's up to your mama, honeybee. I don't think I'd let you out of my sight till the day you turn thirty-one if *I* was your mama, especially after all that's happened."

"Yeah, but my daddy and brother might still be there. *Please*, Miss Priscilla. Tell Mama we'll be careful. Tell her we'll be back."

"Oh, honey, I can't. It has to be your mama's decision."

I went to Mama and looked up at her, knowing that she wasn't gonna let me go. I forgot about anybody else who might've been up in that room with us. Right then it was just me and Mama. I wasn't gonna let myself cry, but I knew the tears were coming anyway. "Mama, please. You *have* to let me go and at least *try* to find them."

Mama shook her head and kept closing her eyes. "They'll find us. I can't let you go."

"Mama, you don't understand. It's because of me that Daddy and Georgie aren't here. Please. Let me go, Mama."

Mama gathered me into her and fought back her own tears. "It is *not* your fault, Armani. It is not your fault." Over and over she said those same words. She let me cry into her till I ran out of tears.

I didn't wanna wipe my nose on my new shirt, so I looked up to ask Miss Priscilla for a tissue, but she wasn't there. Everyone else was gone except for the twins sitting quiet up in their bed, and Sealy standing close by Mama.

"Everyone went for a walk," Mama said. "They'll be back soon."

Mama let out a loud sigh and fell heavy into the rocking chair. She looked about as tiny as I'd ever seen her. I stood there feeling wore down and tired, and ready to go home to find Georgie and Daddy.

"There's something I have to tell you, sweetheart," Mama said, looking at me with eyes as tired as I felt. "Uncle Alvin's here."

CHAPTER 50

A shot of happy zapped through me—till I seen the look on Mama's face. My mouth went dry.

"He hasn't seen TayTay since Monday," Mama all but whispered. *It was Thursday.* "He's been to two other shelters. He can't find her."

I didn't wanna hear no more. *Not TayTay. Not my best friend.*

"I'm so sorry, Armani." Mama patted the top of her leg. "Come here, sweetheart."

I went to her and she pulled me onto her lap. My head went straight to her shoulder and found that cradle spot made for holding heads—a place that felt safe.

Mama held her arm out to my sister. Sealy came over, sat on the floor, and rested her head on Mama's knee. Mama stroked Sealy's head. My sister's hand found mine. I took it and held tight. I closed my eyes and breathed my mama in, wishing that somehow we could stay like that forever.

"Mama," I said calm and quiet, still wrapped in her arms. "Did Memaw die 'cause I snuck her them apple fritters?"

"No, darling, Memaw died because it was her time. There isn't anyone or anything to blame."

"There's no one to blame," Sealy whispered.

Mama took a long, slow breath. "It would make your Memaw so sad if she thought you were blaming yourself, Armani. Please understand that it wasn't your fault. Can you do that for me?"

I lazy shrugged.

"I owe you girls an apology—especially you, Armani."

I lifted my head. Mama gently pushed my head back onto her shoulder. "I shouldn't have left you like I did at the Super Dome. I was so scared and confused and I didn't realize—"

"It's okay, Mama," I said. "You had to get help for Kheelin. We understand. *I'm* the one who's sorry. I should've listened to you and stayed put like you said."

"Oh, sweetheart, you did exactly the right thing. You've taken such good care of my babies. You're an amazing young lady." Mama pulled in a long breath. "Your Daddy's going to be so proud of you—proud of *both* of you."

Sealy sniffled and her thumb rubbed the back of my hand like I used to rub Memaw's.

Mama shifted in the chair when I got up. She stared at me a good long while—into my eyes—studying my face. "You've grown so."

Mama reached behind her neck with both of her hands. She took off the compass-locket and held it out in front of her. Then she reached up under my hair and fastened it back around my neck, the same way Memaw had done up in that awful attic.

"Now," Mama said, "I need you to do one more thing for me."

I blinked, never taking my eyes off hers. "Anything, Mama."

"I want you to go with Miss Priscilla tomorrow."

The air got sucked right out of me.

"But," Mama said. She took hold of my chin and leaned in a little closer. "I don't know what you'll find when you get there. And Armani?"

"Yes, Mama."

"I want you back here tomorrow night."

"That's right," Sealy said, sounding like an echo, "tomorrow night."

Before I had a chance to say another word, I heard the sounds of Miss Priscilla and her ducklings coming down the canvas hallway.

"Knock-knock," Miss Priscilla said in that voice of hers. "Is it all right for us to come in?" She poked her poofy head in, and as soon as Mama said yes, the rest of her and the kids came spilling back into our room. Mr. High Pockets followed behind, toting a pile of paper pillows and scratchy blankets.

I seen the plastic white bag in Matthew's hand and knew right away what it was. Martha snatched the bag out of his hand and skipped over to me. She held the bag out for me to take. "Here, Armani, we found your bag."

"Thanks," I mumbled.

"What's that?" Mama asked.

"What?"

"The bag you're holding."

I looked down at the bag like I was surprised to see it hanging off a hand that belonged to me. "Oh, this? It's nothin'."

Sealy's mouth opened. I shot her a look. She shut her mouth quick. It didn't matter nohow, because my sister's new twin named Martha said all happy, "It's your new shoes, Armani. You know, the ones Miss Priscilla got ya."

"Oh, dear," Miss Priscilla said.

I forced a smile to my mouth that almost hurt. "Martha's right, Mama. It's just some shoes from Miss Priscilla, that's all."

"Can I see the bag?" Mama asked with knowin' in her voice.

She looked inside. She closed the bag and stood up. "Miss Priscilla, I wonder if I can get you to sit with the children for a few minutes longer."

"Well, you sure can, Miss Katherine. Me and Mr. High Pockets here can hold down the fort, can't we, hon?" She winked at the man and he gave her a thumbs-up. "Y'all take as much time as ya need."

I walked with Mama. She had her arm around my shoulder. The white bag swayed back and forth like a floating plastic wall between us while we walked.

"Can you show me where you've been sleeping?"

I led the way to our corner. The MawMaws waved and I waved back. Mama never asked who they were.

I stopped in front of our cots.

"Sit down, Armani."

Without saying one single word, Mama got down on her knees in front of me and took my right foot in her hands. As slow as molasses, my mama pulled the rubber boot off my foot. A tear made its way down my cheek. "Mama—"

276

"Shhh" is all Mama said.

She real careful set the boot on the floor next to her. Then she took my foot and rubbed it between her warm, sweet hands. She brought my foot up to her mouth and she kissed the top of it. She did the same thing with my left foot. When she pulled the new white sneakers with the sky-blue stripes out of the bag, a shiver ran up my spine.

One by one, Mama slipped the new shoes on me. My feet were singing thank you, but my heart was as heavy as a stump. Mama took Memaw's boots and placed them real gentle down inside the plastic bag.

When she finally looked up at me, her cheeks were wet and her eyes let me know her heart was feeling heavy too. She stood up. My hand slid into hers and she helped me to my feet. It felt like I was floating on air. She handed me the bag. We walked the long way back to the clinic.

Now ain't that nice? Memaw whispered in my ear.

CHAPTER 51

I sat on the edge of one of the roll-away beds that a man had brought in earlier. I kept touching Memaw's compass-locket while I watched Sealy braid Martha's long blond hair—the two of them non-stop whisper-gabbing. The twins and little John were sound asleep. Lukey had gone into the hall with Mama and Miss Priscilla. The boy had been hanging on Miss Priscilla's hand all afternoon.

Out of the corner of my eye I seen Matthew staring in my direction. I looked over at him and our eyes locked. He came over and sat down beside me. "Armani, I wanna go with y'all tomorrow."

It was way past lights-out. I noticed that the nighttime lights in the clinic didn't have the same nightmare-gray color like in the rest of the shelter. The buzz was still there, though. I figured I'd always have that buzz stuck in my head—probably even when I was twenty or thirty years old I'd still be hearing that buzz.

I seen the shadow of Mama sleeping in her rocking chair holding Kheelin. I couldn't take my eyes off her. I took hold of the locket and kissed it. *Please help me find my way home tomorrow.*

I tried to force my eyes shut so I could get some sleep, but they kept popping open. My insides were jumpy and my nerves were working me crazy. In the morning I was going home to try and find Daddy and Georgie, and I'd never been so scared in my whole life.

I rolled over onto my side, and that's when I seen it. Khayla had her hand poked out through the metal bars of the crib. I couldn't see her face too good, but I could see her little fingers. Somehow, that baby girl was giving me a perfect "I love you" sign like she'd been doing it all her life.

I smiled into the darkness. I gave Khayla the sign back and her hand disappeared back into the crib.

CHAPTER 52

Friday, September 2, 2005 - 4:23 A.M.

For days I'd been wishing for just a little time to myself away from kids and toilets and noise and shelter. But when the transport people came to take Mama and the twins and Sealy to the hospital, I could barely stand the thought of being away from all of them. Mama surprised me when she didn't cry.

Miss Priscilla promised she'd do everything in her power to get Mama's precious cargo back before lights-out.

"Wait!" Sealy all but hollered directly into my ear after she squeezed the life out of me when we said our byes. She reached into her book sack and pulled out Georgie's glasses.

Mama's hand flew up to her mouth and a tiny gasp squeezed past her lips.

"Here." Sealy handed the glasses to me. "Georgie's going to need these." She smiled. Her wet eyes twinkled. "He's going to be so happy to have them back. And tell Daddy I can't *wait* to see him." She gave me one last hug and held up the plastic bag. "Don't worry about Memaw's boots. I'll keep them safe for you." She looked at me in a way I've only seen a mama or daddy look at a child. "You're the best sister ever, Armani."

I stood there holding my brother's glasses and watched my family leave—not feeling one ounce of brave in my whole entire body.

———

I'd been sitting up in Miss Priscilla's SUV by myself, fiddling with Georgie's glasses on my lap, waiting for Matthew to get back from the bathroom and for Miss Priscilla to come with her friend—the man who'd lost his family. It was strange being outside, even if I was sitting in a big ol' truck. It was mostly dark out. There were buildings all around, like on Canal Street. If I tipped my head and looked up between the black outlines of two of them buildings, I could see the moon working its way across the sky. I'd never been so anxious to see what the sun was gonna look like, and what color blue the sky might be.

"Hey!" I jumped and almost bumped my head when Matthew opened the truck door and hopped into the backseat beside me.

"Hey," I said, looking out the window. I found the moon again. I liked staring at it. I wondered if people in Heaven could see the moon.

Matthew leaned across the seat and shoulder-bumped me. "You all right?"

I shrugged, "Yeah, I guess." I turned to look at him. It was weird the way sitting up in that dark SUV early in the morning like that made our skin look the same nighttime-blue color. "Can I ask you something, Matthew?"

"Sure."

"Are you scared? I mean, you know, about goin' back there."

"More than you know. I honestly didn't think I'd ever go back, 'specially since N'awlins ain't got nothin' left for me anyhow. Martha an' the boys is all I got. I'm grateful to your mama for takin' care of 'em."

Matthew's words about New Orleans not having nothing left stirred up that unsettling feeling in me again. I was fixin' to find my moon when a door opened, allowing Miss Priscilla and her smells to fill the empty driver's seat.

"So how do y'all like my Tahoe? I've had it goin' on a year now and y'all's the first ones to sit in the backseat. Imagine that." She looked up into the rearview mirror and smiled at us. All I could see was her bright cherry-red lips and part of her chin. "Y'all buckle up, now." She went to fluffing up her already big hair.

"Yes, ma'am," me and Matthew said at the same time.

The passenger door opened and a man got in. I blinked and blinked, trying to get rid of the spots left behind by the bright over-head light. I could tell the man was saying "hey" to Miss Priscilla by the way the two of them faced each other. Miss Priscilla let out one of her famous loud laughs and pushed the man's shoulder. She pulled down her sun visor and flipped open the lit-up mirror hidden there. Mama would've loved that mirror.

"Well, we best get goin'," Miss Priscilla said through her smacks. She snapped her visor-mirror shut and started the truck.

"Where are my manners?" Miss Priscilla said and half-turned in her seat so she could look back at us. "Y'all, this here's my friend Alvin that I told ya' about. Alvin, I'd like you to meet—"

Oh, God. It couldn't be. Could it?

The name flew out of my mouth. *"Uncle Alvin?"* I felt half sick to my stomach.

Miss Priscilla flipped down her visor. Her painted mouth was just a-smiling up in the dinky mirror. "Oh! You two know each other?"

Uncle Alvin turned around and looked at me like he was seeing the ghost of the voodoo queen Marie Laveau sitting on the backseat of that SUV Tahoe truck.

"Armani Curtis?"

"You *lost* her? How could you? You're so stupid!" I cried the words.

"Armani, don't . . ." Matthew turned my face so I was looking at him and not my ugly uncle. I fell into Matthew's chest and buried my face there.

Uncle Alvin let out a sob.

"Oh, my," Miss Priscilla said in her worry voice.

My uncle opened his door and got out. He glanced back at me as he walked slowly off.

A zap of angry electricity ran up my back.

He stopped walking and went to hanging his head.

"Honeybee, we need to talk."

"You don't understand." I took in a gulp of air-conditioner air. "He's mean to TayTay."

"Who's TayTay?" Matthew asked.

"My cousin. My best friend," I stifled a cry. "*His* daughter." I pointed out the window. "The daughter he *lost.*"

"Oh," Matthew said.

Without taking the time to think first, I got out of the truck. I grabbed hold of Memaw's locket and walked slow around the backside of the SUV. I stopped when the man I'd been holding hate for looked up. We stared at each other. I didn't realize it till right then that I'd never really looked TayTay's dad in the face before. The man standing in front of me didn't look mean at all. He looked . . . sad.

"I let her down when she needed me the most." His eyes dropped away from mine. "I was passed out drunk when that ol' she-devil Katrina put the Nines under water. I woke up floatin' on the sofa, and my baby girl was *gone*." He was crying. So was I. "I pray every night that God's lookin' after her—"

All the mad left me right then.

"Uncle Alvin." I was calling him by his name for the first time that I could remember. "We're gonna find her, I know we will."

A sob came from him. He slumped so far forward I thought he was gonna tip. His head, covered in gray-black fuzz, went to bobbing up and down.

I slowly wrapped my arms around his middle. At first he just stood there crying, letting me do all the hugging. But then he had his arms around me too. The weight of his head laid up on top of mine.

"I'm sorry," my uncle whisper-cried.

"Me too," I said.

"Do you think my baby will ever forgive me?" He pulled back and looked at me.

I wiped my eyes on my shirt sleeve. "TayTay's the nicest person I know. She loves you—she told me so."

"She said that?"

"Yes, sir, she did."

He sniffed and nodded, standing a tiny bit straighter.

When Miss Priscilla cleared her throat, we looked and seen her standing there dabbing at her face with a tissue.

"When y'all are ready, we really should get a move on," she said all soft.

Right before I opened my door and he opened his, Uncle Alvin said, "Thank you, Armani. You're good people. I know your daddy's proud of you."

I settled into my seat, more tired and wore out than ever. I looked out my window. The moon was gone. I couldn't find it nowhere.

CHAPTER 53

We rode in silence a good while, and slowly the sky changed to dark gray. I sat with my head pressed up against the window watching the shadows of the outside world pass by.

"I'll never forget the day your daddy came to our house."

I lifted my head off the window and looked at Matthew. "My daddy's been to your house? Why? When?"

"Back when Auntie Mama first got her wheelchair. Georgie told your daddy 'bout how she couldn't get in the house without bein' lifted and he came over that next weekend. He sure did."

"I didn't know that."

"Yep. Him an' Georgie showed up with a whole truckload of wood from the old gym floor. Remember when they tore that up? Anyway, it was a cool ramp. Shoot, Filet Gumbo loved it more than anybody."

"Filet Gumbo?"

"Yeah, our dog."

"Y'all named your dog after food?" Little Cricket popped in my head.

Matthew laughed, "Lukey thought the pup was the color of gumbo, and the name stuck. We didn't know she was gonna grow up and be all speckled, y'know? It was a good name. She was a good dog."

"What happened to her?"

"I don't know. Everything happened so fast. The water—"

He didn't have to say nothing else. I knew.

"But anyway," he said after we sat not talking for a few minutes. "I was so embarrassed when your daddy an' Georgie came inside for a glass of Auntie Mama's lemonade." He shook his head all slow.

"Why?"

"'Cause I didn't want 'em to smell the onions."

I know my eyes about popped right out of my head when Matthew Boman said that. I had an instant memory of how them kids smelled walking down the aisle on our bus.

"Onions? What're you talkin' about?" I was more than grateful that the boy was busy staring off into space and not looking my way. It was still too dark outside for him to see the color of embarrassed splashed all over my face, but I was worried he might *feel* it—it was that strong.

"Look, I ain't trying to be disrespectful," he said, "but Auntie Mama, well, she was weird. I mean, she was a real nice lady and all, and she was a good mama to me an' the kids. I think she had a special likin' for Lukey." He looked over at me. I sat quiet and just listened. "She never took us to church or nothin' like I remember our real mama doin', but she prayed all the time and burned so many candles I thought for sure she was gonna burn the house down someday."

"Did the candles smell like onions?"

Matthew let out a loud laugh. "Course the candles didn't smell like onions. The *onions* smelled like onions." He ran his fingers through his hair. "Every night after supper, Auntie Mama and Martha cut up four whole onions—one in a bowl for every room in the house."

"Why? Like some kinda voodoo or somethin'?"

"Naw, it weren't like that. She said it was 'cause the onions would soak up all the germs in the house so us kids wouldn't get sick."

I wanted to say, *Oh, that's why y'all had that smell!* But I didn't. I just said, "Are you serious?" Of course I knew the boy was serious. I'd smelled the proof with my own nose.

"Yeah. Martha came home from school one day cryin' her eyes out, sayin' her teacher pulled her out in the hall to tell her she needed to bathe more. Told my sister she stunk. Martha cried herself to sleep every night for a week."

I swallowed the lump in my throat.

"I wanted to pull that teacher into the hall and tell her that Martha took a bath every single day and that she should apologize. But Auntie Mama told me to let the universe take care of that heartless woman." Matthew's voice took on the sound of remembering. "All I know is, we never got sick—not one time, ever."

"Matthew . . . ," I started to say, but then I heard Memaw whisper, *There's no need, child. Let it be.*

"It's all right," he said. "Some people are just uncaring, ya know what I'm sayin'?"

"Yeah," I said.

I heard the flip of the mirror and the lower half of Miss Priscilla's face lit up. "How y'all doin'?"

"We're good, Miss P.," Matthew said.

"How . . ." I cleared my throat. "How much longer till we get there?"

"Oh, it's gonna be a good while yet, honeybee," Miss Priscilla's lips said up in the mirror. "They've got us takin' alternative routes. Why don't y'all try to get a little rest? Unless you wanna try one of these biscuits we've got in our snack bag."

"No, thank you," I said. "I'm not hungry."

"Me neither," said Matthew.

Just then I seen Uncle Alvin reach his arm out and over the back of Miss Priscilla's seat, like he was putting his arm around her.

"Well, all right," Miss Priscilla said. When she reached up to flip the mirror shut, she looked my way and winked. Her eyes were doing some kind of happy dance. I knew that wink and them eyes had everything to do with the arm resting up behind her. She snapped the mirror shut and the light went out.

I scooched down in my seat. I couldn't keep myself from thinking of TayTay and her clover. My eyes were heavy.

Matthew leaned over and put his face right up close to mine. He whispered into my ear, "I think Miss P. has a boyfriend." His voice-air tickled my ear.

I tried to force a smile, until, finally, slowly, my eyes stayed shut.

"Armani! Hey, wake up." Matthew wiggled his shoulder—the shoulder my head was lying on. I sat up and scooched over toward the window. I'd been all but sitting on top of the boy. Matthew smiled just to where that dimple showed. The light shining through the window behind me caught his face so that the morning honey-colored sky filled his eyes.

"It's all right," Matthew said. He lifted one eyebrow. "I don't mind bein' your pillow."

I play-smacked him across the chest with the back of my arm. "Shut up."

He laughed and took a bite of the biscuit he was holding. My stomach growled. "Miss P's fixin' to stop soon for gas," he said, with his mouth full. "We're gettin' close. You wanna biscuit?"

"Yeah, sure." I looked out my window while he asked Uncle Alvin to pass one back.

"Here ya go," Matthew said, pulling my thoughts out of the clouds. "They're dry as August, but Miss P's got waters if you want one."

"Thanks." I held the heavy biscuit, but I didn't eat it. I looked out my window admiring how beautiful everything looked. "Whenever we were up early in the mornin' to see a sky soaked in them kinda colors, Mama would say, 'It's a blessed day, to be sure, when you wake up under a Louisiana sky with a touch of Heaven shining through.'"

"That's pretty," Matthew sighed. "That's real pretty."

"Yeah, it is," I said in a lazy voice. "Matthew, look!" I pointed over his shoulder to the unsettling sight out his window.

"Aww . . . man."

Army trucks—tons of them—one right after the other for as far as I could see, clogging up the interstate. They took up a whole lane.

"Where's that dern gas station, y'all?" Miss Priscilla asked.

"I don't know," Matthew said. "But look at that, Miss P."

"Sweet Jesus," Miss Priscilla gasped.

"It's the Dome," I said, and tried to wrap my brain around the sight I was seeing.

CHAPTER 54

The Dome looked like a bomb had gone off on top of it. The roof was barely there—huge holes of blackness everywhere. *Was it like that when we were there? Was it like that when Danisha and her family were up inside there—when her mama got attacked?*

After we slowly passed up the Dome, we started seeing Army soldiers with guns. Walking, riding in trucks, standing alongside the road just staring at whatever—most of them with the look of wanting to be somewhere else.

Helicopters buzzed through the air, taking me back to our terrifying night on the roof. The sounds, the soldiers, the smell—the awful, sickening smell. Everything was making my head woozy. I thought I was gonna throw up. *Where was TayTay and Georgie? Where was Daddy?*

We were stuck in a line on the interstate surrounded by Army trucks. The line moved maybe one inch every couple minutes. I closed my eyes and prayed for us to just be there.

The slowness of time made me sick. We crawled along down streets I didn't recognize in a city that sure didn't feel like home.

We were lost. Lost in a place I'd been knowin' my whole life.

CHAPTER 55

Finally we came up on a convenience store that was open—open and all but falling down. A dirt line, taller than me, circled the outside of the building. I didn't have to ask nobody—my good sense told me it was a waterline from where the water had been.

A long row of vehicles, mostly Army ones, sat with us in line for the gas pumps. We stuck out like a zebra in the bayou, sitting up in Miss Priscilla's fancy SUV. There was even people without vehicles in that line, standing around holding gas cans looking wore down and sweaty. I couldn't help but wonder out loud why a person would bother being in a line for gas when they didn't have no car to put it in nohow. Matthew said they were most likely getting it for generators.

"Miss Priscilla," I said after a good while, "can we get out an' stretch our legs?"

She unbuckled her seatbelt and fiddled with the air vent. Then she turned around in her seat and looked at me for the first time in hours without using the mirror.

"I don't know why you'd want to, but . . ." She looked from me to Matthew then back to me again. "I suppose. But y'all stay together and no wanderin'. Ya hear?"

She might've said more, but I was already out the door.

A blast of thick, disgusting, soupy air slapped me in the face as soon as I hopped down out of the air-conditioned truck. I grabbed hold of Memaw's locket.

A smell flew up my nose that I'll never forget. Me and Matthew covered our noses at the same time. It was the same nasty odor that oozed from Mr. Babineaux's broke-down car the summer before, when a cat had climbed up inside the engine and died.

Two helicopters flew by low enough to stir up dirt and whatever else didn't weigh more than a loaf of bread. I squeezed my eyes shut and stuck half my face down inside the front of my shirt till the noisy things passed us by.

A wave of panic burned through me. I looked around every which way and turned in a slow circle. "Matthew?"

"What?"

My heart was up in my throat. "How are we gonna find home when nothin's where it's supposed to be?"

The SUV crawled along like a June bug making its way across concrete. I rubbed the compass-locket between my fingers and stared out the window, trying to recognize where we were. I prayed and waited for that feeling of familiar, but it didn't come. It seemed like we'd come in from the wrong side or something. I was confused and aggravated. It didn't feel or look like we were in New Orleans.

The further we scooched along, the worse the sight was. We passed by a row of leaning shotgun houses with waterlines that looked like the ring left in the tub after the water drains—lines clear up by the tops of the doors. A family with a mama and five or six kids sat there on the ground looking nowhere with that look of nothing on their dirty faces.

"Sweet Jesus," Miss Priscilla said again.

My stomach did a flip-flop.

Walls of stuff were piled high and out of the way on both sides of the messed-up street. Stuff that used to be people's lives. That's when I first knew that we'd lost everything. Everything. Not just the food in Mama's fridge, and Daddy's truck. We'd lost *everything*. How could anyone come out alive on the other side of a storm that had done took away everything? I grabbed hold of Georgie's glasses that were sitting on the seat between me and Matthew. I held them careful with one hand and kept my other hand on Memaw's locket.

"We're getting close to the Lower Nines—I can feel it," Uncle Alvin said.

I could feel it too.

"My, my, would y'all look at that." Miss Priscilla all but stopped the SUV.

Right there, off to the side of the road, mixed in with all the rubble, was ol' Mr. Jasper Junior Sr. and his saxophone, playing a lonesome jazzy song. A lady sitting on top of a laid-down tree smiled sad and swayed, moving her head this way and that. The teenage boy in the wheelchair beside them was tipped up on his back wheels with the front ones in the air. He moved his chair to the sound of the soulful music, dancing in a way I ain't never seen no one dance before.

"That's the spirit of the Nines right there," Matthew said.

He was right. In the middle of all that mess and destruction, the feeling of home was beginning to take over. My heart started thumping a little bit harder and a whole lot faster. I was getting closer and closer to Daddy. It took everything I had to not scream at the top of my lungs for Miss Priscilla to go on and hurry up already and get us to where we were going.

I was fixin' to ask if it'd be possible for us to go faster than new grass could grow, when all of a sudden I seen it.

I knew where we were! Just a little ways off, up higher than any of the piles of rubble, was Mr. Frank's upside-down school bus still sitting on top of the building—the building that was right next to the doughnut shop. Right where it was the last time I'd seen it. When the water was everywhere. When the water was right where we were driving that second. When the bodies had floated by.

CHAPTER 56

Every single house with at least one wall still standing had a big ol' spray-painted X with numbers scattered around it. Somehow I knew our house would have the number *one* up on it. There were lots of X's. And there were lots of numbers.

––––––

We went around a corner, and just like that, the bus was gone. A panic started to take hold when something made me stop and look down at the locket I'd been rubbing on all morning. I opened it. Right away the little needle inside the compass went to moving back and forth before finally stopping with the N situated off to the left.

I couldn't stay stuck up inside the SUV for another second. I asked Miss Priscilla if I could please get out and walk, especially since she was moving along at an armadillo pace anyhow. Matthew got out and walked with me. Miss Priscilla and my uncle followed in the truck behind us.

Where are you, Daddy?

While I walked with Georgie's glasses safe in my hand, I tried to ignore the sound of the whop-whopping helicopters, and the far-off hollerin', and the not-so-far-off gunshot sounds bouncing around in the thick, rotten-canal-smelling air.

Matthew picked up a long stick and swatted at rocks, making them roll out in front of us. I was watching a rock roll when I noticed the dead fish. *Lots* of them—scattered around like it had done rained fish or something. All them dead fish eyes, following me while I walked.

And the smells. The air tasted the way it smelled. I couldn't help but gag and cough.

Matthew asked if I was okay and patted my back the way Mama did when one of us swallowed something wrong.

I shrugged. "I don't know. I guess." I promised myself not to look at no more fish. "I'll be all right soon as I see Daddy and Georgie."

I checked Memaw's compass.

"Armani," Matthew said, "what if we can't find 'em?" He slapped the rock with his stick again. "I just wanna make sure you're prepared in case, well, ya know."

"Yeah. I know" is all I said. I wrapped my hand around the compass-locket. *Please let us find them, God.* Please. Daddy was strong, but that water monster had been even stronger. I knew right then in my heart that no matter what, I'd never hold it against Daddy for not being strong enough to save Georgie—or little Cricket.

I swiped away a hot tear rolling down my cheek before I caught up with Matthew.

———

Concrete steps leading nowhere. The morning of my birthday, them steps most likely led to someone's porch—attached to someone's home. That was a sight I'll carry with me forever. Concrete steps leading nowhere.

"It's something, ain't it?" Matthew said quiet.

"What?"

"The way everything looks when it's gone."

I didn't wanna look no more at the mess the storm had left behind. The trees with nothing but thick trunks, looking all naked without leaves or branches. The layer of swamp mud covering most everything and Miss Priscilla reminding us it wasn't safe to touch nothing with bare hands. All the things that a person calls *home* outside of their home. Everything there but gone at the same time.

We kept on walking. Matthew kept on hitting rocks with his stick. Helicopters kept on flying over our heads. The air kept on stinking. Miss Priscilla kept on following. And my heart kept on growing heavier and heavier.

I looked down at my brother's glasses all covered in my fingerprints. "It's my fault we stayed," I said, my own words catching me off-guard.

"How's that?" Matthew asked and pushed the rock.

"'Cause I wouldn't let Georgie tell Daddy that Mr. Babineaux from next door said we should evacuate." My feet shuffled along. "I didn't wanna mess up my birthday." My throat tried to close up. The air got thicker.

"You had a birthday?"

"Mm-hmm."

Matthew about knocked me down when he shoulder-bumped me and flashed me one of his smiles. "Happy birthday!"

"Thanks." A wave of guilty washed over me, because I knew I would've *never* invited that boy to my house, especially for my party. But there I was, walking down the middle of what used to be my neighborhood, knowing that if there was ever a day worth celebrating again, it wouldn't be the same without Matthew and Martha and the boys right there with us.

"Y'know," Matthew said, "Auntie Mama told us the night of the storm that stayin' was an act of hope. What do you think she meant by that?"

I couldn't speak. I stopped in my tracks and froze solid when I realized where I was. The flashing blue light was gone. Most of the color was gone. But the red paint chips around the edges of the door were enough for me.

CHAPTER 57

"You sure you know this place, honeybee?" Miss Priscilla came up behind me and put a hand on my shoulder.

I could barely breathe. I sure couldn't talk.

Uncle Alvin answered for me. "She knows it. Pete's granddaddy built that shop square and true."

I wasn't expecting the feelings that had took over my whole entire body just from seeing a familiar sight that wasn't nothing familiar no more.

"I—I don't . . . I mean, do you think Mr. Pete might know where Daddy and Georgie . . . ?" My blurry eyes searched the sad, caring faces of Matthew and Miss Priscilla—and Uncle Alvin. Big gator tears rolled down my cheeks. "Georgie didn't know how to swim. He—"

Uncle Alvin reached out to me with a shaky hand. I stared into his black, watery eyes. "We're all storm-tossed children now. Ain't nothin' we can do about that." A tear fell from his eye. "I gotta go find my girl." He nodded at me, then walked past the SUV and kept going on down the road.

"Alvin!" Miss Priscilla hollered after him. "I'm comin' with ya, darlin'. Just hang on." She looked from me to Matthew with all the lovin' a mama can when she looks at her children. "Now y'all listen to me.

I'm gonna go with Alvin. I don't think he should be by himself in the state he's in."

She turned and looked at him getting farther away. She talked faster. "I'm gonna get in my truck and take him where he needs to be, then we're comin' right back here." Miss Priscilla looked at her watch. "It's a quarter to two. I'll be back as quick as I can. Don't y'all go *nowhere* else. I ain't in the mood for no shenanigans." She pointed her finger from Matthew to me. "Do y'all hear me?"

"Yes, ma'am," we both said.

"You can wait for me on that bench over there if y'all want." She pointed at a bright white bench sitting up by the door to Pete's. I knew I'd never seen it there before. It sure did look extra bright and white up next to the faded, water-stained building. "Y'all best not move an inch from this location."

She squeezed us in one lump of a hug, then she walked backward to her truck, still pointing that finger at the two of us. "I'm just so proud of the two of y'all. Honeybee, you're stronger than you know, darlin'. Don't you forget that."

"I won't," I said more to myself than her. I hoped she'd hurry back.

———

"We can do this, Armani. We'll do it together." Matthew let out a poof of air that blew his bangs out of his eyes.

We'd been standing there in the same spot for at least five minutes. I wanted to find out if Mr. Pete knew anything, but I didn't wanna know all at the same time.

"Thanks, Matthew. I don't think I could go in there without you."

I held onto the locket and stared at the knob on that half-red door with the waterline almost to the top, and knew it was time. A little flutter started in the bottom of my belly.

I closed my eyes and imagined the smells that were always waiting on the other side of that door. The thought of warm doughnuts spread through me. I was ready to cross the road. I took hold of Matthew Boman's hand, hugged my brother's glasses to my heart, and headed for the door.

I stopped walking. Matthew stopped too.

I'd never felt the feeling of hope so strong and real in my whole entire life. That new familiar knowin' all but swept me off my shaky feet. A smile took hold on my face.

"What?" Matthew said, staring at me all crazy.

A giggle snuck past my lips. A little bounce found my feet. "That bench! It's our porch swing! Me an' Memaw's—well, really it's Mama's. But whatever. It's *our* swing! I know it is!" If the swing was there, then Daddy had to be too.

"You sure? It looks new."

I let loose of Matthew's hand. I stepped up next to the chair that my PawPaw had built with his own two hands. My finger found one of the grooves I'd been tracing my whole life. The porch swing was painted new and white, but the names were still there—just like always. The storm couldn't take them names away.

"Daddy finally painted it. . . ." The words came out in a choked-up cry. I squeezed my eyes shut. My insides felt tore in half. I didn't know I could be so happy and sad at the same time. The feeling of a person not being there is way stronger than when a person is there. I knew Daddy would be waiting for me up inside that shop, but seeing that pretty white swing reminded me that I'd never sit on it again with Memaw—never.

"You ready to go inside?" Matthew whispered.

I wiped my nose across the top of my sleeve, forgetting altogether that it wasn't polite, especially in front of a boy. I took hold of Matthew's hand again and forced a smile the best I could.

I turned the rough, rusty doorknob. It had never felt scratchy like that before. The door creaked opened like there was sand in the hinges. I pushed a little harder on it, and reminded myself to breathe.

CHAPTER 58

"Hello?" I whispered. My heart raced almost as fast as my brain. The door finally swung all the way open with a stale whoosh, not the happy ding of the bell like always. I right away knew it wasn't the smell of doughnuts burning my nose.

I stood where I was, afraid to take one step into the gutted-out-looking insides of what was supposed to be Mr. Pete's doughnut shop. I fought the urge to run outside and check to make sure—maybe it *wasn't* the right building. My lip started to tremble and the tears were coming on.

There was no way Daddy or anybody else could be up inside that place. There wasn't no lights on, but I could still tell that the orangey-colored floor tile was gone. There was nothing there but cold-looking concrete.

The sound of loud, clunky fans filled the air.

And the smell. The smell was so strong I could *taste* it. A mix of old rain, bleach, mothballs, and canal. Stinking canal.

"Nobody's here."

No sooner did I get the words out of my mouth when a man's voice from somewhere inside the shop hollered out, "Hello? Is some-one there?"

I knew that voice!

Matthew real quick hollered back, "Yes, sir! Can we come in?"

"Course ya can, son. What can I do for ya?"

We stepped inside the shop. After blinking a few times, I could see that it wasn't as dark and awful as it looked when I peered in from outside. But it was still bad. The glass case where Mr. Pete showed off the fresh doughnuts was broke to pieces. A big ol' pile of glass and trash had been swept off to the one side. A huge metal table was set up in the middle of the room with tools and cleaners and rags scattered on it. Two big fans blew at the wet-looking walls.

Mr. Pete popped out from back where the doughnut fryers did their doughnut making. His hands were covered in long yellow plastic gloves. He looked at me and smiled big. It was clear as could be that he was happy to see me.

I was bursting from the excitement I was feeling from seeing him. I ran across the dusty concrete and wrapped my arms around his dough-belly.

"Mr. Pete! I'm so happy to see you!" I wouldn't be surprised if I'd left squeeze marks on the poor man, I hugged him so tight. I pulled back and pointed at Matthew. "This is my friend Matthew Boman." I was smiling so fierce it was beginning to hurt in my jaw.

Matthew and Mr. Pete shook hands.

"It's nice meetin' you, son." Mr. Pete nodded at Matthew.

"Are you serious? You've never been in here to buy doughnuts?" I was wide-open nervous-rambling at that point. "Well, you don't know what you been missin'. Right, Mr. Pete?" I smiled all big and bounced a couple times on my feet.

I didn't like the way Mr. Pete was looking at Matthew—fidgety and uneasy-like.

"Hey, now," another man's voice came from behind us. "Is that you, Armani Curtis?"

I whipped around, and there was ol' Mr. Leroy holding a push broom.

"Mr. Leroy!" I didn't even really know that old man, but I knew he was Mr. Pete's helper and I knew he was Daddy's friend. I went and hugged him like we was kin. I was feeling giggly and jittery the way I feel right before a surprise.

"I don't know what we would've done if I hadn't spotted ol' Mr. Frank's bus and recognized your poor messed-up bell, Mr. Pete. But it don't matter now, right? The important thing is we're here!" I sure wished Mr. Pete would've looked as excited as I felt. I figured maybe he was more quiet with his feelings on account of him living by his-self for so long and making doughnuts all day.

"Armani," Matthew said. "Can you come here?" He motioned with his head for me to come by him. He glanced up at Mr. Pete, and Mr. Pete looked down at the floor.

I stood next to Matthew—still just a-smiling—anticipating the surprise I prayed was coming.

"Leroy," Mr. Pete said. The older man went to him. Mr. Pete whispered something in his ear. Mr. Leroy looked at me. His head went to hanging and he headed for the red door in the corner—the red door that went up to Mr. Pete's living area. The waterline was clear up by the top. Just like the waterline on the outside of the building.

A shiver ran through me.

Footsteps ran across the floor to Mr. Pete's upstairs. It sure did sound like happy feet causing that ceiling to thump. I looked at Matthew and smiled.

But then I froze. All the good I was feeling drained away. In that one tiny second, I noticed the way Matthew and Mr. Pete were looking at each other. It felt like someone reached in and squeezed my heart with both hands.

I stared at the closed red door in the corner and forced myself to keep breathing. The whirly-hum of the fans got louder and louder.

Come on, Daddy, come on. Please Daddy, open the door.

Footsteps pounding down the stairs filled my head. A loud thunk bounced off the other side of the door.

The door swung open and Georgie spilled into the room.

CHAPTER 59

"Georgie!" I ran to my brother and fell into him. We stood there hugging and squeezing each other for the longest time.

"I knew you'd come," Georgie said, not even bothering to wipe the wet mess from his face.

If ever there was a time when I loved my brother more, I don't know when it would've been.

I wiped his glasses the best I could with the bottom of my shirt, then opened them up and slipped them onto his face. He right away took his finger and pushed them up on his nose. Instead of smiling his goofy smile, his eyes fell to the floor.

"Armani," Georgie said. "There's somethin' . . ." He didn't get to finish his sentence, because just then I looked over and seen TayTay standing in the doorway to the stairs, looking more beautiful than ever.

I ran to her across the dirty, sticky floor—crying happy tears the whole time.

Her hands rubbed my head. She shushed me while she did her own crying. "I'm so sorry, Armani," she said through her tears.

"You don't have to be sorry," I said into her neck. "You're safe! You're *alive*. Oh no . . ." I pulled my head off her and wiped my face with the back of my hand. "Your dad's lookin' for you. We gotta tell him you're here! Maybe Matthew can go find him." I turned to look at Matthew, but he had his back to me. Him and Georgie and Mr. Pete were up in a huddle talking in whispers.

TayTay took both my hands in hers. She looked me straight on with heavy eyes and a tilt of her head. I slowly shook my head—my eyes never leaving hers. We stared into each other for a good while in a way that only real friends know how. She told me. She told me the truth without ever saying one word out loud.

New tears filled my eyes but didn't fall. Over her shoulder, I stared at the blurry, empty doorway leading to the upstairs. It stayed empty.

I looked back at TayTay and all the tears of knowin' spilled from my eyes.

"*Daddy* . . ." I barely whispered.

Georgie's arms wrapped around me, catching my fall.

"*Nooooo* . . ." I moaned.

All my feelings of hope turned to dark and concrete, crushing me from the inside out—shattering my heart into a million trillion pieces.

I let myself be held in all them arms. Then I closed my eyes and waited for angels to come and show me the way.

CHAPTER 60

We sat on the porch swing—the four of us—me and Georgie and TayTay and Matthew. None of us saying a word. Swinging and waiting. Waiting for Miss Priscilla to come pick us up in the SUV.

Georgie was the one who'd painted the swing. He said he did it to surprise Mama after him and Mr. Pete found it almost a mile from where our house had been.

I sat there in my usual spot, with my back pressed up against my own name, and let the sadness settle in. Even with everything that was lost and different, I knew I was home. The storm had come and turned everything I cared about upside down and inside out.

Daddy was gone.

Memaw was gone.

Nothing would ever be the same.

But I was home.

I never did hear the truck pull up. All I seen was Uncle Alvin standing there with the look of thankful spread across his face. TayTay ran to him and got wrapped in his arms.

My own arms ached and the feeling of empty took hold of my chest.

Miss Priscilla stayed over by her open truck door with a hand pressed up by her heart. She looked at me only for a second before she dropped her head.

That's when I felt Matthew get up, leaving me and Georgie to ourselves on Memaw's swing.

I rested my head on Georgie's shoulder and ran my finger in the carved-out first letter of my dead uncle's name. I wondered if he was the uncle who needed to be saved that day in the canal, or if he was the one who died trying to save someone he loved.

"I never got to tell Daddy I was sorry." I blinked tears from my eyes and tried to take a normal breath.

"It's okay," Georgie whispered.

"No it's not." My voice was slow and groggy. "I need to tell him that I'm sorry and that . . . that I love him."

"Daddy knows, Armani. I know that for sure—Daddy knows."

A tear ran down my cheek and onto my brother.

The swing looked different—all white and bright. But when I closed my eyes—putting my focus on my ears—my heart took hold and the swing felt and sounded the same.

You'll always be my little girl, Armani.

Now ain't that nice?

Daddy and Memaw were sitting right there beside me. I could feel them.

I kept my eyes closed tight and let my head tilt up toward Heaven. I wrapped my foot around my brother's, gave a push on the concrete, and took in the music of the swing. *High-squeak, low-squeak . . .*

Acknowledgments

First, I need to express my gratitude to the beautiful and brave children whose paths crossed mine at a time when it really did seem that our world had been turned upside down. I am a better me because I had the opportunity to meet each of you.

Quinlan Lee, thank you for believing and paving the way for possibilities. I'm proud to be a member of the Adams Literary family.

Tender thanks to the super talented Karen Smullen. You were my first fan and the consummate cheerleader.

Thank you, Holly Alder, for telling me that my writing was good. You unknowingly gave me that credible sign of consent to be a writer. For this, I will always be grateful.

A ginormous, heartfelt thank-you to my dear, devoted friend and mentor, Shelley Souza, for countless hours of reading those messy early drafts. You never wavered with your ability to ask the questions that needed to be asked, and you helped me to uncover the story that was buried within.

Thank you seems inadequate in reference to my amazing editor, Tamra Tuller. You gave breath to Armani's story. It is a privilege and honor to work with you.

I also want to thank Taylor Norman, Ginee Seo, Kim Lauber, Kristine Brogno, Lara Starr, Wendy Thorpe, Ann Spradlin, Claire Fletcher, and the entire team at Chronicle Books for allowing this one small, important voice to be heard.

And finally, to my husband, Keith, and our joyful kids: thank you for teaching me the true meaning of home.

UPSIDE DOWN IN THE MIDDLE OF NOWHERE

THROUGH WRITING AND DISCUSSION

The following questions may be utilized throughout the study of *Upside Down in the Middle of Nowhere* as reflective writing prompts or, alternatively, they can be used as targeted questions for class discussion and reflection.

- In the opening of *Upside Down in the Middle of Nowhere*, Armani offers readers a window into her neighborhood, the Lower Ninth Ward. She describes the homes adorned with window fans, the local establishments—like Mr. Pete's doughnut shop—and the canal that claimed the lives of two of her uncles. In your opinion, why does her neighborhood play such an important role in Armani's story?

- Consider the cover art for *Upside Down in the Middle of Nowhere*. In what ways are the images represented symbolic of the events that transpire throughout the course of the book?

- In *Upside Down in the Middle of Nowhere*, Armani's nemesis is her cousin Danisha. What do these cousins have in common? How are they different? In your opinion, why do they act the way they do? Though she is cantankerous early in the story, what does Danisha's sacrifice of her spot on the bus tell us about her growth as a person and her understanding of the needs of her cousins?

- Early in the novel, Memaw states, "I sure don't like the looks of that storm." Given that weather forecasters' predictions initially put Hurricane Katrina on a different path, why might Armani's grandmother's life experiences make her likely to be particularly concerned about this storm?

- Armani shares, "Sitting on the porch swing with Memaw was always my favorite time of day. Whether I was doing my homework or finishing my chores, I always did them without dragging my feet if I knew Memaw was waiting for me on the swing," and "We went back to the business of swinging. . . . The high-squeak, low-squeak, high-squeak, low-squeak sound of our rocking just made the feel-good feeling better. Being with Memaw was easy." What is it about their relationship that makes her feel that way? How would you describe their relationship? Do you have a similar one with a grandparent or another special relative?

- Do you think Armani is selfish in wanting her birthday celebration to be uninterrupted? How does she finally reconcile that she wasn't to blame for her family's choice to remain at home and not evacuate?

- Describe Armani. What makes her such a dynamic person? Is she the type of person you would want as a friend? Why or why not?

- Explain the significance of the title, *Upside Down in the Middle of Nowhere*. In your opinion, does it accurately describe the events and relationships portrayed in the book?

- *Upside Down in the Middle of Nowhere* is told in first person; how would the story be different if there were another character besides Armani telling it? Do you think changing the point of view would make the story better or worse? Why?

- How does the death and loss of Memaw profoundly impact and change the lives of each of her family members? Do you think they are ultimately better people because of what she has given them? Why or why not?

- Consider the characters in *Upside Down in the Middle of Nowhere*. Who did you like the most? The least? For what reason? Of all of the characters, who did you feel was most similar to you due to his/her personality or experiences?

- How do Armani's feelings for Matthew Boman change throughout the course of the novel? What does she learn from their shared experiences? Predict what their relationship will be like moving forward.

- After hearing her profess her belief that she was at fault for making her family stay, Matthew Boman tells Armani, "Auntie Mama told us the night of the storm that stayin' was an act of hope." Do you agree with Auntie Mama's sentiment? In what ways do you find this to be true?

- Using the phrase, "This is a story about . . .," supply five words to describe *Upside Down in the Middle of Nowhere*. Explain your choices.

- In *Upside Down in the Middle of Nowhere*, what are the most impressive obstacles Mama has to overcome? Which of these hurdles did you find most challenging? Why?

- Do you think Armani's dad made the right choice of jumping into the water after his son? Why or why not?

JULIE T. LAMANA grew up in a military family, moving frequently throughout the United States and Japan. She and her husband, Keith, eventually chose to make Louisiana their permanent home. Julie was working as an after-school Literacy Specialist in 2005 when Hurricane Katrina tore through her state. She was in a position to help displaced children through one of the most devastating tragedies in U.S. history, giving her a unique insight into the survivor's experience and sparking the idea to write *Upside Down in the Middle of Nowhere*.

Julie currently lives with her family in Greenwell Springs, Louisiana. *Upside Down in the Middle of Nowhere* is her debut novel.